McNally's TRIAL

McNally's TRIAL

Lawrence SANDERS

G. P. Putnam's Sons
New York

G. P. Putnam's Sons
Publishers Since 1838
200 Madison Avenue
New York, NY 10016

Published simultaneously in Canada

Library of Congress Cataloging-in-Publication Data

Sanders, Lawrence, date.
McNally's trial / Lawrence Sanders.
p. cm.
ISBN 0-399-14006-9
1. McNally, Archy (Fictitious character)—Fiction. 2. Private
investigators—Florida—Palm Beach—Fiction. 3. Palm Beach
(Fla.)—
Fiction. I. Title.
PS3569.A5125M38 1995 94-33943 CIP
813′.54—dc20

Printed in the United States of America

1 2 3 4 5 6 7 8 9 10

Book design by Chris Welch

This book is printed on acid-free paper.
∞

McNally's TRIAL

1

It has been said that no good deed goes unpunished, and I can vouch for it. The donee of my act of charity was Binky Watrous, a close pal of mine and a complete doofus who once, deranged by strong drink, brushed his teeth with anchovy paste.

Actually, my tale begins on a coolish night in early October in the Town of Palm Beach. My name is Archy (for Archibald) McNally, and I am employed to conduct discreet inquiries for the law firm of McNally & Son. My father is the attorney, I am the son. My investigations are mainly concerned with solving the personal problems of our prestigious clients before they come to the attention of the police or those supermarket tabloids that might feature the client's tribulations between a truss ad and a story about twins borne by a ninety-eight-year-old Samoan transvestite.

I can't remember the date of the Battle of Actium, but I have almost total recall when it comes to splendid meals I have enjoyed, and dinner that evening was something special. Our live-in housekeeping staff, Ursi and Jamie Olson, had concocted a wondrous salad served in a wooden bowl large enough to hold the head of John the Baptist.

The main ingredients were chunks of smoked chubs enlivened with slices of fennel sausage, and lots of other swell stuff. My father, Prescott McNally, and I demolished a bottle of sauvignon blanc while consuming this feast, but my mother, Madelaine, insisted on her usual glass of sauterne. It was an eccentric habit that papa and I have attempted to convince her is ungodly, to no avail.

After that banquet (dessert was rum cake with a layer of maraschino) I felt so replete that, having nothing better to do, I thought I might make a run to the Pelican Club and perhaps down a postprandial cognac while reflecting that life indeed can be beautiful.

But it was not to be. The lord of the manor stopped me as I was about to ascend to my third-floor mini-suite to change into snazzier duds.

"Archy," he said in that tone he uses when he wishes to couch a command as a request, "were you planning anything special this evening?"

"No, sir," I said, stiff-upper-lipping it. "Nothing of any importance."

"Good. A client is arriving at nine o'clock, and I'd like you to sit in on the meeting."

"Oh?" I said. "Who is he?"

"She," he replied. "Sunny Fogarty. I believe the lady is unmarried, but that's of no consequence."

"It might be," I commented. "To her."

"Yes," he said with his wintry smile. "In any event, she is an employee of the Whitcomb Funeral Homes, the most recent commercial client to be added to our roster."

I tried to raise one eyebrow and failed miserably. That's my father's shtick, and he does it effortlessly. "Is she an undertaker?" I asked.

Again that frosty smile. "I believe the current euphemism is 'grief counselor.' But no, she is not a mortician. Her official title is comptroller of the three Whitcomb Funeral Homes, in Broward, Palm Beach, and Martin counties."

"I hear it's an upscale outfit," I remarked. "Gilt coffins and all that. Someone suggested their advertising slogan should be 'The Deathstyles of the Rich and the Famous.' "

The squire was not amused. He does not appreciate jokes about clients who put osso buco on the McNally table.

"Miss Fogarty phoned this afternoon," he continued. "She sounded somewhat agitated and asked to see me as soon as possible. I said I would be happy to come to her office or she could come to mine. But she preferred to meet at a place where there was no possibility of our being seen conferring together. So I suggested she come here this evening, and she agreed. It was a brief and puzzling conversation, which left me suspecting it might be a situation that requires discreet inquiries on your part."

And that explains why, at nine o'clock on that fateful evening, I was seated in my father's study, prepared to listen to Sunny Fogarty explain the reason for her secretive visit.

At the moment, "Sunny" seemed a misnomer, for the lady was obviously uptight: brows pinched into a frown, lips tightly pressed, fingers clenched. She sat forward in a leather club chair, spine stiff, shoulders back, and she kept crossing and recrossing her ankles.

But despite her angst I thought her attractive. I guessed her age at forty, give or take, and she had the weathered look of a woman who had worked hard all her life and expected the struggle would never cease. We had been introduced, of course, and I had been surprised by the strength of her handclasp. She wore a black gabardine pantsuit with an unexpectedly frilly blouse, closed with a wide ribbon and bow of crimson rep.

Her eyes were a darkish brown with a definite glint, and I imagined they might harden if the occasion required it. Not a woman to be trifled with, I decided, and found myself admiring her sleek russet hairdo. It looked like a helmet worn by one of Hannibal's spearmen.

My father was comfortably ensconced in the swivel chair behind his magisterial desk, and he leaned back, fingers linked across his waistcoat, and asked pleasantly, "Now then, Miss Fogarty, what's this all about?"

The boss had already explained the role I played at McNally & Son and assured her of my discretion since as a flunky of the firm—in addition to being his son—I was as bound by the dictates of attorney-client confidentiality as he. She seemed to accept that, made no objection to my presence, and spoke freely.

She told us she had been employed by Whitcomb for almost ten years, starting as a receptionist in their Fort Lauderdale funeral home and working her way up as secretary, then executive assistant to Mr. Horace Whitcomb, the owner and grandson of the founder. Meanwhile she had studied accounting and business administration, and when the company opened its third mortuary in Martin County she had been appointed comptroller of the whole shebang.

"It's a good position," she said, "and I like the work. My salary is okay; I have no resentment there whatsoever. Two years ago I computerized our entire operation, and it proved so successful I received a large bonus. I'm telling you all this to prove I have no reason for anger against Whitcomb, no reason to seek revenge or anything like that. I want Whitcomb to continue to be profitable, and I want to keep my job. I am the sole support of my mother, who is in a nursing home in West Palm Beach. She suffers from Alzheimer's. The expenses are enormous, so my income is very important to me."

She paused and made an effort to compose herself. Father and I were silent, watching her. I cannot say what his reaction was—his expression revealed nothing but polite interest—but I thought her an honest and disturbed woman, caught in a conflict between her personal welfare and a need to reveal something she felt was just not right.

"Our president, Horace Whitcomb," she went on, "is almost seventy and says he never wants to retire. He's a fine gentleman. He's been very kind and generous to me, but he's that way with all his employees. We love him. He comes to work about four or five hours a day but sometimes skips a day or two for golf or fishing."

"Good for him," my father said unexpectedly.

"Yes," she said with a smile that was faint but transformed her features. I could see then why "Sunny" was not a misnomer after all. "Horace's son, Oliver Whitcomb, is our chief executive officer. He handles the day-to-day operations of all our funeral homes."

"And is he also kind and generous?" I asked.

She ignored my question. "And then we have several other department heads," she said. "In charge of such things as purchasing, maintenance, personnel, and so forth. I can provide their names if you think it's necessary."

"Miss Fogarty," father said gently, "you haven't yet told us the nature of your problem."

She took a deep breath. "About six months ago I became aware—from the weekly reports I receive—that the revenue of Whitcomb was rising dramatically, far above our income of last year. Naturally I was pleased and so were all the other executives who noticed it, including Mr. Horace. During the past six months the number of funerals we handled continued to increase at a really surprising rate."

She looked at both of us, back and forth, as if expecting exclamations of astonishment. But father and I made no comment. Instead we exchanged a swift glance and I suspected we were sharing the same thought: Could Whitcomb's improved bottom line be the sole reason for Miss Fogarty's distress? I began to wonder if this lady had both oars in the water.

"The income of all three mortuaries keep increasing," she said. "I was puzzled because I am a logical woman—and curious, I might add—and I started to question why we were having such an impressive uptick in business."

Father stirred restlessly in his swivel chair. "Surely there must be a simple explanation," he said. "Perhaps it is the result of a new advertising campaign. Or you have enjoyed an unusual number of referrals."

"Or maybe more people are kicking the bucket," I suggested cheerfully.

She shook her head decisively. "We're doing no more advertising than we did last year. Our rate of referrals remains constant. And there has been no extraordinary rise in South Florida's death rate. In addition, I have checked my contacts in the industry, and no other local funeral homes have had the revenue increase we've had. In fact, most of them show flat month-to-month income or a decrease. There is just no obvious reason for our good fortune, and it baffles me."

She stopped, took a small hanky from a capacious shoulder bag, dabbed at her lips.

"Miss Fogarty," my father said kindly, "may we offer you some refreshment? Cola? Coffee? Or would you like a glass of port wine?"

"Yes," she said. "The wine, please."

"Archy," he said, "will you do the honors?"

I rose from my ladder-back chair, went over to his marble-topped sideboard, and poured three goblets of port from his crystal decanter. I'd drink it, but I wouldn't smack my lips. I didn't have the nerve to tell the guv that the last case he bought was definitely corky.

Our visitor took a small sip and sighed appreciatively. "Thank you," she said. "That tastes good."

"Miss Fogarty," *mon père* said, "what exactly is it you wish us to do? From what you've told us it does not appear that anything unethical or illegal has occurred at Whitcomb Funeral Homes. It is merely experiencing exceptional financial success. That is hardly reason for concern."

"Something strange is going on," she stated determinedly. "I just *know* it is. But I can't endanger my own position by poking and prying. People would think me a brainless idiot. I was hoping you might ask a few casual questions—as our attorney, you know—and see if you can discover the reason for our sudden prosperity."

Father looked at me. "Archy?" he said.

I knew what he wanted. I was to express sympathy, ask a question or two, assure our visitor of our willingness to cooperate, and get her out of there as soon as possible.

"We'll certainly look into it, Miss Fogarty," I said briskly. "The situation you describe is certainly odd and may possibly justify further inquiries. Tell me, do you keep records of the cemeteries to which the deceased are, ah, delivered?"

"Of course," she said. "Unless they are cremated. And records are kept of that. We have all our dead on computer."

"Excellent," I said. "Could you provide me with a printout of all the cemeteries Whitcomb Funeral Homes has dealt with in the past six months?"

She hesitated a moment. "Yes," she said, "I could do that. I shouldn't but I shall."

"I'd appreciate it," I said. "It might give me a start for our investigation." I took a business card from my wallet and used my gold Mont Blanc to scribble on the back. "I'm giving you my personal unlisted telephone number. Please feel free to use it if you cannot reach me at our office."

"Thank you," she said, taking my card and tucking it away. She finished her wine and arose. "I can't tell you how much better I feel for having talked to you gentlemen. This thing has been worrying me so much that I've had trouble sleeping. It's nice to know it'll be looked into. I'm ready to provide all the assistance I can."

Father and I accompanied her outside to our graveled turnaround. She was driving a spanking new white Chrysler New Yorker. A lot of car, I thought, for a woman supporting a terminally ill mother. We shook hands and she thanked us for our hospitality and consideration. We watched her drive away.

"Curious," father remarked.

"Yes, sir," I said, "it is that."

"Archy, go through the motions but don't spend too much time on it. I fear the lady is unnecessarily troubled. Mayhap slightly paranoid. It's a matter of no importance."

"I concur," I said.

Lordy, were we ever wrong!

2

Father returned to his study and closed the door firmly. I knew what that meant: he was settling in for the remainder of the evening. He would have another glass or two of port, smoke a pipe or two of his specially blended tobacco ("December Morn"), and read a chapter or two of Charles Dickens. For as long as I could remember, he had been slowly slogging his way through Chuck's entire oeuvre. Lotsa luck, daddy-o.

I glanced at my Mickey Mouse wristwatch, saw it was scarcely ten o'clock and I could still enjoy that brandy if I so desired. I did so desire and dashed upstairs to change to fawn slacks, a madras sport jacket, and Loafers From Hell: acid-green suede—with tassels yet. Then I bounced downstairs, pausing briefly at our second-floor sitting room to give the mater a good-night kiss. Her velvety cheek was wet. She was watching a TV rerun of "Stella Dallas" and tears were leaking.

I was still driving my vintage Miata, a flaming red job of the first model year and still holding its saucy flair. I hopped in and headed for the Pelican Club, my favorite oasis in South Florida. It's a private watering hole and has a membership of effervescent lads and lasses from Palm Beach and environs. It's a pleasantly laid-back joint, serves high-caloric grub, and no one would object if I clambered onto a table and recited "Sheridan's Ride." "Up from the south at break of day . . ."

The place was clanging when I arrived. Roisterers were two-deep at the bar, and couples were to-ing and fro-ing from the dining area. I finally caught the attention of Mr. Simon Pettibone, an elderly gentleman of color who is our club manager and doubles as bartender.

"Rémy!" I shouted to be heard above the din and he nodded.

He was back a moment later with my wallop, handing it to me across the shoulders of club members bellying the mahogany.

"Rushed, Mr. Pettibone?" I inquired.

"Love it, Mr. McNally," he said. "Just love it. Pays the rent."

"So it does," I agreed happily. The Pelican Club, of which I had been a founding member, was a candidate for Chapter 7 until we had the great good fortune of putting our future in the hands of Mr. Pettibone and his family. His wife Jas (for Jasmine) was our housekeeper and den mother. Son Leroy was our chef, and daughter Priscilla our waitress. The energetic and hard-working Pettibones had turned our little enclave into a profitable enterprise, and we now had a waiting list of would-be Pelicanites, eager to wear the club blazer bearing our escutcheon: a pelican rampant on a field of dead mullet.

Glass in hand, I looked about for a place to park the McNally carcass. And there, in a far corner of the pub area, sitting by his lonesome at a table for two, I spotted my goofy buddy, Binky Watrous himself. His head was bowed over a tumbler of an amber liquid. I made my way to his side.

"Binky," I said, "may I join you?"

He looked up and his loopy expression became a beam. "Archy!" he cried. "Just the man I wanted to see. Sit down, sit down, sit down!"

"Once will do nicely," I said, taking the bentwood chair opposite him. "What is that you're drinking?"

"Scotch," he said.

"With what?" I asked.

"More Scotch."

"Binky," I said, "we have been pals for a long time, but I must warn you that I shall not carry you home tonight. I am willing to call an ambulance, but that's the extent of my responsibility. Why on earth are you getting hammered?"

"I've got troubles," he said darkly.

"And pray, who does not?" I said, looking at him more closely.

Binky usually wears a look of blithe unconcern, but now I could see his chops were definitely fallen. He's a fair-haired lad with a wispy growth of blond hair on his upper lip that can be seen in a strong light. He's a bit on the shortish, plumpish side, and if you can imagine a Kewpie doll with a mustache, that's Binky.

Though he may not be physically impressive, he's a generous, good-hearted chap who'd give you the shirt off his back. But you probably wouldn't want it since it was liable to be voile with alternating stripes of heliotrope and mustard. But how can one dislike a man whose bedroom walls are plastered with photos of Lupe Velez?

"Binky," I said, "what seems to be the problem?"

He took a gulp of his drink. "It's the Duchess," he said mournfully. "She demands I get a job."

"A true cri de coeur," I commented.

"What's that, Archy?"

"Something like a kvetch," I explained. "And did the Duchess suggest any particular field of gainful employment?"

He shook his head. "She just said it's time for me to earn a living. Archy, what am I going to do since it's obvious I can't *do* anything?"

I should explain that Binky's mother and father were lost at sea while attempting to sail their sloop to Curaçao. Binky was a mere tot when the tragedy occurred, and he was raised by a wealthy maiden aunt, one of the grandest grande dames of Palm Beach.

Everyone referred to her as the Duchess. She was not a real Duchess, of course, but could play one on TV. I mean, she was imposing, haughty, and rather frightening. Her customary greeting was not "How are you?" but "You're not looking well."

But this Duke-less Duchess did provide for her brother's son and grimly endured his being expelled from Princeton for pushing a pie (chocolate cream) into the face of a banquet guest who made a biting remark about Binky wearing a tie patterned with the crest of the Irish Royal College of Surgeons. Binky was obviously not Irish, Royal, or a sawbones. The target of his pie turned out to be a visiting British VIP, and the resulting foofarah ended with Binky being booted.

Perhaps that was one of the reasons for our palship, since I had endured the same fate for a contretemps committed at Yale Law—a really minor misdeed. I had streaked naked (except for a Richard M. Nixon mask) across the stage during a performance by the New York Philharmonic.

Since his expulsion from Princeton, Binky had spent most

of his time traveling, engaging in harmless mischief, enjoying several romantic dalliances, and generally living the life of a happy drone. The Duchess granted him an open-handed allowance, paid for his profligacies—including gambling debts—and had made no objections other than stiff chidings—until now.

"Archy," Binky said gloomily, taking another swallow of his plasma, "what am I to do? You know I'm a complete klutz when it comes to work. That's just a four-letter word to me."

"Haven't the slightest idea, old boy," I said, sipping my cognac and feeling my toes beginning to curl.

"You work, don't you? Investigations and all that. Like a detective."

"Of course I work. Very diligently, I might add. And yes, my specialty is discreet inquiries."

He looked at me thoughtfully—if such a thing were possible. "You know, I believe I could do that. Lurking about and asking questions."

"There's more to it than that," I assured him. "It requires unique skills, plus curiosity and a keen intelligence."

That pleased him. "Now I'm sure I qualify," he said happily. "I'm inquisitive and no one's ever doubted my brainpower."

"Or even mentioned it," I said, but he could not be stopped.

"I've read oodles of detective novels," he rattled on. "Shadowing villains, threatening suspects, getting beat up and all that. I'm sure I can do it."

"Binky," I said, fearful of what I suspected was coming, "it really is an extremely difficult profession. The tricks of the trade can be learned only by experience."

"You could teach me," he said eagerly.

"I'm not sure you have the temperament for it."

"Look, Archy," he said, trying to harden his cherubic features into an expression of stern resolve, "why don't you let me work with you on your next case. No salary, of course. Just to learn the ropes, so to speak."

"And then what?" I demanded. "The old man would never let me hire a full-time assistant."

"I realize that," he agreed, "but after I catch on how it's done I could set up my own business. Binky Watrous: Private Eye. How does that sound?"

"Loathsome," I said. "Believe me, son, you're simply not cut out to be a sherlock."

"How do you know?" he argued. "I mean, you didn't start out to be a snoop, did you? You were going to be a lawyer and then you became an investigator. And now you enjoy it, don't you?"

I had to agree.

"Give me a chance, Archy," he pleaded. "I'll just tag along, observe and listen, and then I'll get out of your hair. What do you say?"

I sighed. I knew it would be a frightful error, but I could not deny his request. The poor dweeb was really in a bind.

"Okay, Binky," I said finally. "I'll take you on as an unpaid helper. But I'll be captain of the ship—is that understood?"

"Of course!" he said gleefully. "You command and I obey—absolutely! Do you think I should buy a gun?"

I gulped more Rémy. Allowing Binky to buy a gun would be like handing the Olympic torch to an arsonist.

"No, I don't think you'll have any need for a firearm."

"A knife?"

"No."

"Brass knuckles?"

"No weapons whatsoever, Binky. You're not going into combat, you know."

"We'll just outsmart the bad guys," he said. "Right?"

"Right," I said feebly, knowing he was incapable of outsmarting the Tasmanian devil.

I finished my drink and rose. "Got to dash," I said. "I told Connie I'd phone."

"When do we start?" he asked anxiously. "I want to tell the Duchess I'm hard at work getting on-the-job training."

"Call you tomorrow," I promised.

"Great!" he said. "But not too early, Archy. I've got a golf date at noon."

Typical Binky. I believe I told you in previous annals that his main talent was doing birdcalls. His imitation of a loon was especially realistic. I should also mention a formal dinner party we both attended during which corn on the cob was served. Instead of gnawing at the buttered kernels, Binky played the entire ear like a harmonica while humming "America, the Beautiful." The other guests were convinced there was a lunatic in their midst.

But enough about Binky Watrous. I drove home in a remarkably equable mood. I felt certain that by the time the sun was over the yardarm on the following day and the effects of Binky's beaker of Scotch had worn off, my chum would have completely forgotten his determination to become a detective.

It was my second serious miscalculation on that portentous evening.

3

The McNally manse was darkened and silent by the time I returned home. I tiptoed quietly up to my digs, took off the glad rags, and donned a silk kimono I had recently purchased. It was Japanese, and embroidered on the back was a fearsome samurai wielding a long sword and cutting off the head of a dragon that bore a startling resemblance to my barber, Herman Pincus. I suppose that's why I bought the robe.

I lighted an English Oval—only my third that day—and poured myself a small marc. I keep my personal liquor supply in a battered sea chest at the foot of my bed. It holds a limited inventory of brandies and liqueurs—for medicinal purposes, you understand. Much healthier than sleeping pills. Honest.

Then I phoned Consuela Garcia, my light-o'-love. Connie and I have had a thing going for many years. She is Cuban, a Marielito, and a very, very feisty lady. Regrettably, I have been unfaithful to her on numerous occasions, but as I have previously explained, I am genetically disadvantaged and my infidelity is due to faulty DNA.

When Connie discovers my perfidiousness, which she inevitably does, her reaction is usually physical. I dimly recall an incident at The Breakers where I was wining and dining a lissome young miss, a friend of a friend of a friend. To my horror, Connie entered and spotted us. She marched over to our table, plucked a half-full bottle of Piper-Heidsieck from its ice bucket, shook it vigorously and spritzed me from brow to sternum. It was not a night to remember.

"Hiya, honey," I said when she picked up after the seventh ring. "Whatcha doing?"

"Painting my toenails."

"Hey," I protested, "that's my job. Listen, I haven't seen you in ages."

"And whose fault is that?" she asked tartly.

"All mine," I admitted. "I've been an absolute rotter."

"So you have," she readily agreed. "Now make amends."

"Dinner tomorrow night?"

"Can't do it," she said promptly. "Lady Cynthia is having a sit-down for twelve, and I've got to honcho the whole thing."

"How come I wasn't invited?"

"They're all local pols. Want to join the party?"

"No, thank you," I said hastily.

Connie is employed as social secretary to Lady Cynthia Horowitz, possibly the wealthiest of our many moneyed chatelaines. Lady C also holds the Palm Beach record for ex-husbands: six. She's a shrewd operator, a marvelous hostess and a demanding employer. I'm glad she considers me a friend. Her enemies usually end up whimpering.

"How about lunch?" I suggested. "Noon at the Pelican."

Connie considered a moment. "Yes," she said, "I think I can manage it. Wear your puce beret; that always puts me in a hysterical mood. What have you been up to, lad?"

"Nothing," I said. "Life has been bo-*riiing*."

"Not casting a covetous eye about for any available dollies?"

"Not a dolly in sight," I assured her. "I've really been behaving myself."

"You better," she said menacingly. "You know my spies are everywhere."

That was an unpleasant truth.

"See you at noon tomorrow," I said lightly, and we hung up after an exchange of telephonic kisses—energetic sounds that sometimes leave a bit of spittle on the mouthpiece.

When I told Connie there was no temptation of the female persuasion on the horizon, I did not prevaricate. But little did I know of the events that were to ensue from that doomed evening. I had been guilty of three grossly mistaken assumptions in less than two hours—a sad performance even by yrs. truly.

I overslept the next morning, as usual, and awoke to a world of damp gloom. Squalls were gusting in from the sea, and the sky appeared to be swaddled in disposable diapers. I was tempted to crawl back into the sack but stoutly resisted. There were deeds to be done, I told myself, and worlds to conquer.

By the time I clattered downstairs to the kitchen (not forgetting my puce beret), the house seemed deserted and I breakfasted alone. A search of the fridge provided a glass of cranberry juice, an English muffin sandwich containing boneless Portuguese sardines with a dab of Dijon, and two cups of instant black coffee.

Invigorated, I dashed out to our three-car garage and put the lid on my chariot. Then I started driving through a rain that was not vicious but vengeful. I mean, it was steady, resolute, and seemed likely to last forever. Even Sunny Florida has days like that. Tourists stay in their motel rooms, curse, drink beer, and watch television talk shows until their eyes glaze over.

But I was not deterred by the inclement weather, being determined to accomplish all the important tasks I had planned for that day. My first stop was at the salon ("Hair Apparent") of Herman Pincus, where I received a light trim, scissors on the side, nothing off the top. We discussed a possible cure for a limited but definite tonsure that had appeared on my occiput. The bare spot, no larger than a silver dollar, struck terror to my heart, and I had visions of street urchins yelling, "Hey, baldy!"

But Herman assured me a hot oil massage of the affected area would help. So I endured that, wondering if a very small, circular rug might be a better answer for my affliction. Something like replacing a divot, y'see.

My second stop was at a gentlemen's boutique on Worth Avenue, where I purchase most of my threads. I was looking for any new hats that might be available since I have an irrational love of headgear. To my delight I was able to purchase a visored Greek captain's cap woven of straw. It was definitely rakish, added a certain je ne sais quoi to the McNally phiz and, best of all, concealed that damnable loss of hair. I was convinced it signified the looming end of youth, romance, and perhaps even sexual prowess. (All is vanity, the Good Book saith, and I agreeith.)

It was then time to buzz out to the Pelican Club to meet Connie Garcia for lunch. I was a bit early, the place was almost empty because of the downpour, and I was able to sit at the deserted bar and discuss with Mr. Pettibone what I might have to chase my temporary melancholia. He suggested a brandy stinger, but I thought that a mite heavy for noontime refreshment. We settled for a Salty Dog, a lighter potion but rejuvenating.

The reason I have described my morning's activities in such explicit detail is to give you a reasonably accurate account of an average day in the life of a relatively young Palm Beach layabout—at least *this* layabout. I freely confess it was a life of carefree idleness. My only excuse is that at the time I did not think myself engaged in any serious discreet inquiries. In other words, I faced no energizing challenge. Before the day ended I was disabused of that notion.

When Connie appeared it was immediately obvious the miserable day had not crushed *her* spirits. She was her usual bouncy, ebullient self and danced toward me as if the sun were shining and the future unlimited. I know it may sound sexist, but I cannot refrain from describing Connie as dishy. The fact that I am continually unfaithful to her only proves that when it comes to a contest between a man's brain and his glands, hormones are the inevitable winner. It's sad but it's something males must learn to live with.

She was wearing stonewashed denim jeans and vest with a pink T-shirt blessedly free of any legend. Her long black hair swung free, and if it was rain-spangled it was all the more attractive for that. She exuded a healthy physical vigor, and her "What, me worry?" grin would have brought a smile to the face of a moody tyrannosaur.

"Hello, bubba," she caroled, giving me an air kiss.

"Bubba?!" I said, outraged. "Since when have I been a bubba?"

She giggled. "I just wanted to yank your chain. Hey, let's eat; I'm famished and don't have much time."

There was only one other couple in the dining room, so Connie and I were able to sit at our favorite corner table. Priscilla came bopping over to take our order while snapping her fingers. Pris is the only waitress I know who wears a Walkman while working.

We ordered Leroy's special hamburgers, which have no ham, of course, but are a mixture of ground beef, veal, and pork. He also adds other ingredients when inspired by his culinary muse. On that day I believe it was curry powder. Very nice. We also had a basket of thick chips and shared a platter of cherry tomatoes and sliced cukes. Coors Light for Connie and a Heineken for me. It was a delectable lunch as lunches go, and as lunches go, it went—rapidly.

Connie brought me up-to-date on the most recent excesses of Lady Cynthia, including a proposal to issue ID cards to all the bona fide residents of Palm Beach.

"Wouldn't a tattooed number be more effective?" I suggested. "Is the woman totally insane?"

"Not totally, but she's getting there. And what have you been up to, hon?"

"Zilch."

"No discreet inquiries?"

I want to be honest—well, I don't *want* to be, but I must—and I confess that since the meeting with Sunny Fogarty I hadn't given a fraction of a thought to the doings at the Whitcomb Funeral Homes. It seemed ridiculous to investigate a business simply because it was showing a handsome profit. But idly, for no other reason than to make conversation, I asked Connie:

"Ever hear of the Whitcombs?"

"The burying people?"

I nodded.

"Sure, I've heard of them," she said. "Oliver and Mitzi Whitcomb. Socially active—and I mean *very*. You might even call them swingers."

"Oh?" I said, beginning to get interested. "And where do they swing?"

"Here, there, and everywhere. They throw some wild parties."

"In Palm Beach?"

"Boca. But I understand they also have a villa on the Costa del Sol and a condo in Saint Thomas."

"Sweet," I said. "Shows what one can reap from planting people. Do Oliver and Mitzi have children?"

"Nope," Connie said. "Swingers are too busy to breed. Why this sudden interest in the Whitcombs?"

"New clients," I said casually. "I'm just trying to learn more about them."

She stared at me coldly. "I hope that's all it is. I wouldn't care to discover you've been consorting with Mitzi Whitcomb."

"My dear Consuela," I said loftily, "I keep my personal relations with clients to an absolute minimum. It's a matter of professional ethics."

"Son," she said, "you've got more crap than a Christmas goose."

"Zounds!" I exclaimed. "How quickly you've picked up the elegant idioms of your adopted country."

"Oh, stuff it," she said. "Listen, thanks for the feed, but I've got to run."

I signed the tab at the bar and we went out to the parking area. And there, standing in the drizzle, I donned my puce beret. As expected, Connie drove away laughing hysterically. It doesn't take much to make her happy.

I tooled back to the McNally Building on Royal Palm Way. It is a starkly modern edifice of glass and stainless steel. Not at all to my father's taste, I assure you, but the architect convinced him the headquarters of McNally & Son must make a "statement," so mein Vater went along with the express understanding that his private office would be paneled in oak, with leather furniture, an antique rolltop desk, and other solid (and rather gloomy) trappings that would have pleased Oliver Wendell Holmes.

I parked in our underground garage and sat there a moment, thinking of what Connie had told me about the sociable younger Whitcombs. Hardly earthshaking, I concluded, but it was a bit unsettling to learn that the CEO of funeral homes and his wife were swingers. I mean, one does expect somber decorum from people in that profession—not so?

But perhaps my moral arteries are hardening and I'm becoming a young Savonarola.

4

▲

I rode the automatic elevator to my fourth-floor cubicle. It would be gross exaggeration to call it an office. I am not suggesting it was so cramped that you had to enter sideways, but I always thought of it as a vertical coffin and spent as little time entombed as possible. I do believe my liege consigned me to that windowless cubby to forestall accusations of nepotism. If so, he succeeded brilliantly. Fellow employees at McNally & Son referred to my sanctum as "Archy's locker."

I found on my desk a large, bulky package bearing no return address other than the messenger service that had delivered it. My first reaction was that it might be a bomb sent by an enraged husband. But I discounted that possibility although I removed the wrapping rather gingerly.

Within was a handwritten note (in an artful cursive) from Sunny Fogarty. It stated merely that enclosed was the computer printout I had requested, naming the cemeteries to which the Whitcomb Funeral Homes had sent their "customers" for burial during the past six months. Ms. Fogarty also included her address (West Palm Beach) and phone number. She suggested it would be best, if I had further questions or wished to impart information, to contact her at home rather than her Whitcomb office. A very careful lady.

I was looking at the stack of computer bumf with some dismay when my phone rang. It was the would-be Philip Marlowe.

"Greetings, old sport," chirped Binky Watrous. "I'm ready to go to work."

"What happened to your golf game?"

"Washed out," he said. "I'm ready, willing, and able. When do we start?"

"Immediately," I said, eyeing the opened package on my desk. "Come over to my office."

"On my way," he said happily. "Half an hour at the most."

I used the time to phone Lolly Spindrift. He is a gossip columnist (the three-dot variety) at one of our local rags, and his jazzy comments on past, present, and future scandals are read and enjoyed by most of the literate haut monde and hoi polloi of Palm Beach County.

Lolly and I have a mutually beneficial working relationship, a quid pro quo that profits both of us. Occasionally I feed him exclusive items from current discreet inquiries, but nothing, I assure you, that would imperil a client's reputation. In return, the schlockenspieler serves as a database of local rumors and tittle-tattle. He simply knows everything that has gone on, is going on, and will go on in our hermetic social world.

"Hi, darling," he said in his flutey voice. "What have you got for me?"

"Come off it, Lol," I said. "After those tips I gave you on the Forsythe affair, you owe me."

"Very well," he said. "A clear case of noblesse oblige. What do you want, luv?"

"Oliver and Mitzi Whitcomb," I said. "Know anything about them?"

I could almost hear him rolling his eyes. "Do I ever! But why would you be interested in the happy grave diggers?"

"In due time, Lol," I said patiently. "In due time you'll be the first to hear. Now what have you got?"

"Wild ones," he said promptly. "Apparently inexhaustible funds. Chronic party-goers and party-givers. And some of the people they party with are, shall we say, on the demimonde side. A very curious couple. It isn't what I'd call a working marriage, sweetie. They both tomcat around like maniacs, obviously with each other's permission if not approval. I've always thought there's something dreadful and fascinating going on there, but I've never been able to nail them without fear of libel. Keep me informed, dear."

"Will do," I promised and hung up.

I lighted a cigarette while awaiting Binky's arrival. What Lolly had told me only confirmed and sharpened what Connie Garcia had revealed. Of course I had no conception of what the lifestyle of Oliver and Mitzi had to do with the unexplained profits of the Whitcomb Funeral Homes. But I suffer from a bloated curiosity, almost as enlarged as my liver, and it seemed to me further discreet inquiries about the "curious couple" were warranted.

Binky Watrous showed up in a blazer that would have been the envy of Emmett Kelly. He had seen my office before and was not shocked by my teensy-weensy professional crypt. First-time visitors are sometimes stunned speechless. My temporary man Friday flopped into the folding steel chair alongside my desk and helped himself to one of my English Ovals. He gestured toward the stack of computer printout.

"What's that?" he asked.

"That, son," I said, "is the start of a new investigation. It records the names and addresses of cemeteries to which the Whitcomb Funeral Homes have delivered their dear departed over the last six months. You and I must go through this encyclopedia of mortality and compile lists of the cemeteries involved and the number of deceased each of them accommodated."

Binky looked at me with something like horror. "You jest?" he said hopefully.

"I do not jest," I said firmly.

"Archy," he said plaintively, "don't you have anything more exciting for me to do? You know—interrogating predatory blonds, shoot-outs, bloodbaths—that sort of thing."

"Binky," I said at my avuncular best, "you have a totally mistaken concept of what the detective business is all about. It's ninety percent routine, old bean: dull, dull, dull routine. Now either you submit your resignation and endure the wrath of the Duchess or you get to work instanter."

He sighed. "Oh, very well," he said, "I'll do it. Under protest, you understand. Do you have a pencil? And paper?"

I supplied the needed and, after dividing the computer printout into two approximately equal piles, we both got busy. Binky worked in silence for about fifteen minutes. Occasionally he licked the point of his pencil—a despicable habit. Finally he looked up at me in total bewilderment.

"Archy," he said, "why are we doing this?"

"I thought you'd never ask," I said. "We're doing it because the Whitcomb Funeral Homes are making too much money."

He stared at me with that dopey look he always gets when

confronting anything more profound than *Abbott and Costello Meet Frankenstein.*

"Oh," he said.

We continued our donkeywork and finished almost simultaneously. Binky shoved his notes across the desk to me. His handwriting was unexpectedly small, neat, and quite legible. Due to his long experience in signing bar tabs, no doubt. I compared his pages with mine and saw something interesting. I handed the two lists to my new subaltern.

"Take a look," I said. "See if you spot anything."

He studied our jottings with a worried frown. Then, to my pleased surprise, he caught it.

"Hey," he said, "a lot of these stiffs are being shipped north for burial."

"You've got it," I said approvingly. "Of course South Florida has a huge retiree population, and I suppose many of them want to be planted in family plots in their hometowns. But it appears that Whitcomb is handling an inordinate number of out-of-state shipments."

Binky took another look at our computations. "Sure," he said. "And the number is increasing every month. That's crazy."

"Let me see," I said and read over our lists again.

Binky was correct. But then I saw something else. The majority of human remains being sent out of Florida by Whitcomb were airlifted to New York, Boston, and Chicago. The computer printout I had received did not state who was receiving these gift packages at LaGuardia, Logan, and O'Hare.

Binky and I lighted cigarettes and stared at the smoke-stained ceiling tiles.

"You know, Archy," he said, "it's sad. I mean, old geezers retire and come down here to spend their last years in the sunshine. But when they croak, they want to go home. Don't you think that's sad?"

"No," I said, "I don't. Our transplanted oldsters are survivors. More power to them. And when they finally shuffle off, they want their final resting place to be Buffalo, Peoria, Walla Walla, or wherever. It's their prerogative, and who are we to deny their last wishes. That's not what bothers me; it's the enormous number of deceased Whitcomb seems to be exporting. Don't you find that intriguing?"

Binky shrugged. "I'd rather not think about it. Too depressing, old sport. Listen, I think I've done enough hard labor for one day. May I go home now?"

I glanced at my watch. "Almost two hours," I commented. "Well, I suppose I must introduce you to the work ethic slowly and gradually. Sure, take off. Do you plan to be home this evening?"

"I might," he said cautiously.

"Try," I said. "It's possible that I may phone you to continue your education as a detective."

"More of this stuff about people being buried? I'm not keen about it, Archy. Puts a damper on the Watrous spirits—you know?"

"Where do you want to be buried, Binky?"

"On the Côte d'Azur. Under three inches of sand."

And on that lighthearted note he departed. I cleaned up my corral, bundled the printout and the notes Binky and I had made into the original wrapping, and set out for home. I was pleased with my batman's performance. True, he had only slaved two hours at his chosen profession, but he had exhibited enough wit to catch that business of shipping caskets up north. That was a plus, I thought. And somewhat of a shock. Like discovering Mortimer Snerd could explain the Pythagorean theorem.

The weather was still growly, the sea churning, and so I skipped my late afternoon ocean swim. Instead, I went directly to my quarters, plunked down behind the battered desk, and opened my journal to a fresh page.

I keep a record, y'see, of all my discreet inquiries and try to make daily entries while a case is under way. It serves as a jog to my memory, and sometimes a written account of observations, conversations, and events reveals a hidden pattern I might otherwise have missed.

Also, my journal is a sourcebook for the narratives I pen and ensures accuracy. You didn't think I'm making up all this stuff, did you?

I made notes on what had transpired during the first meeting with Sunny Fogarty, what I had learned of the proclivities of Oliver and Mitzi Whitcomb, and what Binky and I had discovered: the perplexing number of defuncts that Whitcomb Funeral Homes were profitably putting aboard airliners for the final trip home.

I finished my scribbling in time to dress for the family cocktail hour, a rigorously observed daily ceremonial of the McNallys. We gather in the second-floor sitting room, father stirs a jug of gin martinis (traditional formula), and we each have one plus a dividend. Then we descend to dinner. If that sounds unbearably Waspish, let me remind you that my paternal grandfather was a burlesque comic, and we are merely obeying the American dictum: Onward and upward. Of course it was dramaturgy. And whose life is not?

After dinner, I rose from the table, returned to my digs, and phoned Sunny Fogarty.

After an exchange of greeting, I said, "I trust I'm not disturbing you."

"Not at all."

"I was hoping I might see you this evening. It concerns the

material you sent to my office. Probably a minor matter but I'd like to get it cleared up. Could you spare me, say, half an hour?"

"Of course," she said.

"Thank you," I said. "Miss Fogarty, would it—"

"You can call me Sunny if you'd like," she interrupted.

"I'd like," I told her. "And I'm Archy. Sunny, would you object if I brought along my assistant, a very personable and competent chap?"

Long pause. "No," she said finally, "I have no objection."

"Excellent," I said. "We'll be at your place within an hour."

I hung up and called Binky Watrous. "What are you doing?" I asked him.

"Just finished dinner," he reported. "You know, Archy, I hate Brussels sprouts."

"Who doesn't?" I said. "Listen, lad, I want you to join me in an hour's time to continue our investigation by interviewing one of the principals."

He groaned. "That business of out-of-state burials?"

"Exactly."

"Do I really have to be there?" he said, wounded. "I rented a tape of 'The Curse of the Cat People' and I was looking forward to—"

"Binky!" I said sharply. "You want to be the new Sam Spade, don't you? Now go get a piece of paper, lick a pencil, and I'll give you the address."

We synchronized watches and agreed to meet at Sunny Fogarty's home at nine-thirty.

"If you arrive before I do," I warned, "don't you dare enter before I show up."

"Wouldn't think of it," he said.

"And when we have our conversation with the lady, I want

you to let me carry the ball. You say nothing unless you're asked a direct question. Is that understood?"

"Absolutely, boss," Binky said. "I shall be nothing more than a flea on the wall."

I was about to remind him that the expression was "a fly on the wall." But then I reflected he probably had it right.

5

Traffic was unexpectedly heavy that night, and by the time I got across the Royal Park Bridge to West Palm Beach I knew I was running late. Also, I had a bit of trouble finding Sunny Fogarty's home. It turned out to be a rather posh condo high-rise off Olive Avenue, almost directly across from Connie Garcia's apartment on Lake Worth. If that had any significance I didn't want to think about it.

I pulled into the guest parking area, disembarked, and looked about for Binky's heap. And there it was. My Dr. Watson drives a 1970 Mercedes Benz 280 SE Cabriolet. It had been beautifully restored when he bought it, but the lunkhead hadn't cosseted it. It was dented, rusted, had a passenger door that didn't quite latch, and generally presented an appearance of sad dilapidation. The vandalism wasn't deliberate, you understand—just an example of Binky's breezy treatment of all his possessions. He wears a gold Rolex that stopped four years ago.

What rattled my cage at the moment was that the Mercedes was unoccupied. That probably meant the idiot owner had disregarded my firm instructions and had barged in on Sunny Fogarty instead of awaiting my arrival. Uttering a mild oath, I hurried to the entrance and found an exterior security system requesting guests to dial a three-digit number listed on a directory, to speak to and be admitted by the residents.

I punched out the number for Sunny's apartment. She answered almost immediately.

"Archy McNally," I said. "May I come up?"

"Of course," she said. "Your assistant is already here."

"Sorry about that."

"No need to apologize. He's entertaining me with birdcalls."

I quailed. Rather fitting, don'cha think?

She buzzed me in, and I rode an art deco elevator to the sixth floor.

The living room of Sunny's apartment was elegant without being lavish. I had no idea of her annual salary or net worth, but she had mentioned the expense of keeping an ailing mother in a nursing home. Still, she drove a new car and apparently owned this charming condo that bespoke moneyed ease. It was enough to give one pause. If not you, then certainly me.

Señor Watrous, wearing his hellish blazer, was sprawled on a couch upholstered in bottle-green velvet. I glared at him and received a sappy grin in response. I turned to our hostess.

"Sunny," I said, "I see you've already met my aide-de-camp. Light on the aid and heavy on the camp."

She smiled. "I think Binky is very talented. May I offer you gentlemen a drink?"

"Oh, don't go to any—" I started, but Binky piped up.

"I'd like something," he said. "How about a vodka rocks? Do you have the makings?"

"I do," she said. "The same for you, Archy?"

I nodded.

"That makes three of us. It'll just take a minute."

She went out to the kitchen, and I whirled on Binky. "Behave yourself," I admonished. "And try to keep your big, fat mouth shut. You promised."

"Right," he said. "Positively. I shall provide nothing but attentive silence."

"That's wise," I said. "Unless you wish to confess to the Duchess that you have been summarily dismissed after one day of unpaid employment."

Sunny returned with a bamboo tray of three handsome crystal old-fashioned glasses containing our vodka rocks. She had put a wedge of fresh lime in each. Much appreciated. She served us, then sat in a facing barrel chair covered in a cheerful chintz.

"Cheers," she said, raising her glass.

Binky hoisted his. "Here's to our wives and sweethearts," he said. "May they never meet."

I could have killed him, but Ms. Fogarty laughed. I vowed to keep my anger in check until we left. Then I intended to flay the goof alive. What a cheeky rascal he was!

"Sunny," I said, "thank you for seeing us on such short notice. But after Binky and I reviewed the computer printout you provided, we found something that puzzles us."

She leaned forward, elbows on knees. "Oh?" she said. "And what is that?"

She was wearing loosely fitted jeans of white denim with leather sandals, and an oversized man's shirt appliquéd with golden stars, this gauzy fabric suggesting an impressive figure. I shall say no more on the subject lest I be accused of indelicacy.

"There seems to be an unusual number of deceased sent up north for burial," I said. "How do you account for that?"

She accepted my direct question calmly. "Archy, all the funeral homes in South Florida do the same thing. So many of the elderly retired are down here, you know. I can't recall the exact figures, but last year about four thousand dead were shipped from Fort Lauderdale alone. That's more than ten a day. And for the entire State of Florida, more than twenty-five thousand deceased are exported for burial, most of them airlifted. That amounts to almost twenty percent of Florida's total death toll."

"Remarkable," I commented.

"Downputting," Binky said. "Definitely downputting."

I ignored him. "Sunny, how many out-of-state shipments would you estimate Whitcomb Funeral Homes makes annually?"

She thought a moment. "Oh, I'd guess about three hundred a year. Perhaps a bit more."

"In other words, one a day on average would be a generous estimate. Is that correct?"

"Oh yes, very generous. I doubt if we do that much."

Binky and I looked at each other.

"Sunny," I said softly, "According to the computer records you furnished, during the past six months Whitcomb Funeral Homes have shipped out almost five hundred dead."

She gave every indication of being astonished. "I can't believe that!" she cried.

"It's true," I said, "if the information you gave us is accurate. You may check it yourself if you doubt it."

"I simply can't believe it," she repeated and took a hurried slug of her vodka.

"In addition," I went on, "the overwhelming majority of those shipments went to three cities: New York, Boston, and Chicago. Can you offer any explanation for that? It does seem odd."

She shook her head without disturbing a hair of that glossy helmet of russet. "I can't explain it," she said. "Are you suggesting that our rise in income is due to a huge increase in the number of out-of-state burials we're handling?"

"It's possible," I said.

"Incredible," she said. "I just can't believe it."

I thought the lady was lying—and amateurishly at that. It wasn't only the thrice repeated "I can't believe it" that alerted me; it was her manner, expressions, and her intense reactions to what I had told her. Too dramatic by half, and she hadn't the histrionic talent to make her passion believable.

Trust my judgment on this, since I am a consummate liar myself. I knew Ananias. Ananias was a friend of mine. And believe me, Sunny Fogarty was no Ananias.

"Archy," she said, "what do you think we should do next? I just can't understand that volume of out-of-state burials."

"Hey!" my acolyte said brightly. "I think I've got it! Maybe there's a serial killer on the loose knocking off scads of people."

"All of whom come from New York, Boston, and Chicago," I said disdainfully. "Binky, Sunny has already informed my father and me that there has been no unusual rise in Florida's mortality rate, and no other funeral homes have had the income increase that Whitcomb has enjoyed."

"Oh," he said.

I turned back to our hostess. "As for what we should do next, I'd like to get the names and addresses of the out-of-state funeral homes or cemeteries to which Whitcomb's shipments were sent."

She stared at me. "Archy, I gave you that. It was all on the computer printout."

"No, ma'am," I said gently, "it wasn't. Names and addresses of Florida cemeteries were noted, but out-of-state shipments were merely listed as being delivered to airports in New York, Boston, and Chicago."

Now she was truly bewildered; there was no falsity in her response. "That's impossible!" she burst out. Her face was suddenly contorted with an emotion I could not quite identify. It was either fury or fear—or a combination of both. "Of course that information is on our computer and it should have been on the printout I sent you."

"It wasn't," I said. "Was it, Binky?"

"Nope," he said. "Just the names of the airports."

I saw in Sunny's hardened eyes an affirmation of my initial instinct that she was not a woman to be trifled with. "I'll find out what happened," she said fiercely. "First thing tomorrow morning."

"If it's missing from the computer," I said, "is it irretrievably lost?"

"No," she said. "It can be restored from the original documents submitted by our funeral directors. A lot of work, but it can be done. I'm more concerned with discovering why it's not computerized as it should have been."

"Please keep me informed," I said. "I'd like to see the names and addresses of assignees in other states as soon as possible. One more thing . . . I think it would help if Binky and I could somehow meet the principals involved. Especially Mr. Horace Whitcomb and his son, Oliver, the chief executive officer, and Oliver's wife, Mitzi."

She looked at me curiously. "How did you know her name is Mitzi?"

"I'm sure I must have read it in the society pages of our local newspapers and magazines," I said without a qualm. "They're very active socially, are they not?"

"Yes," she said shortly. "Very. As for meeting them, that will be no problem. Mr. Horace is having a birthday party for his wife, Sarah, on Tuesday night next week. A black-tie affair. More than a hundred guests are expected. A big buffet, three bars, a band, and dancing. You'll be able to meet all the executive personnel of Whitcomb Funeral Homes. Archy, your parents have already been invited. I'll have invitations sent to both of you."

"Goody," Binky said. "I love huge parties with dancing. Perhaps I'll meet a wondrous lady who can do the turkey trot. As long as no one from Whitcomb follows me about with a tape measure."

"No," Sunny said, smiling, "I don't think that will happen."

I finished my drink, stood up, and motioned to Binky. He rose, obviously reluctantly; he would have been happy to stay for hours, drinking Sunny's booze and schmoozing. We thanked Sunny for her hospitality, and she promised to send me the information I had requested.

In the descending elevator I said to Binky, "A very attractive woman."

"A bit antique," he said. "Too old for me."

"Binky!" I said. "She can't be more than two or three years older than you."

"That's what I mean," he said.

Then my irritation at his behavior that evening faded. I mean, the man was such an utter bubblehead, but if you're going to be a friend of a bubblehead, there's not much point in getting furious because he *is* a bubblehead. That's a bit complicated, but it makes sense, doesn't it?

Outside, we stood a moment in the parking area lighting cigarettes. Mine. Binky never carries coffin nails, claiming he is determined to stop smoking. His pals pay for his firm resolve.

"We're going to that black-tie bash, aren't we?" he asked me.

"Of course."

"Glad to hear it. Things in the detective business are looking up. Archy, do you believe everything Sunny told us tonight?"

"Perhaps not everything," I said cautiously.

"Me neither," he said. "I think she was scamming us—or trying to."

For the second time that day I was shocked by his perspicacity. I wondered if there was a tiny, tiny spark of intelligence in that bowl of lemon Jell-O between his ears.

"Call you tomorrow," I said. "We've got things to do."

"Okay," he said cheerfully, "but not too early. I've got to watch the Cat People tonight so I'll probably sleep in. Make it around noonish—all right?"

I stood there and watched him pull away in his decaying Mercedes, black smoke spewing from the exhaust. Then I climbed into my barouche and headed home.

I slid into bed shortly after midnight, still pondering the events of that hugger-mugger day. Before waltzing with Morpheus I reviewed again everything that occurred and what little I had learned in the curious case of the lucrative funeral homes.

I had an aggravating itch that I was failing to recognize something significant that had happened. But the Z's arrived before I could pinpoint exactly what it was.

6

It sometimes happens that one falls asleep with a problem and awakes with a solution. So it was for me on that Friday morning. I sat on the edge of my bed, and the puzzle that had bedeviled me the previous night suddenly became clear, if not completely resolved.

Question: Why had Sunny Fogarty sought the assistance of McNally & Son in the first place?

She had given us a rather frail excuse for not conducting an in-house investigation on her own: she said she might endanger her job by "poking and prying," and arouse the derision of other employees. After all, who would be silly enough to become concerned because their employer was suddenly making more money?

I might have accepted that if I had not pegged Comptroller Fogarty as an extremely competent executive, a computer maven who kept a sharp eye on Whitcomb's balance sheet and bottom line. I could not possibly believe she had missed the increase of out-of-state burials; it was so obvious that even a couple of computer illiterates had caught it immediately.

Assuming she was aware of what we'd discover before she sent us the printout—and I did so assume—what could be her motive in dumping the mystery into the lap of McNally & Son, her employer's attorneys of record? I could only conclude she had an urgent need for wanting us to investigate rather than the flimsy reasons she had stated.

But what that need might be, the deponent kneweth not. I did know that if something was seriously awry at Whitcomb Funeral Homes, it was doubtful if Sunny herself was involved in any wrongdoing. I mean, since when does a guilty party initiate an inquiry, discreet or otherwise, into his or her own conduct?

After breakfasting on eggs scrambled with chunks of smoked turkey sausage, I phoned Binky Watrous around ten o'clock. I endured his grumbling at being awakened at such an ungodly hour and finally had to cut him short by threatening to tell the Duchess of his distressing lack of ambition. He finally agreed to come to my office in an hour's time.

He was only fifteen minutes late, still yawning, and grasped my packet of English Ovals like an opium smoker reaching for a full pipe. He smoked and listened in silence while I outlined our program for the day.

We were to visit funeral homes in the area and conduct research on exactly how a person who has passed to the Great Beyond is shipped via airliner to the destination of his or her choice, as expressed in his or her will or dictated by close relatives.

"Yuck!" Binky said with a small shudder.

I hope you will not have the same reaction and consider our investigation somewhat macabre. Of course I do not know your attitude toward dying and death. I do know that for many years mine was abject terror.

But then one day at the funeral of a good friend I recalled Aristotle's classic dictum: "A whole is that which has beginning, middle, and end." It is true for a whole life, is it not? That realization has been a great comfort to me, and I hope it may be to you as well.

I explained to Binky that we would canvass funeral homes other than Whitcomb's. Since we were to attend Mr. Horace's party on the following Tuesday, I did not want to run the risk of being recognized by Whitcomb employees, who might question the presence of journalists at the private affair.

"Journalists?" Binky said, puzzled.

"That's what we're going to be today," I told him, "or for as long as it takes. We shall be two writers preparing an article for a national magazine on burial practices in Florida. Do you think you can play the role of a reporter?"

"Of course," he said confidently. "We're looking for a scoop—right?"

I sighed and we started out with two pages torn from the classified telephone directory listing all the local mortuaries.

At this moment I shall not detail the results of our peregrinations, but I promise you will learn them shortly. I do want to mention that although I feared our pavement-pounding might be dreary, it turned out to be unexpectedly fascinating.

We worked all day, pausing only once in mid-afternoon for lunch at a greasery that served French fries limp enough to be bent double. We then continued our labors until 4:30, when we decided we had accomplished enough for one day. We parted company, and I returned home to enjoy a delightful swim in a gently rolling sea just cool enough to give the McNally corpuscles a wake-up call.

Engraved invitations addressed to Binky and me had been delivered, requesting our presence at a celebration to be held on Tuesday evening at the home of Mr. and Mrs. Horace Whitcomb. My father raised one of his brambly eyebrows when being so informed at our family cocktail hour.

"How did you manage that, Archy?" he asked.

"Sunny Fogarty arranged it."

The thicket went up another millimeter. "I hope you intend to dress conservatively," he said.

"Archy always dresses beautifully," mother put in.

"Maddie," the lord of the manor reminded her, "beauty is in the eye of the beholder. But not *this* beholder."

After a ravishing dinner of baked scallops (with braised endives) and a dessert of bread pudding with sabayon sauce, I went upstairs and worked for an hour bringing entries in my journal up to date.

I spent the remainder of the evening planning my weekend and making umpteen phone calls. I lined up a golf game for Saturday afternoon; dinner with Connie at Renato's on Saturday night (playing Benedick to her Beatrice); a tennis match on Sunday afternoon; and a poker joust with a quartet of rapacious cronies on Sunday night. If a whole life really does consist of beginning, middle, and end, I wanted my middle to be as pleasurable as possible. We are all hedonists, but I'm one of the few willing to admit it.

Mirabile dictu, the weekend proved to be as joyous as anticipated. I awoke Monday morning full of p&v and ready for another day of research into the arcane practices of human burial in South Florida. Actually, it was only half a day, for by one o'clock I decided Binky and I had completed the needful. We repaired to the Pelican Club to lunch on barbecued ribs while we compared notes on what we had learned.

If you wish to prepare yourself for this recital, I suggest a sip of schnapps would not be amiss.

The statistics Sunny Fogarty had quoted to us were generally correct: approximately 25,000 dead are exported from Florida each year, most of them to contiguous states but some as far afield as Malaysia and Tibet.

South Florida is especially active in this commerce, with about four thousand corpses being shipped annually from Broward County alone. The large population of the elderly retired accounts for that.

Coffins are packed in cartons, embalmed bodies airlifted in special crates. All containers are labeled "Human Remains" and "Handle with Extreme Care." That's a comfort, isn't it?

The packaged deceased are delivered to airports in unmarked vans, not hearses. This custom demonstrates a nice sensibility. Can you imagine sitting in first class, waiting for your plane to take off, and you glance out the window and see a hearse pull up alongside? "Stewardess, I've changed my mind; I think I'll take the bus."

According to our calculations, Monsieur Watrous and I reckoned that almost every airliner departing from South Florida carried at least one corpus in the cargo bay. As Binky remarked, "That's one passenger who won't worry about a crash."

Of course there was an added expenditure for all this. Funeral homes charged a hefty sum, sometimes two thousand dollars, to prepare a loved one for shipment and delivery to the airport. Airlines billed about three hundred dollars for a domestic destination and at least five times that for one overseas.

A final note: Some religions forbid embalming. In that case, the body is placed in a metal container packed with ice before being airlifted. Remember that before you ask the flight attendant for your third Scotch on the rocks.

After discussing all this wonderful stuff, Binky and I fell silent and stared at each other.

"What does it all mean?" he asked finally.

"It means," I said, "that Whitcomb Funeral Homes is making a great deal of money by shipping an amazing number of dead out of Florida to points west, north, and east."

"Sure, Archy," he agreed. "We knew that before we started. But where are they getting all the inhabitants of those crates?"

I said, "Who knows what evil lurks in the hearts of living men?"

"Hey," Binky said, "you're not The Shadow."

"True, but I'm a reasonable facsimile thereof. Do you have any ideas, wild or otherwise?"

He shook his head. "Haven't the slightest, old boy."

"Nor do I," I admitted. "And there's no point in worrying about it until we get more information from Sunny Fogarty. Let's go home."

"Banzai!" he cried. "There's a rerun of 'Invasion of the Body Snatchers' on the tube at four o'clock. I don't want to miss it."

"Very fitting," I said approvingly. "Maybe it'll yield a clue to what's going on at Whitcomb."

That evening I brooded in my den, staring at the journal notes I had jotted. The entire mishmash seemed to me *Much Ado About Nothing.* But then, I reflected, if there was chicanery afoot, it might be *As You Like It* to the perpetrator. In either case, it was a comedy, was it not?

I recalled the pater's admonition to go through the motions but not spend too much time on the Whitcomb affair. I had already disobeyed him and knew I would continue. I was hooked by the puzzle.

Sgt. Al Rogoff of the Palm Beach Police Department—my friend and sometimes collaborator—constantly complains that I overuse the adjective "intriguing." I suppose I do, but I cannot think of a better word to describe Whitcomb's increased revenue from the departed and deported.

If the truth be told—a painful necessity—I am a nosy bloke. I do like to stick my schnozz in other people's business and learn what's going on. It's a grievous sin, I admit, but more fun than Chinese checkers and also, on occasion, a good deal more dangerous.

Nothing of any great consequence occurred on Tuesday morning except that I had blueberry pancakes for breakfast. The afternoon was similarly uneventful. I did have my quadriga washed and its gullet filled. But other than that, the day was without excitement.

I finished my two-mile wallow in a placid sea and returned home to dress for the Whitcomb party. It was still warmish in South Florida and I decided on a white dinner jacket: a costume my father insists makes me look like the headwaiter at a Miami stone crab restaurant.

We all gathered for a cocktail before setting out for the bash. Hizzoner was wearing his rather rusty black tuxedo with a pleated white shirt (wing collar) and onyx studs. Of course his cummerbund and tie were black, and the bow was hand-tied. He considered pretied bows a portent of the decline of Western Civilization.

I must confess he looked rather regal in his formal attire, not at all like a mustachioed penguin. But mother was the star. She was absolutely smashing in a long brocaded gown and carried an aqua satin minaudière. Her white curls were a halo and she wore a three-strand choker of pink pearls. Momsy has a natural high color and that evening she positively glowed: a teenager ready for the prom.

We emptied the martini pitcher and trooped downstairs,

laughing for no particular reason. Ursi and Jamie Olson came from the kitchen to tell us how magnificent we all looked and to wish us a wonderful evening.

Father drove his big Lexus with mother sitting alongside him. I followed in my flaming scooter, feeling like the skipper of a dinghy trailing the QE2. I think we were all stimulated by the prospect of attending a lavish and crowded revel. The social season in Palm Beach was just getting under way. This was the first big party and offered an opportunity to shed the doldrums of a too long and too hot summer.

I know I was convinced it was going to be a glorious rollick during which I would meet The Girl of My Dreams (Clara Bow) and be universally admired for my skill in executing the Charleston. I would forget about whatever nonsense was transpiring at Whitcomb Funeral Homes and spend a rompish night obeying Herrick's command: "Gather ye rosebuds while ye may." That was my firm intention.

One never knows, do one?

7

The home of Sarah and Horace, the senior Whitcombs, was a palazzo on North Lake Way. It was an aging edifice somewhat lacking in charm. The most amazing feature was the vegetation. I mean, the lot had to be almost two acres and looked like an arboretum with hedges fifteen feet high. You could hardly *see* the house until you were standing at the front door.

Valet parking had been provided; we surrendered our vehicles and stepped up to a portico topped by a wrought-iron balcony. Awaiting my arrival was Signore Binky Watrous, the tyro Mike Hammer. I blinked when I saw his costume.

The idiot was sockless and wearing white mocs, white trousers, and a white shirt with a cascade of ruffles. Worse, his jacket, cummerbund, and bow tie were red checkered linen, looking as if they had been made from the tablecloth of a cheap Neapolitan restaurant. He should have been carrying an empty Chianti bottle wrapped in raffia with a candle stub stuck in its mouth.

"Fetching?" he asked, smoothing the hideously wide lapels.

"I wish someone would," I said. "Binky, where did you get that monstrosity?"

"I had it designed especially for me."

"By whom—the ghost of Liberace? Here is your invitation. I suggest you precede me and for the remainder of the evening let's pretend we are total strangers to each other."

"You want me to ask questions?" he said eagerly. "You know, interrogate people? The old third degree."

"By all means," I said. "If you can find anyone willing to be seen conversing with Bozo the Clown."

My parents had already entered. Binky went inside and I waited a few moments, mortified by the appearance of my henchman. He looked as if he'd be right at home on the stage of the Grand Ole Opry—playing a kazoo no doubt.

I walked through the open front door and surrendered my invitation to a uniformed flunky. I stood a moment to look about and then had to step out of the way as more guests continued to arrive. But the interior of that home was worth close inspection.

If the exterior had been charmless, the inside was something else again. Warm elegance is the only way I can describe it. High ceilings, museum-quality parquet floors, walls papered in an antique trompe l'oeil pattern, furnishings at once attractive and selected for comfort. There were some odd decorative touches that caught the eye: a marvelous model of the first motorcar (an 1886 Benz) in a glass display case; a mysterious Cycladic female figurine; a rattan fireplace screen mimicking a peacock's tail.

There were at least a dozen guests waiting to be received. I took my place at the end of the line and waited patiently. I had expected to be greeted by Sarah and Horace Whitcomb plus son Oliver and daughter-in-law Mitzi. But as the line moved slowly forward I saw that only an oldish gentleman was shaking hands and alongside him, in a wheelchair, was a lady I presumed to be his spouse. There was nothing doddery about either. They spoke animatedly, laughed frequently, and obviously were enlivened by their roles as hosts for this crowded jollification.

"Horace Whitcomb," he said, smiling and holding out a sinewy hand. "Thank you for coming."

"Thank you for having me, sir," I said, shaking that hard paw. "I'm Archy McNally, Prescott's son."

"Of course! So nice to meet you."

"The honor is mine," I said. "You have a lovely home, Mr. Whitcomb."

He gave me a wry-crisp grin. "It's really an ugly heap, isn't it? My father tore a photo from a magazine and had the architect imitate it."

"The exterior may be a bit awkward," I admitted, "but the interior is a sheer delight."

He was obviously pleased, a tall and slender man with the ramrod posture of a drill instructor. His fine hair was silvered and pale blue eyes were startling against suntanned skin. He had a scimitar nose and there was a network of laugh lines at the corners of his wide mouth. A genial patrician. And something majestic about him.

"That's very kind of you," he said. "Perhaps you and I might have a chat later."

"I'd like that, sir."

"Meanwhile I want you to meet my dear wife, Sarah, the lady responsible for the sheer delight you mentioned."

He introduced us and went back to greeting arriving guests. I leaned over the wheelchair and gently pressed the frail hand offered me.

"How good of you to come," she said in a wispy voice.

"My pleasure, ma'am," I said. "I understand it's your birthday."

She nodded. "But I'm not counting," she cautioned.

"I apologize for not bringing a gift."

"Your presence is gift enough," she said.

I suppose she had uttered that line fifty times during the evening, but I still thought it an extraordinarily gracious thing to say.

She seemed shrunken. The skin of her bare forearms was wrinkled as if she had once weighed many pounds more but the flesh had simply sloughed away. There was a waxen pallor beneath her makeup, and she wore a multicolored turban that covered her entire skull. I suspected she was undergoing chemotherapy and had lost her hair. But her spirit was undaunted.

"Are you married?" she asked me.

"No, ma'am, I am not."

"Do you want to be?"

"No, ma'am, I do not."

She laughed and reached up to pat my arm. "I don't blame you one damned bit," she said. "Well, you're a handsome devil. Now go mingle and break a few hearts."

"Before I do that," I said, "I must tell you how much I admire the decor of your home. It's just splendid."

"Yes," she said softly, "it *is* beautiful, isn't it? This home has been my passion. I wanted everything to be perfect."

"You've succeeded brilliantly," I assured her.

She looked longingly at the vast entrance hall, through the lofty archway to the living room. She seemed to be seeing things I had not yet viewed, things no one would ever see and love the way she did.

Her dim eyes glistened. "Thank you," she said huskily. "Thank you so very, very much."

I moved away to explore more of the Whitcomb mansion. There was a grand staircase leading to upper floors, but a velvet rope had been stretched to block use by the evening's guests. I strolled to the enormous living room, pausing occasionally to exchange greetings with friends and acquaintances, kissing a few ladies' hands because I was in a Continental mood. There was a bar set up along one wall, doing a brisk business.

A superb pine-paneled dining room accommodated the buffet boards presided over by the caterer and her crew. What a feast! I shall not detail the viands offered, in deference to calorie-obsessed readers. Well, just one: broiled chicken livers topped with squares of bacon and sharp cheddar.

The enormous dining table was still in place, surrounded by twenty chairs. Additional small tables and folding chairs, obviously rented, had been placed about so guests would not be forced to eat standing while balancing a full plate and a brimming glass. It was in this banquet hall I found the second of the three bars Sunny Fogarty had promised and ordered a double vodka gimlet, believing it would last me twice as long as a single. Silly boy.

Dancing space was provided in a smaller chamber that appeared to be an informal sitting and TV viewing room. Furniture and rugs had been removed, the planked floor waxed, and a trio tootled away in one corner, playing mostly show tunes and old favorites such as "Oh Johnny, Oh Johnny, Oh!" It was here I found my parents at the third bar, looking about amusedly while sipping what seemed to be Perrier with lime slices.

"Mrs. McNally," I said, bowing, "may I have the pleasure of this dance?"

"Let me look at my card," she said, then giggled.

We placed our drinks temporarily on the bar, and father smiled benignly as we went twirling away to the rhythm of "Try a Little Tenderness." Mother is hardly a sylph but remarkably light on her feet, and I think we justly believed ourselves to be the most graceful couple on the floor.

The tune ended, we rejoined the squire at the bar.

"Well done," he said as if delivering a judicial opinion. And then to mother: "The next dance is mine. Unless they play something too fast."

Like "The Surrey with the Fringe on Top"? I wanted to ask—but didn't of course.

I meandered back to the dining room, which I now thought of as Bulimia Heaven. It was beginning to fill with ravenous guests. I was about to join the famished throng at the buffet when I espied Sunny Fogarty standing alone at the bar. I observed her from afar and concluded she was a handsome woman. Not lovely, not beautiful, but *handsome.* There are fine degrees of female attractiveness, you know.

I moved to her side and she looked at me with a tight smile. "Good evening, Archy," she said. "So glad you could make it."

"Wouldn't have missed it for the world. Thank you for the invitations."

"I saw Binky," she said. "Does he always dress like that?"

"Always," I said sadly. "His sartorial sense is gravely retarded. He once wore spats over flip-flops to a beach barbecue."

She laughed—which was a relief for she had seemed tense, almost angry.

"I met Sarah and Horace," I told her. "Lovely people."

"Yes, they are."

"She's quite ill?"

Sunny nodded.

"Cancer?"

She nodded again. "They said it was in remission, but it wasn't."

"I thought her a very brave lady."

"An angel. She's an angel."

I said, "I was surprised that Oliver and his wife weren't also receiving."

Her bitterness returned. "So like them," she said. "So selfish. To be late at his mother's birthday party—that's not forgivable. They arrived just a few minutes ago."

"Perhaps they were unavoidably detained," I suggested.

She looked at me but said nothing.

She was wearing a snazzy tuxedo suit: black satin-lapelled jacket and trousers with side satin stripes. No cummerbund, but she wore a poet shirt of pale pink silk with protruding cuffs of lace. Very debonair. Her only jewelry was a choker of diamonds. They appeared to be of two-carat size at least, and if they were genuine, which I believed they were, it was a costly bauble indeed.

"Sunny," I said, "are you hungry?"

"I could eat," she admitted.

"Suppose you grab us two places at a table and I'll fetch us plates of cholesterol."

"All right," she agreed. "But please make mine finger food; I don't feel like digging into the curried lamb on rice or the beef bourguignonne. While you're gone, can I get you a drink?"

"I have a—" I started and then looked down at my empty glass. "Good Lord," I said, "I had forgotten about the high rate of evaporation in South Florida. Yes, I would appreciate a fresh something. A dry white would be nice if it's available."

Fifteen minutes later we were devouring heaps of the finger foods she had requested. There was an almost infinite variety and I recall fondly the shrimp that had been sautéed in garlic and oil and then chilled. That delight was enough to make me abjure bologna sandwiches for the rest of my life.

"Archy," she said as we nibbled, "will you do me a favor?"

"Of course. Your wish is my command."

She was not amused. "I intend to leave about eleven o'clock," she said. "You stay as long as you like, but would you mind stopping by my place before you go home?"

"No problem."

"There's something important I must discuss with you, and this is not the place to talk about it."

"It concerns the computer printout?"

"Yes," she said.

"Bad?" I asked.

"Very," she said.

8

We finished scarfing (although I could have managed seconds or even thirds) and ordered two more Frascatis at the bar. Carrying our drinks, we began a slow promenade through the crowd of celebrants.

"Sunny," I said, "if you spot Oliver and Mitzi Whitcomb, will you point them out to me, please."

"I'll point them out," she said, "but I won't introduce you."

"Oh? Why not?"

"I don't think that would be smart," she said grimly, leaving me to wonder what on earth she meant.

We looked in at the dance floor and there was Detective Binky Watrous essaying a tango with a rather flashy young woman. The trio was playing "Jealousy," and it was obvious Binky thought himself a reincarnation of Rudolph Valentino. It was an awesome sight and I began laughing.

Sunny permitted herself one soft chuckle. "His partner"—she said—"that's Mitzi."

I took another look. The wife of the CEO of Whitcomb Funeral Homes was a stunner. She wore a tight sheath of silver sequins and her black hair was long enough to sit on. For her to sit on, not you. She was heavily made up and I didn't miss the lip gloss that appeared to be phosphorescent.

I don't wish to be ungentlemanly but there was a flagrant looseness in her dancing as if restraint was foreign to her nature. I confess her sensuousness set the McNally testosterone flowing, but even as I reacted primitively to her physical advertisements I could not help wondering what Horace and Sarah, those aristocrats, thought of their somewhat brassy daughter-in-law.

"Would you care to dance?" I asked Sunny.

"Some other time," she said shortly, and we continued our stroll.

It was in the living room, clamorous with phatic talk, that she stopped me with a hand on my arm. "There's Oliver Whitcomb," she said in a low voice. "At the bar. He's the one wearing a white dinner jacket. He's talking to that heavy man. I don't know who *he* is."

I stared. Oliver was a good-looking chap, no doubt about it, wearing an outfit similar to mine except that his jacket had a shawl collar. I judged him to be about forty, and his fresh complexion suggested he was no stranger to facials. His thick black hair was as glossy as his wife's but artfully coiffed into waves. I wondered who his barber was, knowing it couldn't be Herman Pincus.

"I'll leave you now," Sunny Fogarty said. "Don't forget to stop at my place on your way home."

Then she was gone and I made my way over to the bar. I finished my wine and asked for a cognac. Oliver and the hefty man were close together, speaking quietly; I couldn't catch a word.

"By the way," I said loudly to the barkeep, "I'm looking for Oliver Whitcomb. Have you seen him this evening?"

It was a crude ploy but it worked. Oliver turned to me and flashed absolutely white teeth, so perfect they looked like scrubbed bathroom tiles. The smile was more than cordial. Mr. Charm himself.

"I'm Oliver Whitcomb," he said.

"I've been hoping to meet you," I enthused. "I'm Archy McNally, the son part of McNally and Son, your attorneys."

His handclasp was firm enough but brief.

"Hey," he said, "this is great! You people have been doing a great job."

"We try," I said modestly. "I just wanted to thank you for a magnificent bash."

"Having fun, are you?"

"Loads," I assured him. "And it's only the shank of the evening."

He looked at me with a gaze I can only describe as speculative. "Listen," he said, "why don't you and I do lunch. I have a feeling we have a lot in common."

"Sounds good to me."

"Great!" he said, apparently his favorite adjective. "I'll give you a buzz."

"Fine," I said with what I hoped was a conspiratorial smile. I doubted if he'd ever call, but nothing ventured, nothing gained: an original phrase I just created. I wandered away, gripping my brandy snifter. He hadn't introduced me to his pudgy companion. But there could be an innocent reason for that—or no reason at all.

I had noticed several small, chastely lettered signs posted about: "If you wish to smoke, please step outside to the terrace or dock." And so, in dreadful need to inhale burning tobacco, I looked about for an exit to the terrace. I finally had to stop a passing servitor lugging a bucket of ice, and he pointed the way.

But before I had a chance to befoul the Great Outdoors I came upon a tottering Binky Watrous. His pale eyes were dazed and his checkered bow tie hung askew.

"Binky," I asked anxiously, "are you conscious?"

He gave me a sappy grin. "I'm in love," he said.

I looked at him. What a booby he was! "With Mitzi Whitcomb, no doubt," I said.

He was astonished. "How did you know?"

"A wild guess."

"She gave me her phone number," he said proudly. "She wants to see me again. Archy, I think she's got the hots for my damp white body."

I was about to warn him off, but then I reflected if he was able to form an intimate relationship with the nubile Mitzi he might possibly discover details of the younger Whitcombs' activities that would further our investigation.

"I congratulate you on your good fortune, Binky," I said solemnly. "Keep your ears open. Pillow talk and all that."

I don't believe he grasped what I implied, for he merely shouted, "Party on!" and staggered away in search of the nearest bar.

I found the wide, flagstoned terrace facing Lake Worth, but it was crowded with gabbling guests as intent as I on corroding their lungs. I lighted up and went down a side staircase of old railroad ties to the deepwater dock. I was alone there and could enjoy a brief respite from the brittle chatter.

I would have guessed Mr. Horace Whitcomb owned a fine, woodbodied sloop or something similar. But moored to the dock was an incredible boat: a perfectly restored 1930 Chris-Craft mahogany runabout. It was a 24-footer, a treasured relic of the days when men in white flannels drank Sazeracs and women in middy blouses sipped Orange Blossoms while zipping about offshore waters.

I was admiring the sleek lines of this legendary craft when I sniffed the aroma of a good cigar and turned to find our host. He was holding a lighted cheroot and regarding me with a pleased smile.

"Like her?" he inquired.

"She's a pip!" I said. "Operational?"

"Fully. We used to go out frequently but then my wife became ill and . . ." His voice trailed away.

"Surely your son must enjoy piloting a classic like this."

He took a puff of his cigar. "I think not. My son's taste runs to hydroplanes and Jet Skis. You've met Oliver?"

"Yes, sir. Just a few moments ago."

"And what was your reaction?" he asked unexpectedly.

I was cautious. "I thought him very personable," I said.

"Oh yes, he is that." Horace tossed his half-smoked cigar into the lake, and I heard a faint sizzle. "His mother dotes on him."

I wanted to ask if he also doted on his son, but that would have been an impertinence.

"Tell me, Archy," he said, "do you admire things of the past?"

"Incurably addicted," I confessed. "I'm a nostalgia buff. Two of my favorite comics are Bert Lahr and Ed Wynn, though I never saw either of them perform live."

"I did," he said, "and they were even better than you think. But I was referring to antiques. I collect ship models, mostly sailing men-of-war. I have the *Chesapeake, Serapis, Victory, Constitution,* and several others. They were made by master craftsmen. I thought you might like to see them."

"I would indeed, Mr. Whitcomb. I enjoy reading about old naval battles. Wooden ships and iron men, eh?"

His smile was hard. "Exactly," he said. "Give me a call whenever you'd like to view my collection. And now I must get back to our guests. My wife has already retired and so I shall make the farewells."

"It was a marvelous party, sir," I called after him. "Thank you for having me."

He didn't turn but gave me a wave of his hand in acknowledgment. It seemed obvious he was saddened by his wife's illness. But I also detected an undercurrent of anger that perplexed me.

I smoked another coffin nail, pacing slowly up and down the planked dock, admiring the play of moonlight on the gently rippling surface of the lake. I had many sharp, jagged impressions of that MTV evening but was in too bemused a state to sort them out. I could do that on the morn when, hopefully, I would have slept all befuddlements away and awakened with a clear, concise revelation of the toil and trouble bubbling at Whitcomb's.

I finished my cigarette, drained the last drop of cognac, and went back inside with every intention of leaving immediately and hightailing it to the home of Sunny Fogarty. But there was a short delay.

I attempted to move through the throng of departing guests—all of whom were pausing to pick up their favors: crystal paperweights with a little replica of a Ford Model T encapsulated for gentlemen and, for ladies, a tiny sprig of edelweiss. You may scorn this as kitsch but think of how much more tasteful it was than if the owner of Whitcomb Funeral Homes had handed out miniature caskets suitable for pencils, paper clips, or condoms.

I was about to slip away (I really had no use for a paperweight) when a heavy hand clamped about my left bicep. I turned and faced the chubby gent who had been conversing with Oliver Whitcomb at the bar. He tugged me away from the crowd, his grip still tight on my arm. I finally shook him loose.

"Hey," he said. "Ollie tells me you're a lawyer. Right?"

He was a gloriously rumpled man wearing a wrinkled dinner jacket that looked as if he had been snoozing in it for a fortnight. He wasn't quite obese, but a lot of rare roast beef had gone into that protruding paunch, those meaty shoulders and bulging thighs.

"I'm not an attorney," I told him, trying to be civil, "but my father is. I assist him."

"Yeah?" he said with a wiseacre grin. "Like a gofer, huh?"

I kept my cool; give me credit for that. "No," I said, "not like a gofer. My duties are somewhat more extensive."

"Oh sure," he said. "Just kidding. You got a card? Maybe I can throw some business your way."

I took out my wallet and extracted a card, imagining what my father's reaction would be to a stranger telling him, "Maybe I can throw some business your way."

The fat one examined my card. "Archibald McNally," he said. "What kind of a moniker is that?"

"A serviceable one," I said. "And what is your alias?" He looked at me, startled. "Just kidding," I told him. "Like you were."

"Oh, yeah, sure," he said, and dug a creased business card from his jacket pocket and handed it over.

"Ernest Gorton," I read aloud. "Import-export."

"That's right. But you can call me Ernie."

"Wonderful," I said. "And you may call me Archy. What do you import and export, Ernie?"

"This and that."

"I hope this and that are profitable."

"Sometimes yes and sometimes no," he said. He had twinkly eyes set in a mournful bloodhound face.

"I see your business is located in Miami. That's your home?"

"Yep. You ever been there?"

"Many times."

"Next time you're in town, look me up."

"I certainly shall," I said, thinking never, never, never.

"Maybe you and me can do some business together," he said. "Have a few laughs, make a few bucks."

I had absolutely no idea what he meant and had no desire to find out.

"Nice meeting you, Mr. Gorton," I said.

"Ernie."

"Ah yes—Ernie. Now I've got to dash."

"Love the way you talk," he said. "Real fancy."

"Thank you," I said and fled.

9

Sunny Fogarty greeted me at the door of her condo holding a pilsner of beer. I made a rapid mental calculation of the number and variety of spirituous beverages I had consumed that evening, beginning with the family cocktail hour: gin martini, vodka gimlet, white wine, cognac. I reckoned a beer might push me beyond the point of no return, but then I took solace from the traditional collegiate dictum: "Beer, whiskey: rather risky. Whiskey, beer: have no fear."

Sunny ushered me into her living room, motioned me to an armchair, and brought me a duplicate of her glass of suds.

"It's Budweiser," she informed me. "I have nothing more exotic."

"Bud is fine," I assured her and swilled half my drink to prove it.

"Has the party ended?" she asked.

"It was breaking up as I departed."

"I think it went well, don't you?"

"It went beautifully. I saw no one upchuck, no one was

falling-down drunk, and there were no fights. Ergo, a successful bash. You planned it, didn't you, Sunny?"

She was embarrassed; her gaze slid away. "How did you know?"

"Mrs. Sarah Whitcomb is obviously in no condition to organize a celebration of that magnitude, and I don't believe Mr. Horace has the know-how. And Mitzi and Oliver haven't the talent, time, or the interest in arranging a jamboree like that."

"You're right," she said, "on all counts. You do see things, don't you? Well, I'm happy it went off so well. Did you personally enjoy it?"

"Indeed I did. A very intriguing evening. Binky Watrous has fallen in love with Mitzi Whitcomb."

She gave me a dim smile. "Men usually do."

"Not yours truly," I said stoutly. "I prefer to admire the lady from afar. A strong instinct for self-preservation, I suspect. And Mr. Horace invited me to view his collection of ship models."

She came alive. "Oh, they're incredible! You must see them, Archy."

"I intend to. And I met a curious bloke claiming to be Ernest Gorton. Does the name mean anything to you?"

She shook her head.

"He was talking to Oliver Whitcomb at the bar when you pointed Oliver out to me. They seem to be pals. He referred to Oliver as Ollie."

"Ernest Gorton?" she repeated. "No, I've never heard of him."

"He's from Miami and he's in the import-export business, whatever that may be. Seemed an odd sort to be a close friend of the CEO of funeral homes."

"Mitzi and Oliver have several odd friends," she said tartly. "Let me get you another beer."

"Just one more," I said, "and then I'll be on my way."

She made no reply—which I took for approval. And which only proves how fallible my judgment can be.

She brought my refill, then touched a cushion of the couch on which she was seated. "Sit over here, Archy," she said, and I noted how often her requests sounded like commands. "I have something to tell you, and it will be easier to talk if we don't have so much space between us."

I did as she asked. She had taken off her jacket and kicked away her satin pumps. She looked more relaxed than she had seemed at the party. Her tensity had thawed and her rather schoolmarmish manner vanished. She had softened; that's all I can say. Except that the two top buttons of her poet shirt were undone.

"The last time we spoke about the computer printout," she said, "I told you I could not understand why it did not include the names and addresses of out-of-state funeral homes and cemeteries to which Whitcomb's shipments were made. It was strange; that information is routinely entered on our computer."

"But it wasn't," I said.

She turned sideways to look at me directly. "It *was,* Archy, but it had been erased."

I took a gulp of beer. "You're certain?"

"No doubt about it. I caught it and then called in our computer consultant to verify what I had discovered. He agreed: someone had simply deleted that information from our records."

"Could anyone at Whitcomb's have done it?"

"You need to know a code to access our system. The code is known only by the top three executives—Horace, Oliver, and myself—and by the four department heads and our three chief funeral directors."

"Could a malicious hacker have invaded the system?"

"Of course. That's always a possibility and very difficult if not impossible to prevent. But why would a hacker *want* to delete only those specific items of information?"

"Haven't the slightest," I admitted. "But you did say you'd be able to reconstruct the missing information from the weekly reports of your funeral directors."

"That's correct," she said, "and I'm going to start on that tomorrow. But I wanted you to know that someone made a deliberate and seemingly successful effort to impede the investigation. Archy, I'm now even more certain that something very wrong is happening at Whitcomb's. It may be just dishonest or unethical but it may be criminal, and it's got to be stopped."

"No doubt about it," I agreed. "How soon will you be able to provide me with the missing information?"

She thought a moment. "It shouldn't take longer than two or three days. I'll phone you as soon as I have it."

"Fine. Those names and addresses will provide a good start. Tell me, Sunny, have you informed Mr. Horace of this inquiry and that the computers have been tampered with?"

"I have *not,*" she said explosively, "and I don't intend to. And I forbid you or your father mentioning it to him. Is that understood?"

Overreacting again. I began to wonder if father's and my initial impression had been accurate: this was one squirrelly woman.

"Completely understood," I told her. "You may depend on our discretion."

I finished my second glass of beer (they were only eight ounces per) and started to rise.

Sunny gave me one of her rare sunny smiles. "Must you go?" she said.

Zing! Went the Strings of My Libido.

I set my empty pilsner on an end table and turned back. Then she was not in my arms, I was in hers. She smelled delightful.

"I should tell you," I said, "I don't kiss on the first date."

She cracked up. It was the first time I had seen her laugh with abandon and it was a joy to witness.

"I haven't heard that line since nursery school," she said when she ceased spluttering.

"*Nursery* school?" I said. "I am shocked, *shocked!* I hesitate to think of what went on by the time you got to junior high."

But of course we kissed. And kissed. And kissed. If she had an ulterior motive for coming on to me, and I suspected she had—to insure my loyalty?—I have sufficient male ego to believe what began as a manipulative ploy quickly became a more genuinely passionate experience than she had anticipated.

She was carried away. I was carried away. And we both were carried away right into her bedroom where we disrobed in frantic haste, muttering when buttons were fumbled or zippers snagged.

She owned a body as solid as the figurehead of a Yankee clipper. I don't mean to suggest she could have played noseguard for the Washington Redskins, but there was not an ounce of excess avoirdupois on her carcass. Believe me; I searched.

Our acrobatics became more frenzied, and my last conscious thought was of Binky Watrous attempting the tango with Mitzi Whitcomb. Sunny and I were doing the same thing horizontally rather than vertically. But with infinitely more expertise, I assure you. Then I stopped thinking.

I do recall that at one point during our exertions the bedroom seemed filled with light, really a soft glow. The only way I can account for it is the phenomenon of triboluminescence. Very rare and much to be desired.

I stayed in Sunny's bed until almost 2:00 A.M., during which time we consumed another Budweiser—and each other. What a loverly night that was—a fitting end to an evening of jollity. Such perfect occasions occur all too infrequently and must be sought and treasured. Remember that gem of McNally wisdom the next time someone offers you a beer.

I drove home slowly, hoping my eyelids would not clamp firmly shut before I arrived in the safety of the McNally garage. I made it and stumbled upstairs, undressing as I went, and flopped into bed with a wheeze of content. "Thank you, God," I murmured. A Category Five hurricane could have descended upon the coast of South Florida that night and I swear I would not have been aware of it. I slept the sleep of the undead.

I awoke the following day a sad Budweiser man. Listen, I know it's an ancient pun, but I was not in a creative mode that morning. Physically I felt fine, having had the foresight to pop a couple of Tylenols before collapsing into the sack. But mentally I was totally flummoxed. The Whitcomb case seemed to be growing steadily like some horrid fungus that just keeps getting larger and larger until it devours acres. The Blob That Ate Cleveland.

In addition, I was suffering from an attack of the guilts. My unfaithfulness to Connie Garcia, of course. I had committed a disloyal act and could not deny it. Well, I could to Connie but not to myself. Sighing, I blamed those treacherous genes of mine. I tell you a faulty DNA can really be hell.

I had slept a good eight hours, and by the time I finished my morning routine, breakfast was out of the question; luncheon loomed. Determined to do something—anything!—purposeful that day, I phoned Sgt. Al Rogoff at PBPD headquarters. I was told he was on a forty-eight. They wouldn't give me his unlisted home phone number, of course, but that was okay; I already had it.

I called and he picked up after the third ring.

"Archy McNally," I said.

"Good heavens!" he said. "I haven't heard from you in a week or so. I hope I haven't offended you."

"Oh, shut up," I said. "I hear you're on a forty-eight. Have anything planned for today?"

"Why, yes," he said. "I thought I might play a chukker of polo this afternoon or perhaps enjoy an exciting game of shuffleboard—if my heart can stand it."

"Funny," I said, "but not very. Al, why don't you have lunch with me at the Pelican?"

"Oh-oh," he said. "Every time you invite me to lunch I end up getting shot at."

"You know that's not true."

"It's half-true," he insisted, "and half is enough for me. I refuse to lunch with you at the Pelican Club or anywhere else. And that's definite."

I told him, "We'll have Leroy's special hamburgers with a basket of matchstick potatoes and perhaps a few pale ales."

"What time do you want to make it?" he asked.

Before leaving home I called Binky Watrous, hoping the Duchess wouldn't pick up the phone. She didn't but their houseman did, and he informed me Master Binky was still asleep and had hung a Do Not Disturb sign on his bedroom door. (I happened to know that sign had been filched from the Dorchester in London.) I requested that Master Binky be asked to phone Archy McNally as soon as he reentered the world of the living.

"I don't know when that will be, Mr. McNally," the houseman said dubiously. "He just arrived home about an hour ago."

"Whenever," I said and hung up, wondering where my vassal had spent the night. Deep in mischief, no doubt. The apprentice shamus was becoming even more of a trial than I had expected.

10

I arrived at the Pelican Club in time to enjoy a Bloody Mary (with fresh horseradish) at the bar before Sgt. Rogoff showed up. The dining area was filling rapidly and I peeked in to see if Connie Garcia was present. Thankfully she was not. The horseradish had invigorated my spirits but not to the point where I was ready to face Connie's wrath if she had learned—as I was certain she would—that I had attended the season's first big social affair and did not invite her to accompany me.

Sgt. Rogoff finally came trundling in, wearing casual, off-duty duds. Al is a truculent piece of meat, built along the general lines of a steamroller. For career reasons he projects the persona of a good ol' boy, and he drives a pickup to aid his public image. But he is brainy, a very keen investigator, and also happens to be a closet balletomane. One never knows, do one?

We snagged a table for two in the dining room and, after some repartee with the sassy Priscilla, ordered the lunch that had lured the sergeant. Knowing our predilection, Pris served the Bass ales first, and we both took palate-tingling swigs.

"I'd like to be floating in a tank of this stuff," Al said. "Trying to drink the level down. Wasn't there an English lord or someone who did something like that?"

"Drowned in a vat of malmsey," I said, but then my mind went blank. "I can't remember who it was," I admitted.

Al looked at me reproachfully. "That's not like you, Archy," he chided. "You usually have instant recall of useless information."

"True," I said, "but that bowl of Cheerios I call my brain is not up to cruising speed this morning. I've got problems."

"Yeah? Like what?"

"Well, for starters I've taken on an unpaid assistant who wants to learn the discreet inquiry business, and he's driving me right up the wall. Binky Watrous. Do you know him?"

Rogoff took a gulp of his ale. "That twit? Sure, I know him. Last year he was charged with committing a public nuisance for riding a mule up Worth Avenue. He got off with a fine. Screwballs like him make me question the purpose of evolution. How come you tied up with an airhead like Watrous?"

"Well, he *is* a friend of mine," I explained lamely. "And he has to get a job or his aunt is liable to end his freeloading career."

"The Duchess!" Al said, laughing. He's not totally ignorant of the intricacies of Palm Beach society. "That lady is a fruitcake, too. Every year she sends the Palm Beach Police Department a subscription to *National Geographic.* How does that grab you?"

But then Priscilla brought our burgers and spuds along with a complimentary platter of sliced tomatoes and onions. The sergeant and I wasted little time in talking while we absorbed all those tasty calories. It was only when the plates were completely denuded and we were quaffing our second ales that Rogoff leaned back and said, "All right, let's have it."

"Have what?" I inquired innocently.

"Come on, Archy," he said, "don't jerk me around. Daddy taught me a long time ago that there's no such thing as a free lunch. What do you want?"

"Well, there is one little thing you can do for me."

"A little thing? Like immolation? Ixnay."

"Al, it's just a routine inquiry. One of our clients thinks someone is dipping into the till. He has his suspicions but doesn't want to risk a lawsuit for defamation if he goes to the police and it turns out he's wrong. So he asked McNally and Son to look into it first. It's really a very low-key investigation."

I wasn't exactly lying, you understand—just dissembling.

"Oh sure," he said. "That's how all your discreet inquiries begin. Then they end up on my desk. I always think of you as Archy the Jonah."

"That's not fair," I protested. "Some of your greatest successes were initiated by my preliminary labors."

"Granted," he said. "But do they all have to finish with some coked-up zombie coming at me with a machete? All right, what do you want?"

"Our client believes one of the villains ripping him off is a gent named Ernest Gorton. He runs an import-export business in Miami. I hoped you'd be willing to run a trace on him."

The sergeant finished his ale. "I can't do it officially. It's got nothing to do with the Department. But I could make some phone calls to a few compadres in Miami, who might be willing to take a look at this guy."

I fished Ernie Gorton's business card from my wallet, and Rogoff took out his little notebook closed with a rubber band.

He copied Gorton's full name, address, and telephone number.

"Don't expect an answer tomorrow," he warned. "You'll be lucky if I hear back in a week or two."

"I understand that, Al," I said. "And thanks for your help."

"It was the sliced tomatoes and onions that did it," he said.

We waved goodbye to Priscilla, and I went to the bar to sign the tab while Rogoff departed in his pickup. Then I headed for the McNally Building, feeling I should at least stop briefly at my office to see if Binky had regained consciousness and had phoned to report on his previous night's misadventures.

But there were no messages on my desk and so I had little choice but to light an English Oval (first of the day) and ponder my next move. I decided it would be wise to take a nap. I had slept well but felt the McNally batteries could benefit from a short recharge. I had just finished my cig and settled down for a brief slumber when the phone shrilled me awake. Binky's call, I thought mournfully, and perfectly timed to disrupt my snooze.

But it was Sunny Fogarty, and she wasted no words.

"I'm at a pay phone outside the office," she said, speaking rapidly, "so I can talk. This morning I started checking the funeral directors' weekly reports covering the past six months. They're supposed to include invoices for out-of-state shipments with the assignee's name and address—the information missing from the computer printout I sent you. They're gone."

"Gone?"

"The shipping invoices—just vanished. Obviously someone went into the files and removed them. Damn! Now I'm sure something crooked is going on."

"It would appear so," I said carefully.

"Archy," she said, and I thought I detected a note of desperation, "what are we going to do now?"

I reflected a moment, and the McNally brain began to function on all two cylinders. "Sunny, when Whitcomb airlifts a deceased out of Florida, surely the airline keeps a copy of the invoice: nature and weight of the cargo shipped, number and date of flight, names and addresses of the shipper and the assignee."

I heard her sharp intake of breath. "Double damn!" she cried. "I should have thought of that but I'm so upset by finding our invoices have been stolen that I'm just not thinking straight. Of course the airlines will have copies."

"I'd volunteer to request that I be allowed to examine them," I said, "but I doubt very much if they'd cooperate with an outsider. I'm afraid you'll have to do it, Sunny—acting as Chief Financial Officer of Whitcomb Funeral Homes."

"You're right and I'll get on it at once. It's going to take time, Archy."

"I realize that. Meanwhile there's something you can do for me. I'd like the names and addresses of your four department heads and three chief funeral directors."

A short pause on her part. Then: "You think one of them may be involved?"

"One or more."

"I'll get the list to you immediately," she said. "Even before I start contacting the airlines. I can't tell you how relieved I am that you're on my side. We'll get to the bottom of this, won't we?"

"Absolutely," I said with more confidence than I felt.

"And Archy," she added, her voice suddenly soft, "thank you for last night."

"The pleasure was—" I started, but she hung up before I could finish.

I knew what I had to do next. Since there would be heavy expenses incurred, I felt it prudent to get the pater's permission before running up a humongous bill. I called his office. Mrs. Trelawney, his private secretary, was absent that day, sitting at the bedside of an extremely pregnant niece, and the honcho answered the phone himself.

"Father," I said, "may I see you for ten or fifteen minutes?"

"Now?" he said testily. "Can't it wait?"

"No, sir," I said. "Time is of the essence."

"What a brilliant expression, Archy," he said dryly. "Original, no doubt." He allowed himself a short chuff of laughter. "Very well, come on up."

A few minutes later I was in the sanctum sanctorum, seated in one corner of a chesterfield covered in bottle-green leather. His Majesty sat upright in the oak swivel chair before his antique rolltop desk.

"All right," he said, "get to it."

I told him everything that had happened regarding the goings-on at Whitcomb Funeral Homes since we had first been alerted by Sunny Fogarty. His expression didn't change as he listened without interrupting. I believe mein Papa considers duplicity as natural a part of human nature as hope.

"You suspect there is criminal activity taking place at Whitcomb's?" he asked when I had finished.

"Yes, sir, I do."

"And what is Sunny Fogarty's role in all this?"

"Equivocal," I admitted. "She is very intent on finding out what's happening, but she is equally insistent that Mr. Horace Whitcomb not be informed of the investigation. Curious."

"Exceedingly," he concurred. "Do you think she has fears of his involvement in illegalities?"

"I simply don't know, father."

"And what do you propose doing next?"

"Sunny is going to provide me with the names and addresses of Whitcomb's executive personnel: four department heads and three chief funeral directors. I'd like to purchase their credit dossiers."

"Of all seven?"

"Actually, sir, of ten. I'd like to commission reports on Horace Whitcomb, Oliver Whitcomb, and Miss Fogarty as well. It will be costly, and because I have promised we shall not inform our client of the inquiry, it would be awkward if we billed him for an investigation of which he apparently is not aware and has not approved."

One hairy eyebrow went up as I anticipated, and the master began mulling. As I have described in previous tomes, this is a process of silent and deep reflection during which he slowly—oh, so slowly!—arrives at important decisions, such as whether or not to spread cheese on a fresh celery stalk.

"Very well, Archy," he said finally, "go ahead with the credit dossiers. If nothing comes of them, we'll eat the expense."

"Thank you, sir," I said gratefully, and escaped.

There was nothing more I could accomplish at the office and so I drove home in a surprisingly felicitous mood, warbling aloud another of my favorite songs: "Ac-cent-tchu-ate the Positive"—not only a frisky tune but an appealing philosophy as well. Much more meaningful than "Sam, You Made the Pants Too Long."

I took an early ocean swim, returned to my cell, and donned my latest acquisition: a luscious kimono of vermilion pongee. Then I set to work on my journal, for there was much to record about the affair I was now calling The Case of the Flying Dead.

I had to interrupt my labors to dress for the family cocktail hour, but after dinner I returned to work and finally, close to nine o'clock, had brought my professional diary up to date. I read everything I had scribbled, but it yielded no hint of what was transpiring at the Whitcomb Funeral Homes.

That was one mystery. Another and (to my way of thinking) more fascinating conundrum was the behavior of Sunny Fogarty. I was convinced the lady was sincere in wanting to uncover whatever skulduggery might be under way. But a sneaking suspicion also lurked that she was not telling me the whole truth, especially about her motives for sparking the inquiry.

I love puzzles like that. The conduct of *Homo saps* is a source of infinite wonder, glee, and gloom—don't you agree? I mean, there's no end to the complexities of human passions. A study of the way people act, particularly when tugged by wants and needs they cannot control, is immeasurably more captivating than, say, a game of spin the bottle.

I was brooding on the enigma of Sunny Fogarty when my mental gymnastics were brought to an unwelcome halt by a phone call. I picked up, expecting the worst. It was.

"Hi there, Archy!" Binky Watrous said in tones so excessively cheerful I wanted to throttle him.

11

I snidely remarked to Binky that I was gratified he had found time to report to his mentor, since it showed he was rapidly adopting the work ethic. Of course the chucklehead took it as a compliment.

"Well, I didn't spend the whole night carousing, you know," he said righteously. "A gang of us left the party and went down to Mitzi and Oliver Whitcomb's place in Boca. We had a real riot, Archy, but I never forgot I was on duty, and I observed."

"Did you now?" I said. "And what did you observe?"

"Scads of swell stuff. Listen, suppose I pop over to your digs and fill you in. I've got some primo scoop."

That hooked me. "Sure, Binky," I said, "come ahead. Meet you outside."

I pulled on a nylon golf jacket and went downstairs to our graveled turnaround. I lighted an English Oval and paced slowly back and forth, watching the stars whirl overhead. It really was a super evening. The moon wasn't full but it was fat enough, and there was a cool ocean breeze as pleasurable as a lasting kiss.

About twenty minutes later my disciple pulled up in his dinged MB and promptly bummed a cigarette. Then we crossed Ocean Boulevard and went down the rickety wooden staircase to the beach. We walked close to the water to be on firm sand and headed south.

"What a crazy night that was," Binky started. "Mitzi invited me, so I couldn't refuse, could I, Archy?"

"Of course not."

"There must have been twenty of us, and no one feeling any pain. Mitzi and Oliver have this lush layout with a lot of lawn. I figure two mil at least. Marble floors, mirrors everywhere, and all the furniture is stainless steel, white leather, and tinted glass. Not exactly my cup of pekoe, you understand, but it shouted bucks."

"Do they have a staff?" I asked.

"I spotted two: a butler type and a Haitian maid, but they had to have more. I mean, that mansion is gigantic."

We strolled slowly in the moonlight, jumping back occasionally when an unexpectedly heavy wave came washing in. We saw the lights of a few fishing boats, but otherwise the sea was glimmering ink broken by a few vagrant whitecaps.

"Mucho drinking?" I inquired.

"Mucho mucho!" Binky replied enthusiastically. "I mean, they've got a wet bar that just doesn't end. But booze was only half of it."

"Oh?" I said, guessing what was coming. "What's the other half?"

"Joints and nose candy. Maybe there was heavier merchandise available, but grass and coke were what I saw. Archy, you know alcohol is my poison of choice. I smoked pot once and fell asleep, but I've never snorted. Anyway, supplies were plentiful and only a few of us were sticking to liquid refreshment."

"What about Mitzi and Oliver?"

"Higher than kites," he said. "But not as bad as some of the others. What a wild scene that was."

"Sounds like real whoopee."

"It was," he affirmed. "And it went on and on. When I finally staggered out of there a half dozen people were still partying and organizing a game of strip poker. Not my favorite sport, Archy."

"I should hope not. Binky, do you happen to recall if a man named Ernest Gorton was there?"

"Ernie? Sure he was. Hey, he's a lot of laughs."

"Was he doing drugs?"

Binky thought a moment. "I don't think so," he said. "Always had a glass in his fist, but maybe it was only one drink because I don't remember him getting smashed."

"Did he have a date?"

"Did he ever! A carrottop. Couldn't have been much more than twenty years old. Pretty enough, but to tell you the truth, Archy, she looked like a hooker to me. Naturally I didn't ask her."

"Naturally," I said gravely.

We paused, lighted fresh smokes, turned around, and began to walk back.

"Binky," I said, "I congratulate you on your keen eye. Are you going to see Mitzi and Oliver again?"

"You betcha!" he cried. "Especially Mitzi. She promised to call me and said we'll have a few giggles together."

"That's encouraging," I said. "No objections from her dear hubby?"

"Nope. He was standing right there when she said it and all he did was shake a finger at us and say, 'Naughty, naughty!' I think they have an understanding. You know? I saw him coming on to Ernie Gorton's redhead, and the two of them disappeared upstairs. Live and let live—right?"

"Right," I said, dismayed by his description of the younger Whitcombs' marital concordat. "Binky, who were the other guests? I mean, what kind of people were they?"

"Young swingers," he said. "*Rich* young swingers. Lots of Jags and Lexi parked outside. Everyone seemed to know everyone else. Just one big private club."

"Did you tell them who you were?"

"Oh sure," he said. "I told Ernie I was your assistant. He said that was interesting and invited me to visit him in Miami. Wasn't that nice of him?"

What a naif! "It certainly was nice," I said. "And did Oliver Whitcomb ask who you were and what you did?"

"Yep," he said brightly. "He wants to have lunch with me."

I said nothing. What was the use? We returned to the McNally driveway and I praised him again for the skillful job of detecting he had done, refraining from mentioning that he had let his tongue waggle too much to strangers.

He positively glowed when he heard my commendation and said that discreet inquiries were proving so enjoyable he was now firmly convinced he would make them his lifetime career. I concealed my shudder, gave him what few cigarettes were left in the packet, and sent him on his way. A cuckoo, I agree, but a lovable cuckoo, and I acknowledged his fumbling efforts might prove useful.

For the remaining waking hours of that night I resolutely refrained from ruminating on the tidbits of information divulged by my Sancho Panza. The mound of lasagna I call my brain was flaccid with the complexities it had absorbed that day, and so I treated myself to a wee marc and listened to a tape of Jimmy Durante rasping some wonderful tunes, including "Inka Dinka Doo."

I recall that just before I fell asleep I murmured the Schnozzola's famous sign-off: "Good night, Mrs. Calabash—wherever you are."

I awoke Thursday morning so chockablock with the Three Vs (vim, vigor, vitality) I was convinced the day would be a triumph for A. McNally, detective nonpareil and implacable righter of wrongs. This loopy attitude lasted for almost a half hour when disaster struck in the form of a phone call from Consuela Garcia. Before breakfast!

"You didn't invite me," she accused in the tone she uses that illy conceals her desire to transform me into a soprano. "To the Whitcombs' party."

"Connie," I pleaded piteously, "it was a business obligation. As I told you, the Whitcombs are clients. I attended with my parents and we departed early. A very dull affair."

"That's not what I hear."

My leman has a network of spies, informers, and snitches that would be the envy of the CIA. I mean, she has the uncanny ability to learn about my peccadilloes before the sheets cool off. Rarely—*very* rarely—have I been able to misbehave without news of my conduct eventually coming to her alert ears. It is a cross I have learned to bear.

"Connie," I said sincerely (I can do sincere when it's required), "I attended the party with my parents to fulfill a professional duty. We put in the requisite appearance and that's all there was to it."

"We shall see," she said darkly. "Reports are still coming in."

And she slammed down the phone. There went my ebullience. I breakfasted in a subdued mood that even buttermilk pancakes could not lighten. I drove to the office thinking of my totally unexpected and unplanned pas de deux with Sunny Fogarty on Tuesday night. I convinced myself that despite her espionage organization there was no possible way Connie could learn of my infidelity. I should have remembered Mr. Seneca's observation: "What fools these mortals be!"

I found on my desk a small sealed envelope that had been delivered by messenger. The single sheet of paper within, unsigned, listed the names, home addresses, and Social Security numbers of the four department heads and three chief funeral directors of Whitcomb's. Sunny Fogarty was prompt, organized, efficient—and had freckled shoulders.

Several words of explanation are now necessary. When I received permission from my father to commission credit dossiers on the individuals involved in the Whitcomb affair, you may have thought, in your innocence, we were merely seeking reports on their net worth, income, liabilities, and general creditworthiness. That may have been the limits of information available to us a few years ago, but no longer.

New agencies now exist—some legitimate, some a bit on the shady side—which are capable of supplying skinny of an incredibly personal nature: Your unlisted phone number. Your marital and medical history. Your shopping habits, including the brand of corn flakes you prefer. Your taste in collectibles. The types of investments you favor. The make, model, and cost of the car you drive. The size and value of your condominium or house. The name of your pet cat or dog, and how much you spend annually on said feline or canine. The duration and destinations of your vacations. Your annual expenditures on food, liquor, and clothing. Your preferences in entertainment: movies, video tapes, sporting events, theater, ballet. The extent of your gambling in casinos.

All that and more is available to interested inquirers—at a

hefty price, of course—through the magic of computerized bank accounts, credit cards, mail order purchases, bar codes, and the energetic exchange of mailing lists. Surely you know that privacy is an antiquated concept. Recently, for the fun of it, I had ordered a complete dossier of myself. I was staggered by the intimate nature of the report I received—including the name of the Danbury, Conn., hatter from whom I had ordered my puce beret, the price I had paid, and the date of the purchase.

We may rail against this electronic intrusion into our private lives, but I do not believe it can be stopped. I foresee the day when anyone requesting a complete dossier on yrs. truly will be informed that on August 18, 1997, at 8:36 A.M., I trimmed my toenails.

Hello there, Big Brother!

I added the names and addresses of Horace Whitcomb, Oliver Whitcomb, and Sunny Fogarty to the list I had received and took it upstairs to the office of Mrs. Trelawney, the boss's private secretary. I requested it be faxed to the investigative agency we used with an URGENT label affixed thereto.

(You may feel that after caterwauling about the loss of privacy and the indecency of electronic prying, I was something of a hypocrite to take advantage of what I claimed to despise. You are correct, of course; I was acting shamefully, and in the very near future I fully intend to commit several kind and generous acts in atonement.)

"It'll cost," the beldame observed, examining my list. "Is your father aware of this, Archy?"

"He is," I assured her. "I made certain to obtain his permission."

"Smart boy," she said approvingly. "He's on his annual cut-the-costs campaign."

"I know, I know. I've been trying to reuse staples but it's difficult."

"That's no joke. He's composing a memo to all employees suggesting ways to limit the use of paper towels in the lavatories."

"From now on," I promised, "I'll dry my hands on my pants, and I suggest you do the same."

"Dry my hands on *your* pants?" she inquired sweetly. She really is a delightfully raunchy old lady.

I returned to my closet wondering how I might profitably spend the remainder of the day. The problem was solved when our lobby receptionist called to inform me that Mr. Horace Whitcomb had just phoned and requested I get back to him as soon as conveniently possible.

I called at once and identified myself to a male staffer who quavered, "The Whitcomb residence." Mr. Horace came on the line a moment later and we exchanged civilities.

"Archy," he said, "it's such a pleasant afternoon I simply cannot bring myself to make an appearance at the office and pretend I'm working. Would you care to lunch with us at twelve-thirty, say, and later I'll be happy to show you my collection of ship models."

"I accept," I said at once. "It sounds like a delightful prospect, and I thank you. I shan't be late."

I hung up, happy I had been asked but curious as to why the invitation had come so promptly. I mean, he had mentioned it casually at the party, but I had taken it as a generalized courtesy: "We must get together sometime."

But now, two days later, he had made it definite. Perhaps I too often look for ulterior motives, but if I didn't I really should be in another line of work.

12

▲

The table had been set on the flagstoned terrace and since it faced westward we were in blessed shade. There was a flotilla of sails taking advantage of a splendid day and the ripply lake. Hobie cats were everywhere, plus a few trim sloops and one majestic trimaran. Mercifully there was not a cigarette boat in sight—or sound.

I was dressed informally, as usual, but my peony-patterned jacket didn't even elicit a snicker; these were very polite people. Mr. Horace wore a navy, brass-buttoned blazer with gray flannel slacks. Mrs. Sarah, her wheelchair pushed up close to the table, was clad in something gossamer and flowing that looked like a morning robe. A jaunty turban decorated with a single lavender orchid covered her pate.

We were waited upon by an aged servitor, he of the quavery voice, introduced to me as Jason. He moved slowly and carefully, apparently not wishing to disturb us with the creaking of his bones, but his hands were steady enough and his solicitude for Mrs. Whitcomb was admirable.

We started with kir royales, an excellent choice for lunching alfresco on such a brilliant day. I complimented my hostess on the success of her recent party. "A night to remember," I told her, and she brightened. I suspect she might have brightened even more if she had known how my memorable night ended.

"It *was* fun, wasn't it?" she said. "Everyone seemed to have a good time. Did you meet our son?"

"I did indeed. He suggested we might have lunch one day."

"Do it," she urged. "But you'll have to phone him. He's so forgetful—isn't he, Horace?"

"Yes," her husband said.

"Such a scamp!" Mrs. Sarah said and laughed. "Sometimes I wonder if he's ever going to grow up. He still gets into mischief just as he did when he was a little boy. Remember, Horace?"

"I remember," he said. "I still wish we had sent him to a military academy, but you couldn't see it."

"It would have crushed him," she said firmly. "He's such a free spirit."

I had the impression this contention was nothing new but had existed since Oliver was a mischievous little boy and would continue until he became a mischievous old geezer—if his parents lived to witness it.

Jason brought an ice bucket chilling a bottle of excellent South African Pinot blanc, a wine to die for—which, I reflected, the Whitcombs' customers were doing. Then came individual wooden bowls of lobster salad (endive and watercress) and a communal basket of focaccia with saucers of garlic-infused olive oil for dipping. That lunch, I may say without fear of serious contradiction, was superior to a Big Mac.

Mr. Horace and I ate heartily. Mrs. Sarah made a valiant effort but really just toyed with her food, forking out a few chunks of lobster meat but ignoring the greens and focaccia. One glass of wine.

"Horace," she said almost timidly, "I don't want to spoil your lunch, but I do think it best if I leave you men alone now. I better rest awhile."

He rose immediately to his feet, as I did.

"Of course, darling," he said. "Archy, continue your lunch. I'll be right back."

He wheeled her away. I slid back into my chair and poured myself another glass of that fragrant wine, wishing it was something stronger to dull a sudden onslaught of grief. The host returned in a few minutes, walking briskly, his Ronald Colman features revealing nothing of what he felt.

"She'll be fine," he told me, pulling up his chair and attacking his salad again. "We have a nurse's aide who'll take care of her. Sorry for the interruption."

"Sir," I said, then stopped, not knowing what to say.

"She insisted on joining us for lunch," he went on. "I feared it might be too much for her. But she keeps trying—which is important, don't you think?"

"Absolutely," I said. "A very brave woman, Mr. Whitcomb."

He nodded. "She is that."

"How long has your wife been ill?"

"Too long. It's been a dreadful ordeal. For everyone."

He shook off his despair and called, "Jason!" The ancient one appeared immediately and Mr. Horace gestured toward the ice bucket. "Supplies running low," he said, and a few moments later we were supplied with a second bottle along with goblets of lime sorbet and a plate of crisp anise cookies.

We finished all the edibles in sight. Even the sadness of the Whitcomb household could not blunt my enjoyment of that lunch; I gave it my 2-R rating (Ripping Repast).

"Shall we take a look at my ships now?" Mr. Horace suggested. "Bring your glass along and we'll finish the bottle upstairs."

"Sounds good to me," I said.

"My study used to be on the ground floor," he remarked as we entered the house. "But when my wife became ill and needed a wheelchair, we converted the den into her bedroom and I moved my junk upstairs. It's worked out very well."

He said it blithely, but I didn't believe him. (My father would be outraged at having *his* den moved.) I guessed Mr. Whitcomb's dispossession had been wrenching, but he struck me as a man who stoically endured setbacks and disappointments without grousing. I wish I could.

He carried the wine bottle, wrapped in a napkin to prevent dripping, and preceded me as we traipsed up that grand staircase to the second floor. The room we entered was androgynous. Even if he hadn't told me, I'd have known it had originally been designed as a lady's bedchamber; the walls were papered in a flowered pattern, the balloon drapes were chintz, and the plastered ceiling was painted with vignettes of rosy cherubim gamboling in golden meadows. I thought it all a trifle much.

But the furnishings were starkly masculine: desk, tables, and bookcases in burnished oak, all the chairs upholstered in maroon leather with brass studs. And an enormous pine étagère obviously custom-built to fill one wall. The long, heavy shelves held Mr. Horace's collection of ship models.

Lordy, they were handsome. Not a bit of plastic to be seen, but all carefully crafted of oak, teak, mahogany, ebony. The sails looked to be fine linen, and I was certain the rigging was accurate down to the tiniest belaying pin and the exquisite miniature anchor chains.

We sipped our wine while Mr. Whitcomb gave me a short

history of each ship, enlivened with a few details about the craftsmen who had built the models, working from original plans. Some of the reduced-scale copies were quite old, some of recent vintage, and I was delighted to learn there were still artisans capable of such devoted and painstaking work. The model of the clipper *Flying Cloud* was my favorite. What a beauty!

Then, the tour completed, we sat in facing club chairs to finish our wine. A civilized afternoon.

"A remarkable collection, sir," I said. "Any museum would love to have it."

His laugh was short and, I thought, rather bitter. "I expect one of them shall," he said. "Eventually. I'd hate to see it broken up and sold off piecemeal after I die. I've spent a great deal of time and money, but it's been a labor of love. I can't tell you how much pleasure these models have given me over the years. They've provided the perfect antidote to the somewhat depressing routine of my particular business."

"Your son doesn't share your enthusiasm?" I ventured.

"No," he said shortly, "he does not. Oliver has hobbies of his own."

I didn't dare ask what those might be, but I could imagine. I could also guess that despite his urbanity, Horace Whitcomb was a troubled man.

But his conversation remained light and pleasing. He related several anecdotes of sea battles between men-of-war, all of them interesting and some amusing. He was a skilled raconteur, but I had the impression he was merely repeating thrice-told tales and his thoughts were elsewhere. I presumed his wife's condition was distracting him.

But suddenly he broke off his account of the bloody engagement between the *Bonhomme Richard* and the British frigate *Serapis* off Flamborough Head. He fell silent and stared at me in what I can only describe as a contemplative, almost broody, manner.

"Archy," he said, "I understand you conduct private investigations for your father's firm."

I was startled and tried not to show it. I was certain poppa hadn't said a word about my duties to Mr. Whitcomb, and I couldn't recall mentioning them to him, his wife, son, or anyone else at the party. The fact that my profession is discreet inquiries is hardly a secret in Palm Beach, but it was a mite unsettling to learn my host was aware of it.

"That's true, sir," I said. "Occasionally I do quiet investigations when discretion is required, rather than take inquiries to the authorities and risk unwanted publicity."

"Quite understandable," he said. "You must have had many unusual experiences."

It was obviously an invitation to gab, and I was offended. Did he think me a babbler—or was he testing me?

"Most of what I do is exceedingly dull," I told him. "I wouldn't want to bore you—and naturally I must respect client confidentiality."

It was a mild reprimand and he accepted it.

"Naturally," he said, and we smiled at each other.

Wine finished, we walked down the long stairway to the ground level.

"I'll leave you here," he said. "I want to look in at Sarah. Jason will see you out."

"Thank you for a lovely luncheon," I said, shaking his proffered hand. "And for letting me view those incredible models. Please give my best wishes to your wife and my hopes for her speedy and complete recovery."

"We all hope for that," he said, but there was little hope in his voice. "Archy, you're good company. I look forward to seeing you again."

He left me and the archaic majordomo appeared out of nowhere bearing my snazzy pink panama with a snakeskin band.

"Thank you, Jason," I said. "It was a super luncheon."

"Thank *you,* sir," he quavered. "I am happy you enjoyed it."

I looked around that magnificent entrance hall, a shining vault that seemed to go on forever.

"What a wonderful home," I marveled.

"It was," he said in such a low voice I could hardly hear him. But that's what he said: "It was." Of course I thought he was referring to Mrs. Whitcomb's illness.

I drove slowly back to the McNally Building, pausing en route at a florist's shop to have a cheerful arrangement of mums delivered to Mrs. Sarah with a note of thanks. The Whitcombs were, I knew, people who honored traditional etiquette, mailed birthday and Christmas cards, and never failed to visit sick friends. My parents are similar types. I, regrettably, am not.

I hadn't been at my desk more than five minutes when Binky Watrous phoned.

"You'll never guess what happened to me," he burbled.

"You're enceinte?" I inquired.

"Better! Mitzi Whitcomb called and wants to see me tonight. Her lesser half is going down to Miami on business and she's all by her lonesome. Wants me to buy her a pizza and then we'll go dancing. How about that!"

"Sounds like you've made a conquest, laddie," I said. "Have fun but promise me one thing."

"What's that?"

"Not a word to Mitzi about our investigation of the Whitcomb Funeral Homes. Is that understood?"

"Of course."

"Not one single word," I warned him. "The lady may try to

extract information in a friendly, offhand way, but you know nothing."

"About what?" he said.

I sighed. I had feared he would be a trial; he was rapidly becoming an inquisition. "About *anything*," I told him. "Just chat her up and keep the conversation frothy and inconsequential. Do your birdcalls for her."

"Oh yeah!" he said happily. "I've got a new one—the yellow-bellied sapsucker."

"That should enchant her," I assured him. "And Binky, in the most casual way possible you might inquire what business is taking Oliver to Miami tonight. You understand?"

"Oh sure. I'll ask her."

"Don't *ask* her. Say something similar to 'Your husband must be a very busy man, driving to Miami at night.' And then wait for her reaction."

"I get it," he said. "You want me to be subtle."

"Yes, Binky, I want you to be subtle—right after you imitate the call of a yellow-bellied sapsucker."

"I can do it," he said eagerly. "I'll get the goods on Oliver."

"Call me tomorrow," I said, stifling a groan, "and tell me how you made out."

I hung up and put my head in my hands. He was going to commit a monumental balls-up, I just knew it. What concerned me most was not that Binky might reveal to Mitzi and Oliver Whitcomb that they were subjects of an inquiry by McNally & Son, but that my father might learn I was employing a certified bedlamite in one of my discreet inquiries.

I could easily envision his reaction: *both* tangled eyebrows twitched aloft, the bristly mustache drooping, and I'd get a stare that shared pain and incredulity: "Have I raised my only son to be an utter dunce?"

I felt it best to leave the McNally Building and seek solace in a slow ocean swim and the comfort of the family cocktail hour and dinner later. I'm sure it was an excellent feast, but I could not help but regard it as a condemned man's last meal.

I retired to my quarters and phoned Connie Garcia. You know, I do believe I half-hoped she had learned of my recent joust with Sunny Fogarty. If so, Connie would be aflame, steam spouting from her ears, and she would threaten me with physical punishments I don't wish to detail here, not wishing to offend your sensibilities.

No, I am not suicidal. In hoping my one-and-several might condemn me, vociferously and at length, I was merely seeking normality in a world suddenly gone awry.

13

But apparently my Dulcinea had not learned of the recent moral boo-boo I had committed, for she couldn't have been more affectionate. We chatted for almost twenty minutes, and our conversation was all bubbles. We ended by agreeing to meet for dinner on Saturday night and exchanged vows of love and fidelity everlasting before hanging up.

It was a puzzlement. I mean, I loved the woman, I really did, but my devotion obviously wasn't sufficient to restrain me from casting covetous eyes on others of the female persuasion. Are all men like that? I suspect we may be, and it's disheartening. Certain absolutes, such as courage, are expected of the male gender, but faithfulness is not one of them. What's worse, it's usually treated with cynical amusement while a woman's infidelity is roundly condemned.

I scribbled in my journal for the remainder of the evening, recording my impressions of the luncheon with Sarah and Horace Whitcomb. They were true patricians, I reckoned, whose breeding and bravery were being sorely tested. I thought they were enduring their trials with exemplary fortitude—which only proves how mistaken first impressions can be.

I awoke the next morning with the nagging suspicion it would prove to be an unproductive day. I was in a waiting mode: waiting for Sunny Fogarty to retrieve names and addresses from the airlines' shipping invoices; waiting for our credit agency to return dossiers on the individuals listed; waiting for Sgt. Al Rogoff to report on what he had learned about Ernest Gorton from his police pals in Miami. It was, I decided, going to be a vacant day. Hah!

Nota bene: The following times are approximate.

9:30 A.M.:

I had overslept, as was my custom, and finally clattered downstairs to a deserted kitchen, where I prepared a solitary breakfast. If memory serves—and mine usually doesn't—I found a cold pork chop left over from our previous night's dinner. I trimmed it carefully of fat and bone, and then inserted the round of meat between two toasted halves of an English muffin, with a dab of mayo. You might try it sometime. Chockful of goodness.

10:30 A.M.:

I arrived at the McNally Building to find on my desk a message that Mr. Ernest Gorton had phoned and asked that I return his call as soon as possible. I debated a moment, fearing he might invite me to visit him in Miami. I had no intention of doing that, of course, but I was curious as to why he should follow up a casual meeting at a crowded party with a call three days later. I assumed he had a motive of which I wot not. And so I phoned.

"Archy!" he said heartily. "How's by you?"

"Very well, thanks, Ernie," I said. "And you?"

"Seventh heaven," he proclaimed. "Listen, let me get right

to the point." He didn't exactly say "pernt," but it was close. "When we met the other night at the Whitcombs' party, you hit me as a guy who likes wine. Am I correct?"

"Well, yes," I said cautiously. "I enjoy a glass of good wine now and then."

"I'll bet you do," he said with a sound halfway between a chuckle and a chortle. "You know anything about it?"

I was briefly nonplussed. "About wine, you mean? I do know a little, but I am no oenophile."

"Whatever the hell that is," he said. "Look, in my import-export business sometimes I luck on to a great deal and naturally I think of my close friends first."

"Naturally," I said, wondering when and how I had become his close friend.

"Suddenly I got this shipment of 1990 Chateau Margaux. That's a good wallop, isn't it?"

"An excellent drink," I assured him.

"I can let you have it for a hundred bucks," he said.

"Ernie," I said as gently as I could, "the 1990 Margaux is a fine wine, but I can buy a bottle for less than a hundred at my local liquor emporium."

"A bottle?" he said indignantly. "Who's talking bottles? I'm offering you a case."

Holy moly! I was stunned. A case of 1990 Chateau Margaux for a hundred dollars? Incredible. "Did it fall off the truck?" I said feebly.

"What do you care?" he demanded. "I got two cases left. If you want one you'll hafta tell me now. And you'll hafta pick it up. No delivery."

"Ah, what a shame," I said. "My car's in the shop, and there's no one I can trust to make the pickup. Ernie, I'll have to skip on this one, but I do appreciate your thinking of me.

Perhaps we can get together if you have any marvelous bargains like that in the future."

He took rejection cheerfully. "All the time, Archy. For instance, right now I'm working on a deal for diamond-studded Rolex wristwatches. The real thing, not ripoffs. And the price will be right, believe me. Interested?"

"I may be," I said carefully.

"Great," he said. "I'll be in touch." And he hung up abruptly.

I sat there staring stupidly at the dead phone in my hand. What was that all about? Even if the Chateau Margaux was genuine and had been stolen, which I presumed it was and had been, a hundred dollars for a case was simply a ridiculous price, even for thieves attempting to fence their loot.

The only reason I could imagine for Gorton's call was an effort to concretize our relationship. But I still could not fathom his motive. I did know the man made me uneasy. I did not think him simpleminded. No stumblewit he. I was convinced he was sure of what he was doing—and I'm not sure of anything except that you can't put too much garlic on buttered escargot.

Then it occurred to me that maybe he had been testing my cupidity, just as Horace Whitcomb had tested my discretion. I was beginning to feel like a lab rat condemned to run a maze. I could only hope I would find the exit and the reward awaiting me: a nice wedge of ripe Brie.

11:15 A.M.:

I phoned Binky Watrous, eager to learn all the juicy details of his evening with the supercharged Mitzi Whitcomb. He sounded hoarse, as if he had spent too many hours imitating the call of a hypertensive parrot.

"Sore throat?" I inquired solicitously.

"Sore everything," he rasped. "Archy, I am unraveled, totally unraveled. All I want is a quick and merciful end to my suffering."

"What a shame," I said. "I was about to ask you to join me for a burger and a bucket of suds at the Pelican, but we'll make it another—"

"I accept," he interrupted hastily. "Give me an hour to get my bones in motion."

"I gather you had a riotous night."

"Times Square on New Year's Eve. I asked Mitzi to divorce Oliver and marry me."

"You didn't!"

"I did."

"And what did the lady reply to that?"

"She said, 'Let's practice first.' "

"See you in an hour," I said.

1:30 P.M.:

We had finished lunch and were dawdling over our second beers. Color had gradually returned to the pallid cheeks of my helot. When he arrived at the Pelican Club he had looked like something the cat dragged *out.* But a rare burger, a basket of FFs, and icy Rolling Rock had worked wonders; he was now his normal dorky self.

Unasked, he told me of his night with Mitzi Whitcomb. I shall not repeat the salacious details since I know you're not interested in that sort of thing. "What an orgy it was!" he concluded.

"Binky," I said, "can two people have an orgy? I thought it required a multitude."

"We had an orgy," he insisted. "Just the two of us. Archy, that woman scares me."

"But you want to marry her."

"That was last night. This morning I wanted to take a slow boat to Madagascar."

"And where was Mitzi's husband during this alleged debauch?"

"He called and said it was too late to drive home from Miami, so he was going to spend the night at Ernie Gorton's place."

Thick as thieves, those two, was my immediate reaction, and then I wondered if "thick" in that cliché meant intimate or stupid.

"Binky, did she toke during the evening?"

"Constantly," he said gloomily. "Had a pack of neatly rolled ganja. No filters."

"And what did you talk about?"

"A lot of nothing. She was flying, and I really shouldn't have had that fifth vodka. Archy, I've never met such a harum-scarum female. I've done a few irresponsible things in my life, as you well know, but she makes me look like Albert Schweitzer."

"Are you going to see her again?"

"Wild horses—" he started, but I halted him with a raised palm.

"Binky, I *want* you to see her again. As often as Mitzi wishes. I think she may prove to be a valuable source of information pertaining to the Whitcomb case. Your role will be that of a mole, boring from within. And I select my words carefully."

"Must I?" he cried. "Another night with her and I'll be calling 911 for the paramedics to come and take me away."

"Nah," I said. "You're in the full flower of young louthood and I'm certain you're capable of coping with the lady's demands. Meanwhile you will ever so cleverly be extracting delicious nuggets of inside skinny that may possibly solve the mystery."

"It will be the death of me," he pronounced gloomily.

"Rubbish!" I said sternly. "You're the lad who wants to become the Dick Tracy of Palm Beach. Here is an opportunity to prove your mettle."

"But Archy," he whined piteously, "she *bites!*"

"Bite back," I advised, and we drained our beers and left. I had a twinge of remorse watching him totter to his rusted heap, but I consoled myself with the thought that he would live to imitate the yellow-bellied sapsucker again.

2:30 P.M.:

I drove back to the McNally Building wondering about the inexplicable friendship between Oliver Whitcomb and Ernest Gorton. They seemed so unlike, and yet they were close enough to enjoy each other's hospitality—and share other goodies as well, including Gorton's carrot-topped lady friend.

I was musing on this riddle at my desk when Mrs. Trelawney called from m'lord's office.

"Archy," she said briskly, "your father is conferring with Horace and Oliver Whitcomb at the moment. The son wants to come down to your locker before they leave, just to say hello. Thought I'd alert you."

"Thank you, luv. I don't have many visitors. Perhaps I should change my socks."

"But it's only October," she said.

Oliver breezed in about ten minutes later. If he was shocked by the diminutiveness of my professional quarters he gave no evidence of it—from which I could only conclude he was extraordinarily polite (doubtful) or had seen even less prepossessing offices, hard as that was to believe.

"Great to see you again!" he said, shaking my hand with excessive enthusiasm. "Listen, I just stopped by for a minute. Father and I are having a powwow with your father."

"Oh?" I said. "No problems, I hope."

He laughed. "The opposite," he said. "We're planning an expansion to the west coast of Florida. The Naples–Fort Myers area."

"Sounds like business is booming."

"Couldn't be better," he said merrily. "People do insist on dying. Hey, how about that lunch?"

"Of course. What's a good time for you?"

"Next Tuesday," he said promptly. "Twelve-thirty at Renato's."

"I'll be there," I promised, impressed by his forcefulness. Another man sure of himself.

"Great!" he said and shook my hand again. Monsieur Charm in action. "I've got to go collect pops. I'm driving my Lotus Esprit today."

Then he was gone, leaving me to ponder his last unnecessary remark: "I'm driving my Lotus Esprit today." A bit on the vainglorious side, wouldn't you say? Similar to asking, "How do you like my eighteen-karat-gold Cartier Panther with a genuine alligator leather strap?" Too much.

But I had learned to deal with clients who possessed egos as inflated as the Goodyear blimp. Some people define their worth by their toys. I, of course, do not, although I take justifiable pride in my original Pepe Le Pew lunch box.

3:45 P.M.:

I closed up shop and cruised home in time to sluice my angst away with a leisurely ocean swim. Actually, I was not apprehensive or anxiety-ridden. But I must confess to a vague, indefinable premonition of disaster. Did you ever bite into a shrimp, taste, swallow, and get a slightly queasy feeling that you might soon be connected to a stomach pump at a local hospital?

That's the way I felt as I plowed through the warm waters of the Atlantic. I was convinced there was a clever plot in motion that was wreaking mischief, and I could not endure the thought of being hornswoggled.

14

▲

7:00 P.M.:

Family cocktail hour.

8:45 P.M.:

Finished dinner (chicken piccata), anticipating a peaceful evening alone with my thoughts and Billie Holiday.

8:50 P.M.:

Father stopped me as I was about to ascend to my nest. "A moment, Archy," he said and motioned toward his study. He did not invite me to be seated or offer a postprandial brandy. I stood motionless as he paced, jacket open, hands thrust into his hip pockets. Our conversation became a rat-a-tat-tat interrogation.

"Any developments in the Whitcomb matter?" he demanded.

"No, sir. Nothing of any significance."

"Oliver stopped down to see you this afternoon?"

"For a few moments."

"What did he have to say?"

"That the Whitcombs are planning an expansion to the west coast. And he invited me to lunch next Tuesday."

"You accepted, of course."

I nodded.

"I presume you met Horace at the party."

"I met him then," I said, "and had lunch with him yesterday."

He stopped pacing to stare at me. "For any particular reason?"

"He said he wanted me to see his collection of ship models. I suspect he may have had another motive. He is aware of my investigative activities and seemed anxious to verify my discretion."

The guv resumed his pacing. "Curious family," he remarked. "During your conversations with Horace and Oliver, did you get the feeling of enmity between father and son? Well, perhaps 'enmity' is too strong a word. Did you sense a certain degree of estrangement?"

"Yes, sir, I did. In their thinking, their lifestyles. They're really not on the same wavelength."

"I'm glad to hear you say that, Archy. I have the same impression. Regarding their expansion into the Naples–Fort Myers area, Horace appeared to be very dubious about that project. But then Oliver began to talk of a nationwide chain, perhaps converting Whitcomb Funeral Homes into a franchise operation."

"McFunerals?" I suggested.

He allowed himself the smallest of smiles. "Something like that. Horace was outraged at the suggestion, and I had to play the role of peacemaker to keep father and son from shouting at each other. Their argument ended only when Oliver left to go down to your office. But I had a very distinct feeling there was more to their spleen than merely a difference of opinion on business strategy."

I said, "Perhaps it's partly generational and partly an attitudinal clash: young, energetic, ambitious son versus aging, conservative, risk-adverse father."

He stopped pacing again, and this time his look was almost a glare, as if I had been referring to *our* relationship. "Do you really believe that, Archy?"

"I do, sir, but I also believe there's more to it than that."

"Yes," he said, "I do, too."

He gave me a nod of dismissal and I started upstairs. I stopped at the second-floor sitting room where mother was seated at her florentine desk busily writing letters. In addition to talking to her begonias, one of the mater's favorite pastimes is corresponding with old friends, some of whom she hasn't seen in fifty years. There was one case of a school chum to whom she continued to pen chatty missives before discovering the woman had passed away two years previously.

"Mrs. McNally," I said, "I suggest you and I steal away tonight to a tropical isle. You will wear a muumuu and a lei, and I shall wear a breechcloth of coconut shells and strum a ukulele."

She looked up brightly. "Oh Archy," she said, "that sounds divine. But I can't leave tonight. On Wednesday I have an appointment with my chiropodist."

"Whenever you're ready," I said and swooped to kiss her downy cheek. Splendid woman.

10:15 P.M.:

Sunny Fogarty phoned.

"Archy," she said, "I know it's late and I apologize."

"No need," I said. "I hadn't planned to go beddy-bye for—oh, ten minutes at least."

Her laugh was tentative. "Could you manage to come over for a few moments?" she asked. "I know it's an imposition but I think it's important, and it's not something I want to write or tell you on the phone."

Paranoia again?

"Of course," I said. "I can be there in twenty minutes or so. Do you need anything? Vodka, beer, Snapple, ice cubes?"

"No, no," she said. "I've got everything."

I could have made a leering rejoinder to that but restrained myself. I combed my hair, slapped on some Romeo Gigli, inspected myself in the bathroom mirror and saw nothing to which anyone could possibly object. I loped downstairs and exited into an overcast night. There was a streaky sky with occasional flashes of moonlight, but mostly it was dark, dark, dark with rumbles of thunder to the west.

When I was a beardless youth my mother assured me thunder was the sound of angels bowling. Listen, if you don't have family jokes, who are you? And on that night, hearing the angels bowling, I wished them nothing but strikes.

10:45 P.M.:

I arrived at the Chez Fogarty wondering if Sunny's urgent summons was merely a ploy to lure me within grappling distance. Let's face it: I am a habitual fantasizer.

Do you remember those nonsensical romantic movies of yore in which a secretary (usually played by Betty Grable) removes her eyeglasses, and her bachelor boss gasps in amazement? He had always considered her a plain-Jane but now, seeing her sans specs, he realizes she is a Venus de Milo—with arms of course.

The reverse happened when Ms. Fogarty opened the door of her condo. She was wearing brief cutoffs and a snug tank top, but those were of peripheral interest. What caught my attention and set the McNally ventricles aflutter was that she wore eyeglasses, and those amber frames and glistening lenses somehow made her appear softer and unbearably vulnerable. You explain it; I can't.

She provided me with a vodka and tonic (weak) and led me into a smallish room obviously used as an office. It was dominated by what seemed to be a gigantic computer with monitor, keyboard, printer, modem—the works.

"Are you computer literate, Archy?" she asked.

"Not me," I said hastily. "I'm a certified technophobe. I have trouble changing a light bulb."

"Then I won't attempt to describe my setup here except to tell you it enables me to access the mainframe at Whitcomb's headquarters in West Palm. I frequently work at home in the evening and sometimes during the day when I need to get away from the hectic confusion at the office. Why are you smiling?"

"Your use of the term 'hectic confusion.' It's difficult for an outsider to visualize the activities of funeral homes in quite that way."

"But that's what it is," she said seriously. "Like any other business. Naturally we make certain our clients see none of it. We provide them with a quiet, dignified atmosphere."

"Naturally," I said.

"I'm still checking shipping invoices at the airlines, and I have nothing definite to report on the names and addresses of consignees to whom all those out-of-state shipments were made by Whitcomb. But this evening I started reviewing our records of the past six months. I was trying to discover how and by whom the information we want was deleted from the main computer."

"Any luck?"

"No," she said, and I could see the failure angered her. This was not a woman who took defeat lightly. "But I did find something so extremely odd I thought I better tell you about it. Would you like another drink?"

"Please," I said, holding out my empty glass. "A bit less tonic would be welcome."

"Sorry about that," she said, grinning at me. What a *nice* grin.

She returned with a refill that numbed my uvula. "Wow," I said, "that'll send me home whistling a merry tune. Now tell me: What did you find on your handy-dandy computer that was so extremely odd?"

"As I'm sure you're aware, we require a death certificate signed by the doctor in attendance before we prepare the deceased for burial, cremation, or shipment elsewhere. Whoever fiddled the weekly reports from our three chief funeral directors neglected to remove copies of the death certificates from the records. I scrolled through them and noticed one physician had signed an extraordinary number of death certificates for all three funeral homes."

"Remind me not to consult him," I said.

She ignored my tepid attempt at levity. "His name was on a surprising number of certificates," she went on. "We deal with a large number of doctors, of course, but none of them even came close to providing the volume of certificates this man has."

"In other words, a lot of his patients are turning up their toes? And they're all being delivered to the Whitcomb Funeral Homes?"

"It appears so. After noting that, I did some cross-checking and discovered that all the deceased whose death certificates were provided by this particular physician were being shipped out of Florida for eventual interment elsewhere."

I took a gulp of my drink. A big gulp. "Do the certificates

signed by this one doctor account for all the increase in Whitcomb's out-of-state shipments?"

"Not *all,*" she said. "But most. We're talking, like, ninety percent."

We stared at each other, and I drew a deep breath. "You're right," I said. "Extremely odd. May I have the name and address of Dr. Quietus."

"I wrote it out for you," she said and handed me a slip of paper. The first thing I saw was that it was written in lavender ink. I would have guessed Sunny Fogarty used jet black, but she was a woman of constant surprises.

The medico's name was Omar K. Pflug, and his office was in Broward County.

"Odd name," I commented.

"Is it?" she said offhandedly, and once again I had the impression she knew more than she was telling me. But I simply could not conceive a reason for her secretiveness.

"I shall visit Dr. Pflug," I said. "Not for professional advice, I assure you. I wouldn't care to end up on your computer."

She smiled. "Let's move into the living room, Archy. We'll be more comfortable there."

And so we were, sitting at opposite ends of that long couch, turning to face each other. It was then I decided to confront her. It wasn't a sudden resolve or surge of bravado. She had slugged my second drink; it was really her fault. (Are you familiar with Henry Ford's comment about a colleague?: "He took misfortune like a man. He blamed it on his wife.")

"Sunny," I said boldly, "I must tell you I have the feeling you're not revealing all you know about this matter. I'm not implying you're lying, only that you are deliberately holding back certain things that might possibly aid the investigation."

She slowly removed her eyeglasses and became once again the sovereign and rather bristly woman I had imaged.

"That's nonsense," she said sharply. "I've told you all you need to know."

"Why don't you let me be the judge of that?" I said. "Try telling me *everything*. I'm quite capable of separating the raisins from the rice pudding."

She turned her head away. "I want to protect my job," she said. "I told you and your father that from the start."

"So you did. It's a valid reason for your reticence, Sunny, but I don't believe it's the entire reason. You're stiffing me and I'd like to know why."

There was a silence that seemed to last for an hour, although I don't suppose it was more than a few moments. Then she sighed and faced me again.

"There are some things, Archy," she admitted. "But I swear to you they have absolutely nothing to do with your inquiry. Will you trust my judgment?"

"I'd rather trust mine."

Then she flared. "Impossible!" she almost spat at me. "If you insist on knowing, perhaps we should end this right now."

I drained the vodka bomb she had prepared. "Perhaps we should," I said, rising. "I'll inform my father that I've been unable to discover any evidence of wrongdoing at Whitcomb's and recommend we close the case."

It shook her.

"Archy," she said pleadingly and held out a hand to me. "Don't do that. Please. I admit I haven't been as forthcoming as I might have been, but I do have a good motive, believe me. And it doesn't affect the investigation; I swear it doesn't. Don't leave me in the lurch now, Archy. I don't know what I'd do without you."

What red-blooded American boy could resist an appeal like that? Not this boy.

"All right, Sunny," I said. "I'll stick around awhile and see what happens."

She gave a little yelp of relief, bounced to her feet, and rushed to give me a chaste peck on the cheek. I was glad she hadn't replaced her specs or I might have thrown myself upon her with a hoarse cry of brutal concupiscence.

But I knew there was to be no nice-nice that evening. She promised to inform me of the results of her inspection of the airlines' shipping invoices. I promised to tell her whatever I could uncover about Dr. Omar K. Pflug.

Just before I departed she donned those damnable eyeglasses again, and my final vision was of a stalwart spectacled woman wearing brief cutoffs and a snug tank top.

Midnight:

Fantasy, fantasy, all is fantasy. But what would life be like without sweet dreams?

15

It was a very virtuous Saturday. I awoke in time to breakfast with my parents. I played eighteen holes with a trio of cronies and never did I request a mulligan. I lunched at the country club, returned home for an energetic ocean swim, and dressed for my dinner date with Consuela Garcia. And not once during those active twelve hours did I imbibe an alcoholic drink. I was so proud—and so thirsty.

Connie and I met at La Veille Maison in Boca, and because the snowbirds had not yet arrived in any great numbers we were able to snag that snug little room (one table) to the right of the entryway. We immediately ordered champagne cocktails, just to get the gastric juices flowing, and Connie studied the menu while I studied her.

As usual, she looked smashing. She was wearing a black slithery something held aloft by spaghetti straps. It wouldn't have been out of place in a boudoir. In a cozy public dining room it unnerved our waiter and added zest to my already ravenous appetite. We ordered sautéed pompano with pecan sauce but I knew, looking at my companion, that delightful dish would leave my hunger unassuaged.

Our conversation was casual and gossipy during dinner. But then, while we were lolling with espresso and tots of B&B, Connie remarked, "By the way, your pal Binky Watrous was seen dancing up a storm with Mitzi Whitcomb at a local disco. My informant reports both of them looked zonked."

"No kidding?" I said. "Old Binky is moving in fast company."

"Too fast for him," Connie said. "I know Binky. He's a sweet boy but nebbishy. Mitzi will chew him up and spit him over the left field fence."

"A barracuda, is she?"

"I don't really think so, Archy. Not from what I hear. I mean, she doesn't deliberately set out to destroy men. She just doesn't care. You know? She flits hither, thither, and yon, and thinks all her temporary partners do, too. But some of them get hurt."

"Not Binky. He's a bit of a flit himself."

"I hope you're right."

I thought I was but I began to wonder. Could my bird-calling chum have surrendered his heart to this Blue Angel? He was a mental flyweight, but I didn't want him wounded. My good deed—accepting him as an apprentice in the arcane profession of discreet inquiries—began to give me an attack of the Galloping Guilts. I decided I better attempt to cool Binky's ardor and turn him to more profitable pursuits. Tatting, for example.

We strolled out to our cars. You may think it curious that we both drove separate vehicles and met at the restaurant, rather than my calling for her at her home as a gentleman should. But Connie preferred the two-car arrangement, I suppose, because it gave her independence. It certainly served her well on those occasions when our dinner dates ended in turbulent conflicts—usually the result of her having learned of my misconduct.

"Archy," she said, "don't bother following me home. I'll be okay. And I want to get to sleep early. I've got a family thing in Miami tomorrow. One of my cousins is getting married. Sorry about that, pal."

"Sorry about the marriage?"

She laughed and punched my arm. "You know what I mean: sorry I can't ask you up for fun and games."

I was tempted to quote the remark attributed to Voltaire: "I disapprove of what you say but will defend to the death your right to say it." Instead, I just caroled, "We'll make it another time."

"Of course we will," she agreed and gave me a warm, sticky kiss before we parted.

And so I drove home alone on that virtuous Saturday. I'm sure you know what was giving me the glooms. No f&g with Sunny Fogarty on Friday night. No f&g with Connie Garcia on Saturday night. I feared the small tonsure on the crown of my noodle might be more serious than I had imagined. You'll admit two spurns in a row can be daunting to an always hopeful lothario.

But I am happy to report the day ended on an uptick. I arrived home, disrobed, and phoned Connie to make certain she was safe, sound, and behind a bolted and chained door. She was.

"Oh Archy," she wailed. "I made such a horrible mistake tonight."

"You didn't order a second B and B?"

"No, silly. I didn't insist you come home with me. Stupid, stupid, stupid! I wish you were here right now."

"Another time," I said grandly. "I've just undressed and am deep in volume three of 'The Decline and Fall of the Roman Empire.' Exciting stuff. Otherwise I'd be happy to pop over. But another night awaits us."

"Promise?"

"Of course," I assured her.

We had no sooner hung up when my phone jangled. I thought it might be Ms. Garcia demanding to know the exact date of that promised night, but it was Sunny Fogarty.

"Archy," she said, "I want to apologize."

"Whatever for?"

"Last night. I acted very foolishly and knew it the moment you walked out. I should have asked you to stay. Am I forgiven?"

"Of course," I said grandly. Magnanimous me!

"I suppose it's too late to invite you over now. Isn't it?"

" 'Fraid so," I said. "I'm unclad and engrossed in the seventh volume of 'The Original Journals of the Lewis and Clark Expedition.' Fascinating stuff. But there will be other nights."

"Promise?"

"Absolutely," I assured her.

And then grinning, I drank a marc, smoked an English Oval, and listened to the original cast recording of "My Fair Lady." I went to bed with my self-esteem healed and intact.

Continuing my righteous weekend, I accompanied my parents to church on Sunday morning. I was rewarded by the sight of an awesome contralto in the choir and immediately lost my senses. She was quite tall, broad-shouldered, with hair cut so short it might have been razored by a Parris Island barber. Fascinating woman, and I kept staring at her while listening to a sermon exhorting us to seek the beauty of God's work on earth and be comforted thereby. Oh, how true, how indubitably true!

I thought I might audition for the choir the next time they had a casting call, but then I realized my chances were nil. I mean, my singing voice is serviceable for barroom ballads, but when it comes to such tunes as "Lead, Kindly Light," you want a tenor with a better instinct for pitch—and more religious fervor than possessed by your humble scribe.

I arrived home still pondering how I might wangle an introduction to that impressive contralto. Ursi Olson told me Mrs. Sarah Whitcomb had phoned and asked I return her call. Father had retired to his study to begin excavating the national edition of *The New York Times,* and so I trudged upstairs to take off my Sunday go-to-meeting costume and call Mrs. Whitcomb.

"Archy," she said, "I do hope I'm not disturbing you."

"Not at all, ma'am. I just returned from church."

"Oh? Do you attend regularly?"

"No," I said.

She laughed delightedly. "Didn't think so," she said. "I've given it up since I've been anchored to this ridiculous chair on wheels. But the pastor insists on dropping by regularly to provide what I'm sure he thinks of as 'spiritual solace.' Dreadful man. Archy, I called for two reasons. First, I want to thank you for the lovely flowers you sent."

"A very small token of my gratitude for a marvelous luncheon."

"Well, it was very thoughtful of you. The second thing is a request. Horace has gone to his club for an afternoon of golf that will take hours. I'd dearly love to have a chat with you—just the two of us—and I wondered if it might be possible for you to come visit for an hour or so."

"Of course," I said promptly, figuring I could return home in time for our Sunday dinner—an early afternoon feast usually followed by a major nap by all the McNallys. "I'll be there in half an hour, Mrs. Whitcomb."

"Sarah," she said. "You *must* call me Sarah. I'll have Jason chill a bottle of this year's Fleurie Beaujolais. Will that do?"

"I'll be there in twenty minutes, Sarah," I vowed, and her giggle had a girlish quality.

I hurriedly pulled on informal duds and bounced downstairs. I paused at the kitchen to see what Ursi and Jamie were preparing. I began to salivate, for they were working on quarters of glazed duckling to be served with a cider sauce.

"Don't you dare serve dinner without me," I warned them. "Be back in an hour. And would you put out some of that cranberry relish, please."

I was at the Whitcombs' palazzo in slightly more than twenty minutes, but the trip seemed to take much less time because I was dreaming about Amazonian contraltos and glazed ducklings. I admit my mind doesn't always work in lucid ways—but neither does yours.

The arthritic Jason met me at the door and slowly—oh, so slowly!—conducted me to the terrace where Mrs. Whitcomb was seated in her wheelchair at a shaded table covered with a jazzy abstract-patterned cloth. An ice bucket, complete with uncorked bottle, was set nearby, and my hostess's glass was half full—or half empty.

She gave me a winsome smile and turned up her face. "Kissy," she commanded, and I leaned to buss her cheek.

She was wearing her usual turban, in an indigo denim this time, and another of her voluminous, filmy gowns that stirred occasionally in a breeze coming off the lake. I took the chair opposite her. Jason, swaddling the dripping bottle in a napkin, added to Mrs. Whitcomb's glass and then filled mine. He departed and I sipped the nectar.

"How do you like it?" Sarah asked.

"Heaven," I pronounced.

"Well, you did go to church this morning," she said mischievously, and I realized again this woman might be ill but her wit hadn't dulled.

"Archy," she said, "tell me something: Are all men idiots?"

I considered that query very, very carefully while savoring another taste of the young Beaujolais. "Perhaps 'idiots' is too harsh a condemnation, Sarah," I said. "But I agree that most men are limited."

"Limited," she repeated. "Yes. Exactly. I knew I could depend on you."

Then she was silent, staring out over the water. It was a thousand-yard stare, and I knew she was not seeing lake, shore, or tacking sailboats.

"I shouldn't bother you with my problems," she said finally.

"If not me—whom? If now now—when?" I tried to say it lightly and was rewarded with a wan smile as she turned to face me.

"All right," she said. "Archy, I love my husband dearly, and I love my son dearly. The two are so unlike—really from different planets—but up to about six months ago they had a—what's it called? A modus something."

"Modus vivendi?" I suggested.

"That's it! They had a sort of unspoken compromise. A live-and-let-live thing. They accepted and loved each other, I believe, even if their lifestyles are so opposite. Horace is a very stiff-necked man. He has his standards."

"I am familiar with the type," I murmured, thinking of my liege.

"Oliver is a hell-for-leather boy. Always has been. And yet the two of them managed to coexist. Horace took Oliver into the business and he's performed brilliantly. Of course there have been disagreements, I can't deny that, but nothing serious. Until, as I said, about six months ago when their relationship became cold and nasty. Their trivial arguments have become rancorous. Spiteful. Sometimes they say things to each other that frighten me. Archy, I'm not asking for your sympathy or pity, but I know I'll be gone soon and I want my son and his father to be close and cherish one another when I'm no longer here to serve as umpire or referee or whatever you want to call it."

She stared at me: a very resolute stare. I had the impression I was listening to this doomed woman's last will and testament.

"Sarah," I said softly and reached across the table to clasp her hand, "I'm sure this is a very real problem that's troubling you. But it's such a personal family matter. How can I possibly help?"

"I know my son is a charming rascal," she said. "But I refuse to believe he could do anything seriously wrong. Nothing unethical or illegal or anything like that. He just *couldn't.* He's my son and I know he's incapable of evil. And yet his father is now treating him with what I can only call suspicion and contempt, as if Oliver might be committing some horrible crime. That's just absurd!"

Her distress was obvious. Hers were not merely the fretful complaints of a dying woman; she was deeply concerned and sharp enough to sense that what was occurring between husband and son was a preliminary tremor that might presage a destructive quake.

"Archy," she said quietly, and our conversation became a whispered dialogue on a drowsy, sunlit midday, "I understand you do investigations for your father's firm."

"Yes, Sarah," I said just as lazily, "that's true."

"I'd like to employ you," she said, looking at me directly. "At whatever rate you name. To see if you can discover what is happening between Horace and Oliver. Neither will talk to me about it; they treat me like a brainless invalid, which I definitely am not! Since both are unwilling to answer my questions, I want you to find out what's going on. I don't expect you to make recommendations on how their quarrel may be resolved; that's my job. But I can't begin until I know the cause. I need information. Will you try to provide it? Our arrangement will be known only to us."

I finished the bottle into her glass and mine, knowing as I poured that I was about to do something exceedingly foolish. But I really had no choice, did I?

"I shall do as you ask, Sarah," I said. "With the understanding it will be an attempt with no guarantee of success. And I want to hear no more mention of rate, charges, or billing. This is a small service for a beautiful woman I love."

Her smile was radiant as she lifted her worn face to me. "Kissy," she said, and so I did.

I drove home in a contemplative mood, musing on the promise I had just made to that wounded woman. Naturally I believed the conflict between Whitcomb *père et fils* was rooted in the financial matter my father and I had discussed: Oliver wanted to create a national chain of funeral homes as rapidly as possible; his father thought it a loony idea not worth discussing. I had mentioned nothing of this to Sarah, of course, respecting client confidentiality.

At that moment I really thought I had two discreet inquiries in progress: investigations into the exceptional profits of the Whitcomb Funeral Homes and into the enmity between the president and the chief executive officer.

Exactly what do people mean when they speak of "a pretty

kettle of fish"? I've never seen one—have you? This entire Whitcomb affair was rapidly becoming an ugly kettle of fish.

Fortunately I arrived home in time for the glazed duckling. With cranberry relish.

16

▲

I started phoning Binky Watrous early Sunday evening, called every half hour, and eventually found the lad at home shortly after 10:30 P.M.

"Archy," he said, "if you value our friendship, make this brief. I am flogged, utterly flogged, and if I don't get some shut-eye I doubt if I shall live to see the sun rise over the yardarm tomorrow."

"Binky, old sod, what have you been up to?"

"We flew to Ocala early this morning."

"Who is 'we'—or who are 'we,' whichever is grammatically correct."

"Me, Mitzi, Oliver, Ernie Gorton, and some other people whose names fortunately escape me."

"You *flew* to Ocala?"

"We did. On a private jet that belonged to someone."

"And why did you fly to Ocala?"

"Oliver wanted to looked at a horse."

"He could have stayed in Boca and looked at a poodle."

"You don't understand, Archy. He's thinking of buying this horse."

"Ah," I said. "And did he?"

"He was impressed. It's a two-year-old with good bloodlines. It was a nice horse. I fed it a carrot. And then we partied. At the home of the guy who owns the horse and then on the flight back to Palm Beach. I can state definitely that the grape and the grain are not a marriage made in heaven. Good night, sleep tight, and don't let the bedbugs bite."

"Wait a minute," I said hurriedly. "I expect to see you in my office at ten o'clock tomorrow morning."

His moan was piteous. "Could we make that noon, Archy?" he pleaded. "You want me up to speed, don't you? And I figure twelve hours' sleep will do it."

I agreed to noon on Monday, but I wasn't certain sleep would bring Binky Watrous up to speed. A frontal lobotomy might do the trick.

As I expected, he didn't show up at noon on Monday, but by one o'clock we were heading south. We took my Miata since I didn't feel Binky was in any condition to navigate even a Flexible Flyer. He had the look of a man brought low by excess. Even the bags under his eyes had bags, and his natural pallor exhibited a greenish tinge that suggested mal de mer. But I was not displeased with his appearance; it fitted the scenario I had devised.

"Where are we going?" he croaked. "And why?"

"We are driving to Broward to see a doctor."

"To cure me?" he said hopefully.

"No, Binky, not to cure you. Only a vow of lifelong abstemiousness might do that. This particular doctor has signed an immoderate number of death certificates submitted to Whitcomb Funeral Homes. And all his allegedly defunct patients have been shipped elsewhere for burial."

"Beautiful. I don't suppose he has much chance of being voted Physician of the Year. What's his name?"

"Omar K. Pflug."

"Impossible."

"Certainly improbable," I agreed. "Although I once heard of a professor of anatomy named Lancelot Tush. Now here's the script I have planned for our visit to Dr. Pflug. You are to play the starring role."

I explained the scam I had devised. Binky was to claim to be a visiting tourist who had arrived from New Jersey with his elderly father only two days ago. They were staying at a nearby motel and the father, who had a long history of heart problems, had unfortunately passed away. Since there had been no physician in attendance, Binky was ignorant of how he might obtain an official death certificate that would enable him to ship his father's remains home to the family plot in Metuchen. The people at the motel had recommended he consult Dr. Pflug.

Binky listened as we sped southward on Federal Highway. It was a so-so day: a lot of greasy clouds with occasional flashes of sunlight. The breeze was right out of a sauna and smelled of sulfur. We drove through one sprinkle of rain but it didn't last long.

"Archy," Binky said, "why are we doing this?"

"To test the bona fides of Dr. Pflug. We are dangling bait to see if he bites. You are to tell him that money is of no importance; your only concern is to get your deceased father home to his final resting place as quickly as possible. All you want from the doctor is a signed death certificate and the recommendation of a funeral home that can handle the details. Think you can play the part of a bereaved son?"

"Of course I can," he said, perking up. "I'll do it just as you told me. No problem."

It took some scouting to find the office of Dr. Omar K. Pflug, and both Binky and I were startled by its location. It occupied the rearmost unit of a grungy strip mall on Copans Road, and I would not care to shop there after nightfall (or even at high noon) unless accompanied by a heavily armed platoon of Army Rangers or Navy Seals.

We didn't stop immediately but made a short tour of the neighborhood until we found a rather decrepit motel, the name and address of which could be used in our planned deception. We then returned to Dr. Pflug's office, parked, and marched up to the door.

I halted Binky for a moment. "Remember," I instructed, "you are a grieving son whose beloved father has just departed for realms where the woodbine twineth. You are racked with grief. If you can manage to stifle a sob or wipe away a tear, it would help."

"Trust me," he said. "I can handle it. I'm a great actor. I once impersonated the Shah of Iran at the Pierre in New York."

"Did it work?" I asked.

"Nope," he said cheerfully.

We pushed in, ignoring a large, hand-lettered sign that declared "By Appointment Only." The waiting room was definitely not designed to soothe nervous patients. The furniture seemed to have been hastily constructed of unpainted plywood except for two chairs and a couch of dented tubular steel upholstered in an acidic green plastic that made my molars ache. I found the wallpaper of screaming parrots especially loathsome.

There was a young woman lounging behind a makeshift desk. She was painting her fingernails a violent crimson, and although dressed in a nurse's whites she was totally unlike any nurse I had ever seen. Her cap was perched atop a pile of orangy hair and her jacket was carelessly (or deliberately) unbuttoned to hint at the bounties within.

I heard Binky gasp and thought it no more than his usual reaction to any charlotte russe of legal age. I found the lady comely enough but considered her sharp features a mite off-putting.

"Yes, gentlemen," she said, looking up with a vacant smile. "What can I do for you?"

I waited for Binky to demonstrate his claimed histrionic ability.

"My pop died," he blurted.

I could have strangled the sap. He had, I realized, all the thespian talents of Popeye, and my hopes for a successful investigation of Dr. Pflug went into deep six.

But the nurse didn't seem discombobulated. "Sorry to hear that, sir," she said chirpily. "But if your father passed, there's not much we can do for you. I mean, it's too late to consult a doctor, isn't it?"

"It's a private matter," I said hastily. "Could we talk to the doctor? It'll only take a few minutes."

She stared at me, obviously debating whether or not to give us an immediate heave-ho.

"I'll see if the doctor is available," she said finally, rose, and sashayed into an inner office. A googly-eyed Binky watched her go.

"Imbecile!" I hissed at him, but he paid no attention.

In a moment we heard a sudden shout of male laughter from within, followed by what I can only describe as a torrent of giggles, male and female. We waited patiently and eventually the nurse emerged adjusting her starched cap, which was hanging rakishly over one ear.

"The doctor will see you now," she said primly.

We entered an inner office which had all the warm ambience of a subway loo. There were a few medical machines in white enameled cases. I could not identify them, although one might have been a cardiograph. The most striking furnishing was a life-size skeleton of plastic, held upright on a metal support that seemed to have sagged, for Mr. Bones appeared to be dancing a jig.

The man seated behind the bare desk had a head that looked like a huge matzo ball: totally hairless, and the face was soft, doughy and dimpled. But it was the eyes that caught my attention. His gaze wavered and never stopped: up and down, left and right, directly at us and then sliding away. He looked as if he was trying to follow the path of a housefly.

This man, I immediately concluded, was stoned out of his gourd. I couldn't guess his drug of choice, but I had no doubt he was gone and drifting.

"Dr. Pflug?" I inquired.

It took him a beat or two to remember who he was. "I am Dr. Omar K. Pflug," he said at last, smiling with triumph. "And who are you?"

Binky launched into his spiel, and to my delighted surprise he delivered it in earnest tones just as he had been coached: His elderly father had died suddenly and a death certificate was needed as well as the name of a funeral home that would facilitate shipping the deceased to a family plot in Metuchen, New Jersey.

Dr. Pflug tried hard to concentrate on Binky's tale of woe.

"Your father?" he asked.

"Yes, sir."

"Croaked?"

"A few hours ago."

"Where is the corpus now?"

Binky explained the body lay in a nearby motel suite. It had been the motel owners who suggested we consult Dr. Pflug.

That flickering glance swung to me. "And who might you be?" he said, not much interested.

"A close friend of the family," I answered. "Eager to provide any assistance I can."

"Air-conditioned?" he said.

"Pardon?" Binky said, totally bewildered.

"Where the deceased presently resides."

"Oh yes," I assured him. "The motel suite is very chilly."

"Good," he said. "Then he'll keep awhile. I'll be very busy this afternoon. At the beck and call of my dear patients, you know. Perhaps I can make it in an hour," he added vaguely. "Maybe two or three. Give me the address. Meet me there and I'll make it official."

"We'll get a signed death certificate?" I pressed.

"Why not?" he said. "If he's as dead as you say. And I suggest Whitcomb Funeral Homes. Lovely people. Very efficient. Very understanding. Write down the name and address of the motel. And the room number where the departed lies at rest."

I took out my gold Mont Blanc but there was a moment of embarrassment because he had nothing to write on, not a single scrap of paper, not even a prescription pad. Finally he dug into the wastebasket beneath his desk and came up with a *Daily Racing Form.* I scribbled the name and address of the motel on the margin of the front page.

"What time, doctor?" Binky asked.

Pflug's flickering stare settled on him again. "Time?" he said. "For what?"

"When we can meet at the motel," I explained slowly. "And you can sign the death certificate."

That unfocused gaze shifted to me and he floated away. "Surely that's not necessary," he said and began to yawn, great jaw-cracking yawns. He shook his head and the flesh on his fat face waggled. "If you say he's gone, he's gone. I don't take credit cards. Or out-of-state checks."

Binky was completely confused, but I knew where the doctor was coming from and I was delighted. Druggie or not, he had been suckered.

"How much, doctor?" I asked him.

"A thousand," he said, squinting at the ceiling.

"We'll be back here with the cash in an hour," I lied. "And to pick up the death certificate. Thank you for your kind cooperation, doctor."

"Thank you, doctor," Binky said humbly.

"Twenties and fifties," Pflug said, glaring at that droopy skeleton. "Jacksons and Grants."

We left, never having shaken his hand, and moved out to the waiting room. The nurse had finished lacquering her nails and was talking animatedly on the phone. She flipped a hand at us as we departed. "Ta-ta!" she sang out.

We stood alongside the Miata in the parking area.

"Got him!" I said exultantly. "The guy is a dyed-in-the-wool wrongo. Strictly a doc-for-rent. Binky, I despaired of you at first, but then you performed brilliantly. I congratulate you."

"She shook me at the start," he said. "The nurse."

"Yes, I saw you making goo-goo eyes at her. But she's not that attractive."

He looked at me with a shaky grin. "Archy, you don't understand. She's Ernest Gorton's carrottop. His date at the wild party Mitzi and Oliver had at their place after his parents' reception. Oliver went upstairs with her later."

"Ah-ha," I said. "The plot curdles."

17

▲

We stopped at a Deerfield joint for an enormous platter of barbecued ribs and a carboy of beer. While enjoying an hour of unalloyed gluttony we discussed which addiction it was that caused Dr. Pflug to act in such an irrational manner. Binky thought it might be cocaine. I thought it might be the nurse.

On the drive back to Palm Beach I gave Binky his next assignment.

"Look, gramps," I said, "you acquitted yourself with distinction this afternoon, and as a natural progression in your on-the-job training I think it's time you take on an independent inquiry with no assistance from yours truly."

"You want me to interrogate the nurse?" he said eagerly. "Force a confession?"

"No," I said sternly, "I do not want you to cozen Ms. Carrottop at all, except possibly to learn her name, which may prove useful in the future. What I want you to do is run a trace on Dr. Omar K. Pflug. Is he licensed to practice in the State of Florida? What are his antecedents? Where is he from, and has he ever been disbarred elsewhere? What was his education, and where did he receive his medical training? Any malpractice suits against him? Any criminal record? Where does he live? Is he married? In other words, I need a complete dossier on that reprehensible quack."

"Archy," he said plaintively, "how do I find out all that?"

"Ask questions," I told him. "You and the Duchess have a family physician, do you not?"

"Oh sure. Old Doc Fellows. He's a bit of a codger but a nice man. Every time I have a checkup he gives me a Tootsie Roll."

"He knows you," I said. "Start with him. Tell him a friend of yours wants to investigate the legitimacy of a new doctor he's thinking of consulting. Ask your family physician how this imaginary friend should go about it. What State licensing boards to phone, what professional organizations to contact, how he can get a report on the new doctor's medical education and competence."

"I guess I can do all that," Binky said doubtfully. "But isn't there an easier way to handle it?"

"No," I said, "there isn't."

There was, of course, but I didn't want to tell a beginner national agencies could provide all the poop required in twenty-four hours—for the payment of a substantial fee.

I was not being mean or trying to create unnecessary labor for my freshman student. I merely wanted him to learn the nitty-gritty of investigation before he discovered how modern technology has rendered obsolete the role of the literary PI. Computers have replaced Lew Archer, the Continental Op, and their brethren. And the Compaq DeskPro/M Pentium doesn't drink bourbon.

We separated in the garage of the McNally Building. Binky chugged away in his bruised Cabriolet, and I went upstairs to my office, dreaming that the chore I had off-loaded onto my lieutenant would keep him out of my tousled locks for at least a week.

I found on my desk a plump FEDEX envelope from the agency I had faxed, requesting financial reports on the principals involved in the Whitcomb ragout. I lugged the bundle down to the garage, tossed it into the Miata, and headed for home, sweet home. It was then twilightish and what started as a so-so day had definitely become melancholy. It wasn't raining, but the pewter sky looked ready to weep at any moment. I decided against an ocean swim and instead went directly to my dormitory and flopped onto my bed for a short snooze. First a balding spot and now an afternoon nap! What was happening to the debonair, vigorous A. McNally we all know and love? Was I becoming a young geezer? Perish forbid!

Morale had been rejuvenated by the time I awoke. I showered, pulled on casual duds, and galloped downstairs in time for the family cocktail hour. That went well and a dinner of broiled Maine lobster went even better. The noble crustacean was nestled on a couch of Ursi Olson's special risotto with just enough saffron to banish my blahs completely. I returned to my desk ready to labor, convinced I would unravel the Whitcomb tangle *tout de suite,* my temporary attack of alopecia would disappear, and I might become the Peter Pan of Palm Beach.

Fortunately, the dossiers I had received were succinct, resembling computer printouts in their use of abbreviations. I mean, they weren't novellas—just précis of the information requested, factual and exact to the penny.

I started with the reports on the four Whitcomb department heads, in charge of purchasing, maintenance, personnel, and merchandising (including public relations). Their records were brief and I went through them swiftly.

All four (three men and one woman) were earning generous salaries, and their annual expenditures and investments seemed commensurate with their income and net worth. There were no suggestions of wild profligacies, although one gentleman, the maintenance supervisor, had made a great number of recent purchases from L. L. Bean. I couldn't understand what need a South Florida resident would have for heavy wool mackinaws and fleece-lined boots. Then I noted his age; he was sixty-four and nudging retirement. I reckoned he was planning to spend his remaining semesters in the Maine woods or thereabouts.

When I turned to the dossiers on the chief directors of the three Whitcomb Funeral Homes, it was a nag of a different hue. Each of the trio (all men) was also earning a more than adequate salary, but their current net worth seemed excessive when linked to annual income.

It didn't take long to discover that the good fortunes of all three were of recent vintage, like the past six months. The bank deposits of the first had increased appreciably. The second had made a large cash down payment on a million-dollar Boca Raton town house. And the third had purchased a Lexus, a customized hot tub, not one but four gold coin Corum wristwatches, and similar costly doodads.

I stared at those records in amazement. Where on earth was their loot coming from? The funeral director who was banking his cash was acting prudently, if not cautiously, but the other two were plunging and taking on heavy debt as if their newfound income was just going to go on and on.

I put this puzzle aside for the moment and turned to the balance sheets of the individuals who interested me most: Horace Whitcomb, son Oliver, and Sunny Fogarty. But before I could focus my gimlet-eye on their journals, my phone pealed and the caller was one of the objects of my curiosity—and possibly the object of my affection.

"I trust I am not disturbing you, Archy," Sunny Fogarty said formally.

"You trust correctly," I assured her.

"I now have information I believe is significant. I think you will be interested. Could we get together? Not tonight of course; it's too late. But I was hoping you'd be free tomorrow evening."

"Never free," I said loftily. "There's always a price to pay. But yes, I'll be available tomorrow evening. What time and where?"

She hesitated half a mo. "Could you come over to my place at nine o'clock?"

"Sounds fine to me."

"I'll expect you then," she said crisply and hung up.

I sat staring stupidly at the dead phone. It had not been the warm, intimate conversation of a female and a male who had recently shared one of life's sublime gifts. I wondered if she now regretted our joust. It was a discomfiting thought, and I resolutely cast it from my mind—with as much success as one might ignore a hangnail.

I took up the reports on the three principals.

Horace Whitcomb wasn't yet a decamillionaire but inching close. In addition to his handsome salary, he was also drawing a hefty annual bonus. Total income, I figured, more than covered his basic living costs. And he had wisely invested in a large portfolio of tax-exempt municipal bonds, the income of which, in the form of dividends and capital gains, he promptly reinvested, obviously believing in what Wall Street likes to call "the miracle of compounding."

Our client's personal ledger showed a heavy outlay for

medical expenses which, considering his wife's condition, was understandable. I had a vague feeling that his periodic cash withdrawals, in various sums ranging from five hundred to five thousand dollars, seemed excessive. But they could be explained by the upkeep on that palazzo he had inherited as well as the purchase of his museum-quality ship models.

All in all, I found nothing in Horace's management of his wealth that ran up red flags and set bells ringing.

I began scanning the analysis of son Oliver's financial health. I must confess I expected to find the heir to Whitcomb Funeral Homes in deep doo-doo. From what I had learned about his lifestyle, I had assumed he'd be in hock up to his nostrils with a balance sheet revealing wild and careless expenditures that had him teetering on the edge of personal bankruptcy.

I couldn't have been wronger—or more wrong, whichever Mr. Webster prefers.

Oliver had a net worth in the neighborhood of three million—which is a pleasant neighborhood if you're thinking of moving. Yes, he had liabilities—mortgages, loans, and such—but they amounted to less than twenty percent of his assets: no reason for panic. And while he seemed to be a free-spending bloke with a taste for big-ticket items, he was quite capable of paying his bills from Whitcomb salary and bonus plus investment income.

I won't say I was shocked, but I was certainly surprised. He proved not to be the profligate I had anticipated. In fact, I thought he was managing his money remarkably well: no splurging on real estate in the Australian outback or on ostrich farms in Texas. I mean, the lad appeared to be a semi-conservative investor with a keen appreciation of the risk-benefit ratio.

I had obviously misjudged him. He was not the pot-smoking resident of hippiedom I had imagined. Instead, his balance sheet presented a portrait of a knowledgeable businessman. It was a puzzle.

I put his record aside, took up the dossier of Sunny Fogarty, and encountered another puzzle.

That perplexing lady had never exactly talked a poor mouth, but she had emphasized how important her job and salary were to her, how horrendous the expenses were of keeping her mother in a nursing home, and had generally given me the impression that the legitimate prosperity of Whitcomb's was her sole concern.

But her ledger painted a somewhat different picture. I don't wish to imply she was loaded. She was far from that, but she was also far from hurting. Her salary and annual bonus from her employer easily covered her expenditures with enough left over to build a small but profitable portfolio of Treasury notes and bonds.

There were a few things in her report that baffled me—or rather things that were *not* included. Her new car was listed under her assets, as was her condominium. But there was no mention of a loan on the former or a mortgage on the latter. In addition, Sunny's credit card charges for new clothes, accessories, and jewelry were practically nonexistent. Yet I knew how smartly she dressed, and not cheaply, I assure you.

I stacked all the credit accounts, bound them with a thick rubber band, and slid the whole pile into the bottom drawer of my battered desk. Then I spent a half hour ruminating on everything I had just read.

I admit I felt like a voyeuristic CPA, but what I had done—although it may seem to you a shameful invasion of privacy—was necessary if I was to discover what offenses were occurring that threatened our client's well-being. I now had no doubt there was frigging in the rigging at the Whitcomb

Funeral Homes, but as to what crimes were being committed, by whom and for what purpose, I hadn't the slightest.

I would love to be able to tell you that at this point, almost halfway through my narrative, I began to get an idea of what was going on. Unhappily, I didn't have a glimmer. I was as befuddled as I had been the first evening the investigation began.

But from long experience I have learned how to deal with befuddlement. You disrobe, take a hot shower, don a silk robe, light a cigarette, and enjoy a small nightcap while listening to a tape of Sinatra singing "One for My Baby . . ." Then you go to bed.

Your befuddlement remains, but you just don't care, You sleep well and dream of a holiday weekend at Veronica Lake.

18

Occasionally I have been accused—unjustly, I aver—of devoting entirely too much wordage in these accounts to rhapsodic delineation of meals I have enjoyed. It is true that I believe good food is the second-greatest pleasure life has to offer. It is also true there is a hand-lettered and framed inscription hanging on the wall of my study that declares: "Nutritious Ain't Delicious!"

But I assumed everyone feels the way I do, and it comes as something of a stun to learn I have calorie-conscious readers who count grams of fat and the sodium content of their daily nutriments—and probably prefer a nibble of tofu to a peanut butter and jelly sandwich on Wonder bread.

It is out of respect for the convictions of these demented few that I shall limit the description of my luncheon with Oliver Whitcomb at Renato's on Tuesday to a single comment: The salmon parisienne was heavenly. I don't wish to titillate anyone's taste buds by extolling the splendor of the brandy Alexanders we drank as dessert. You must seek your own heaven; I found mine.

Of more significance to this magnum opus is the conversation that took place during our feast. Oliver showed up clad in black suit, white shirt, black tie—quite a contrast to my glad rags.

"I have an important funeral to supervise this afternoon," he explained.

I thought it curious phraseology. I mean, *all* funerals are important—are they not?—and especially to the star.

He wasted little time on small talk: nothing about the weather, sports, or the inflated cost of a good bagel.

"I'm really excited about our expansion to the Naples area," he said. "I figure if our business—or any business—isn't growing, then it's falling behind. Don't you agree?"

"Perhaps," I said cautiously. "But there can be dangers in too-rapid expansion. It's meant taps for a lot of healthy companies."

He waved my warning aside. "We'll be able to afford it out of current profits," he said confidently. "They're increasing enormously. And opening on Florida's west coast will be only the first step in establishing the nationwide chain I see as our future. I have a plan all worked out, and believe me, it makes sense."

Then he was silent as our food was served, and I had an opportunity to observe him more closely. He had inherited his father's patrician handsomeness, but Horace's features had a certain craggy strength while son Oliver's face was softer. I don't wish to imply it was weak, but there was a discernible fleshiness testifying to a good life that included much rare roast beef and fortified wines.

"Y'see," he continued, "the mom-and-pops are finished. Bigness is the name of the game. Look at how the giant discount chains have put so many local stores out of business."

There was no doubting his seriousness. It was obviously a

subject to which he had given a lot of thought. What amazed me was that I now saw no evidence of that easy charm he had exhibited at our previous encounters. It made me wonder if that genial warmth was not a natural attribute but a role he played to win what he sought.

That might be true, I reckoned, unless his present performance as an earnest, intent businessman was the façade and he really was the lightweight charmboy I had presumed him to be. People are endlessly fascinating, are they not? I mean, even the dullest are Chinese puzzles. Sometimes they can be solved—but not always.

"I owe it to my father," he went on solemnly. "As well as my grandfather. They built the family business with a lot of hard work and by taking risks to expand. I want to do the same thing."

He paused and looked at me expectantly, as if waiting for praise.

"Mmm," I said, finishing my salmon.

"It's doable," he said with conviction. "I want to establish a national network of brand-name funeral homes, either company-owned or franchises. I've met with some very smart moneymen, we've crunched numbers endlessly, and everyone believes we can swing it."

My plate was now empty. His was not but he seemed to have little interest in those wonderful viands. I was now convinced he had prepared a business presentation for me, a script, possibly even rehearsed, all to persuade me, to win my acquiescence. It was a selling job he was doing, and doing well. But why he needed my approval I could not have said.

That was when he ordered the brandy Alexanders and continued his spiel.

"The brokers I have selected worked out a three-part program. The first requires start-up or up-front money for fees to get this thing rolling. Those funds will be provided by Whitcomb's current cash flow without the need of a bank loan. The second step will be a private placement of stock to interested investors. And the third move will be a public offering of stock, probably initially listed on the NASDAQ exchange. How does that sound to you?"

"It appears you have gone into this very thoroughly," I said diplomatically.

"I have," he said, slapping a palm down on the tabletop for emphasis. "But there is one rub. A fly in the ointment, so to speak. As I'm sure you know, Whitcomb's is a privately held corporation. Shares are owned by my mother, father, myself, and small amounts by longtime employees under a profit-sharing plan. But what I hope to accomplish means going public: selling a portion of the company on a stock exchange. My father is dead set against it. He wants the business to remain strictly within the family. I've tried to explain to him that a public offering doesn't mean we'll lose control; we'll still hold a majority of voting shares. But he's a stubborn man."

Oliver shook his head sorrowfully and finished his dessert. He drew a deep breath, and I anticipated the "hook": the final closing of his eloquent and well-reasoned sales pitch.

"What I'm hoping you might do," he said carefully, "is help me out. I'm sure my father will discuss my project with your father. It would be dad's way to ask his attorney for advice. I'd like to think I could depend on your understanding and cooperation if your father brings up the subject."

I gave him a rueful smile. "My father rarely asks my opinion on legal counsel he gives to clients."

"I know," Oliver said, "but he *might.* And if he does, I'd like to think you're in my corner."

He said no more while he called for a check, paid the bill

with plastic, and we moved outside. I thanked him for a splendid luncheon, but I don't think he was listening.

"By the way," he said, not looking at me, "when it comes time for our private placement—shares of stock sold to a limited number of investors—I'll be happy to put your name on our preferred list. After we go public you could make a mint."

"Thank you," I said, trying to keep any trace of sarcasm out of my voice. "That's very kind of you."

We shook hands and he departed for the "important funeral" he was to supervise. I stood there a moment realizing I had just been the object of an attempted bribe. I wasn't insulted. Amused really, because I knew what little effect I could have on the decisions of Horace Whitcomb or my papa.

Oliver's pitch to me, I decided, revealed a woeful ignorance of my influence, which was practically nil. Either he was misinformed or he had become aware of my investigation into Whitcomb's recent unexplained prosperity and was essaying a measure of damage control.

Whatever his motive, I had learned he was a very determined chap, much deeper than I had originally thought. And that he was intensely ambitious I now had no doubt whatsoever. But as we all know, ambition is a two-edged sword.

I drove away with the conviction that I had just lunched with a three-dimensional man, not the cartoon of a lint-headed, high-living prodigal I had first believed him to be. And what bewildered me most about his chameleonic personality was his marriage to Mitzi, that panther. Was it love that drove him to such an unlikely union or could it have been a deliberate desire to offend his conservative father and by so doing declare his independence?

An intriguing enigma—and I loved it.

If you've devoured previous tales of my adventures, I'm

sure you're aware that occasionally I dabble in stocks. Nothing enormous, I assure you; just a hundred shares here and a hundred there. *Pour le sport,* you might say. I mean, I don't go to Las Vegas, and everyone knows Wall Street is the biggest casino in the world.

My broker is a jolly chap of Chinese ancestry named Wang Lo. I've tried to convince him that if he expects to succeed as a stockbroker he should change his name to Wang Hi, but he won't hear of it. He's a popular member of the Pelican Club, and it was he who taught me how to bolt tequila straight with a lick of salt and a bite of fresh lime.

I'm sure my account is Wang's tiniest, but he's unfailingly polite and willing to spend time shooting the breeze even if it means no commissions for him. Anyway, when I arrived back at my office I phoned him and, after an exchange of pleasantries and genial insults, I requested his advice.

I outlined Oliver Whitcomb's business plan, without mentioning any names of course. I merely told Wang an acquaintance of mine was trying to get a new project moving and wanted me to invest. Should I or shouldn't I?

"That three-step plan is fairly conventional," Wang told me. "A lot of new companies get started that way. Some make it, some don't. Very chancy, but there's always the possibility of a new McDonald's or a new Xerox. This pal of yours—is he asking for up-front money?"

"No, he says he can manage that himself. He's just asking if I'd be interested in the private offering."

"Well, that sounds a little better, Archy; the risk is somewhat reduced. If he's got his start-up funds, it shows he's probably not peddling emu ranches or rhinestone mines. I really can't tell you what to do unless I know more about it. It's not another new chain of pizza joints, is it?"

"No, Wang, it's a chain of noodle palaces."

"Hey," he said, "I might put a few bucks into that myself. But only if they promise to serve curried rice stick noodles, my favorite."

"I'll tell him that," I promised, and we hung up laughing.

About all I had learned from that consultation was that Oliver Whitcomb had a viable business plan and was apparently not running an out-and-out swindle. I'm no financial wizard, but I could see that what Oliver termed "a rub, a fly in the ointment"—id est, his father's objections—might doom the project before it got off the ground.

Just to make certain, I phoned Mrs. Trelawney and asked if our honcho was present and could grant me an audience of no more than five minutes.

"Oh Archy," she said, "I doubt that; he's so busy."

"Inspecting his briefs again, is he? Be a luv and ask, will you?"

She came back on the line and told me I could have five minutes, no more.

I went leaping up the back stairs to poppa's office and found him seated at his antique rolltop desk reviewing a humongous stack of legal documents.

"Yes, yes, Archy," he said irritably, "what is it now?"

"Sir," I said, "something curious has come up concerning the Whitcomb Funeral Homes investigation, and I need to know who actually owns the business. I presume Horace Whitcomb holds a controlling majority of the stock."

He stared at me. "This is important to the successful conclusion of your inquiry?"

"Yes, father, it is."

He paused a moment, then drew a deep breath. "In that case I shall reveal that you presume incorrectly. The majority of shares are held by Mrs. Sarah Whitcomb."

I was astonished. "How can that be?"

"Very easily," he said testily. "The shares were legally transferred to his wife's name by Horace Whitcomb for tax purposes. Of course her shares are always voted as her husband recommends since she has little knowledge of or interest in the business affairs of their privately held corporation."

"I see," I said, beginning to get a glimpse of what was going on. "Thank you for the information."

He thawed briefly. "Making any progress, Archy?" he asked.

"Yes, sir. A little."

He nodded. "Keep at it," he commanded and went back to his bumf.

I returned to my office just long enough to pick up my panama and then set off for home. I decided an ocean swim was needed to soothe the day's rigors I had endured, to say nothing of restoring me to fighting trim for my meeting that evening with Sunny Fogarty.

My slow wallow had the desired effect, and the family cocktail hour followed by a light dinner of veal marsala completed my rejuvenation. I dashed upstairs to make entries in my journal concerning recent events. I was about to close up shop and prepare for my tête-à-tête with Ms. Fogarty when a phone call stopped me.

"Archy," Sunny said, "I'm glad I caught you before you left. Could we make it ten o'clock instead of nine?"

"Of course," I said manfully. "No problem. But would you prefer another night?"

"No, no," she said hurriedly. "I want to see you tonight. It's important. But a neighbor asked to stop by for a while to ask me about her investments, and I couldn't very well refuse. I hope our meeting an hour later won't inconvenience you."

"Not at all," I said. "I'll be there."

"Thank you, Archy," she said gratefully.

I hung up absolutely certain the female neighbor seeking investment advice was a fabrication. Sunny's voice had taken on the deeper, more solemn and intent tone prevaricators use, thinking it will convince the listener of their honesty and sincerity.

I had no doubt the lady was lying.

19

I make no claims to possess ESP and I trust you don't either. But have you ever entered a room and had the definite impression it was recently occupied by a visitor now departed?

That was the feeling I had when Sunny Fogarty led me into her condo. She had told me she expected the visit of a female neighbor, but I had a distinct notion that her guest had been male. Later that night, when I analyzed my reaction, I realized there were rational reasons for it: the down cushion of an armchair was still deeply depressed and, although I am no supernose, I did detect an ever-so-faint odor of cigar smoke plus another scent difficult to identify. My best guess was that I had sniffed a man's rather spicy cologne.

Naturally I made no mention of my suspicions to Sunny. She had welcomed me graciously and almost immediately supplied me with a tot of iced vodka, for which I was thankful.

She was dressed smartly, as usual, wearing a loose charmeuse T-shirt and silk jeans dyed to resemble denim. I thought the latter amusing. Similar to people who install gold bathroom fixtures but insist they must be tarnished. There are such odd creatures, you know.

"Sorry for the delay, Archy," she said. "But I really couldn't help it."

"No problem," I assured her again. "You're looking mighty perky this evening, Sunny."

"Am I?" she said, genuinely surprised. "Thank you. I wish I felt perky, but I don't. The deeper we get into this mess, the more depressed I become. And frightened."

"Frightened? How so?"

"Because I know now that someone is trying to destroy Whitcomb or at least use the funeral homes in a criminal scheme. Archy, in effect I am the chief financial officer and feel I have a fiduciary duty to make certain our business is conducted in a legal and ethical manner. And I find this matter a cause for grave concern."

I think I successfully hid my amazement. I mean, that rather pompous speech was so obviously rehearsed she lacked only a promptbook. I merely nodded encouragingly.

"As you know," she continued, "I've been checking the invoices of the airlines which handle Whitcomb's out-of-state shipments, trying to discover the names and addresses of the consignees."

"The information missing from your files."

"*Stolen* from my files," she said angrily. "As you discovered, most of those shipments went to New York, Boston, and Chicago. At LaGuardia in New York, practically all of the caskets were picked up by the Cleo Hauling Service."

I looked at her, puzzled. "Sunny, isn't that a bit unusual, to deliver human remains to a hauling service?"

She was drinking an amber liquid with bubbles. I guessed it might be ginger ale or something similar. Now she took a great gulp of it as if she needed whatever strength it might give her. "Unusual?" she repeated. "Archy, it's practically unheard of. The coffins are customarily picked up by local funeral homes or cemeteries. Sometimes by relatives or churches when a service is to be held. But by a hauling company? That's just ridiculous! Would you like another drink?"

"I think I need one," I said, holding out my empty glass.

"You will," she said. "The worst is yet to come. I'll have one, too. I've had enough diet cream soda for one night."

She returned with our drinks, and I noticed mine was larger this time, and it turned out to be gutsier. But hers was the same size and, I hoped, of the same toughness. I mean, I did not believe Sunny was trying to paralyze me.

She seated herself on the couch close to me. She continued: "It's definite that the majority of shipments going to LaGuardia in New York were consigned to the Cleo Hauling Service. Now would you care to guess who picked up most of Whitcomb's shipments to Logan in Boston and O'Hare in Chicago?"

I groaned. "Don't tell me it was the Cleo Hauling Service."

"You've got it," she said, and we stared at each other. "Archy, what on earth is going on?" she burst out. There was fury in her voice and, I thought, an undertone of fear.

"We'll find out," I promised, "and bring it to a crashing halt. I'm as convinced as you that there's a nefarious plot afoot aimed at your employer and our client."

She gazed away, looking at nothing. "If I let anything bad happen to the company I'd never forgive myself. Never! Horace Whitcomb has been so good to me. He's helped me so much. He's given me a chance to be happy."

"Like a father, is he?" I said casually. It was perhaps an intrusive thing to say, but as you well know, I'm a nosy chap.

She turned to look at me directly. "A father?" she said. "I wouldn't know. My real father deserted my mother and me when I was three years old."

"Oh," I said, an admittedly vacuous comment. "Well, I think Horace Whitcomb is a splendid gentleman."

"Yes," she said, "he is that. And I can't have him hurt. I simply won't stand for it."

Suddenly she had become too heavily emotional. She was falsifying again, just as she had when Binky and I first visited. After that encounter the would-be Hercule Poirot of Palm Beach had declared the lady was scamming us—or trying to. I thought his judgment was accurate.

I believed she was sincere in her professed loyalty to Whitcomb, but I still sensed she was not revealing all she knew. That troubled me. Not because I suspected she might be involved in the caper—whatever it was—but because what she was holding back might enable me to write "Finis" to this case a lot sooner. Now I had to spend time and the racking of my poor, deprived brain in an effort to tweak out the mystery she kept hidden.

"Something bothering you, Archy?" Sunny asked.

"Pardon?" I said. "Oh no. Just woolgathering." And then, because I have a talent for improv, I forged ahead. "I was thinking of your comment that Horace Whitcomb had given you the *chance* to be happy. That was well said. The Declaration of Independence lists 'the pursuit of happiness' as one of our unalienable rights. What a wonderful phrase! 'Pursuit' is the key word. I suspect Tom Jefferson used it ironically or at least slyly, meaning to imply that the chase after happiness is more important than its capture."

Sunny smiled and took my hand. "Let's go see if we can capture it," she said. We finished our drinks and off we went to the tourney.

I won't label Sunny Fogarty as Rubenesque, but she was abundant and all the more stirring for it. Her body was vital, overwhelming. I hung on for dear life and, in addition to my pleasure, had the added delight of being a survivor.

But I must admit that despite our yelps of bliss I could not rid myself of an aggravating unease that there was a dichotomy in her motives and in her actions. Just as during our first tumble, I had the antsy feeling that she was a Byzantine woman, very complex, and quite capable of giving mouth-to-mouth resuscitation without becoming emotionally involved.

I sensed there was a deep and muffled part of her that she would never surrender, ever, to anyone.

But I cannot deny it was a joyous evening. For me at least. And before I departed, Sunny clutched me in a hot, almost frantic, embrace, and I began to believe she was a woman torn.

I promised I would investigate the Cleo Hauling Service and report the results to her ASAP. She gave me a brave smile and walked me to the door, clutching my hand tightly as if she feared to let me go. No doubt about it; she was a riddle, a troubling riddle.

I was home shortly after midnight with absolutely no desire to jot notes in my journal, smoke a coffin nail, listen to music, or have a nightcap, no matter how tiny. In truth, the McNally carcass was totally drained, wrung out, and hung up to dry. All I sought was blessed sleep, hoping the morn would bring roses back to my cheeks.

I had a delayed breakfast on Wednesday morning, having enjoyed a few extra hours of catalepsy. I found Jamie Olson alone in the kitchen, puffing on his ancient briar, which had a cracked stem bound with a Band-Aid. He was also nursing a mug of coffee, and I had no doubt he had added a dollop of aquavit to give him the push to face the rigors of another day.

Jamie offered to scramble a brace of eggs for me, but I settled for an OJ, a bran muffin, and black decaf. Very abstemious and totally unsatisfying. Why do all healthy meals remind me of wallpaper paste?

I sat across from Jamie and thought it a propitious time to start redeeming the promise I had given Mrs. Sarah Whitcomb: to discover the reason for the enmity between her husband and son.

"Jamie," I said, "do you know Jason, houseman for the Horace Whitcombs?"

"Yep," he said. "One year younger than God. Got the arthritis."

"I noticed. Nice man?"

"Jase? The best. Him and me have a belt together now and then."

I was about to observe that "He and I" would have served even better but restrained that pedantic impulse.

"There seems to be a quarrel between Horace and his son Oliver. The next time you have a belt with Jason you might inquire as to the cause."

Jamie considered that a moment, staring at his fuming pipe. "Couldn't ask straight out," he said finally.

"Of course not," I said hastily. "Didn't expect you to. But you might hint around. Gently, you know. Tell him you've heard gossip. Something like that. He may tell you something he wouldn't reveal to me."

"Yep," he said. "Jase don't blab when it comes to his family. But I can buy him a Bushmills. That's his favorite, and it would be a treat for him."

I took a twenty from my wallet and slid it across the table. "Buy him two Bushmills," I said, "and see if he'll loosen up about Horace and Oliver."

"With two Bushmills in him," Jamie said mournfully, "he'll tell me again about Peaches and Daddy Browning."

I was preparing to depart when the phone rang and I picked up in the kitchen.

"The McNally residence," I said, figuring it was probably a call for mother.

"Archy?" Binky Watrous said. "Why aren't you in your office?"

"Because I'm here," I explained. "What's on your mind, Binky?—if you'll forgive a slight exaggeration."

"How about buying a fellow lunch?" he asked eagerly.

"And what fellow do you suggest?"

"Come on, Archy," he said. "You don't pay me a salary, and the least you can do is feed me for all my hard work. I've got a lot of neat stuff to tell you. Besides, the Duchess has canceled my credit cards. Archy, I'm *starving!*"

"All right," I relented. "Meet you at the Pelican Club around twelve-thirty."

"Can't we go somewhere tonier?" he said plaintively. "And more expensive."

"No," I told him.

I drove to the McNally Building, went directly to my office, and got on the horn. I phoned Operator Assistance in New York, Boston, and Chicago. I called vehicle license and registration bureaus, trade associations, and even chambers of commerce. And by noon I had my answer.

Or rather I had no answer. None of the sources I contacted had any record—past, present, or applied for—of the Cleo Hauling Service. Apparently it did not exist.

I can't say I was shocked. After all, it would be a fairly simple scam to finagle. One truck for each of the three aforementioned cities, the trucks purchased secondhand or stolen.

Ditto for the license plates and registration. No insolvable difficulties. Then you painted whatever you wished on the truck sides, added a phony address, and you were in business.

But *what* business?

20

Leroy Pettibone, our esteemed chef at the Pelican Club, occasionally grew bored with preparing his special cheeseburgers or seafood salads for luncheon. Then he switched to what he called a Deli Delite: a hot corned-beef sandwich on sour rye with a heap of coleslaw spiked with coarsely ground black pepper, and a plate of kosher dill spears. Leroy had also discovered a hot mustard made in Detroit, of all places, that made your eyes water.

The Deli Delite was not the equal of masterworks from the Stage or Carnegie in Manhattan of course—but then what is? But it was as yummy as anything of the genre I had tasted in South Florida.

And that's what Binky Watrous and I had for lunch, with enough cold beer to keep our palates from charring.

"All right, Binky," I said as we scarfed, "what's the neat stuff you said you had to tell me?"

"About this Dr. Omar K. Pflug," he said, mumbling through a mouthful of corned beef. "He was kicked out of

New York and New Jersey. And now he's working in Florida. Also, he's a druggie."

"Why was he kicked out of New York and New Jersey? Was his license to practice revoked or was he just accused and is under investigation? And for what? Has he been licensed to work in Florida?"

"Well, those are just minor details, aren't they? I mean, the guy is obviously a wrongo."

"Binky, did you check with your family physician or contact professional associations and the state licensing board as I suggested?"

"Well, ah, no," he said, taking a chomp of a pickle. "I thought there really wasn't much point in going through all that folderol. So I just asked Mitzi Whitcomb and she told me."

I tried to repress a groan and didn't quite succeed. I looked at him, saw a brain sculpted solely of cottage cheese, and wondered if I had suddenly become a victim of synesthesia.

He must have sensed my outrage, for he immediately became defensive. "You can depend on what Mitzi told me," he said. "Absolutely!"

I took that *cum grano salis.* With a heap of *salis,* if the truth be known.

"Binky," I said, "did it ever occur to you the lady may be lying?"

He was astonished. "Why should she do that?"

I sighed. "People usually lie for reasons of self-interest of which you wot not."

"Well, Mitzi wouldn't lie to me."

"Oh? Give me a because."

"Because she's in love with me."

"She told you that?"

"Not exactly. But she let me paint her toenails."

This surreal conversation, I realized, was getting me precisely nowhere.

I asked, "Did Mitzi Whitcomb reveal any other nuggets of information?"

He pondered a moment, pale brow furrowed, a shred of coleslaw hanging from his chops. Then he brightened. "Sure she did! The carrottop, the nurse you saw in Pflug's office—well, she's no nurse. She's not exactly a hooker, but she's sort of a call girl and uses the doctor's place as a home base."

"Some home," I said. "Some base. Did Mitzi tell you her name?"

"Rhoda. Mitzi didn't know her last name."

"Is Ernest Gorton managing her?"

"I don't understand."

"To put it crudely, is Gorton her pimp? Providing customers?"

"Oh," he said, and I think he actually blushed. "I don't know anything about that."

I finished my second beer and sat back. The Deli Delite had more than adequately compensated for that wretched bran muffin I had for breakfast.

"All right, let's assume Mitzi Whitcomb's information is accurate. Then what we've got is a rogue doctor willing to sign fake death certificates, presumably to finance his drug addiction. He also shares working quarters with a call girl who may or may not be the girlfriend and/or employee of Ernest Gorton, a Miami hustler who claims to be in the import-export trade. Is that how you see it?"

"See what?" Binky said.

There was no point in screaming at the pinhead. He was a good-hearted chap, no doubt of that, but his thought processes were so sluggish as to be almost immobile.

"Binky," I said gently, "discreet inquiries demand the ability to deal with complexities and complications. You must be able to endure total confusion temporarily with the faith that eventually you will be able to bring order out of chaos. You follow?"

"Oh sure," he said, "Hey, let's have a kirsch at the bar. Just to cut the grease, you know."

Later we were in the parking area when, emboldened by the cherry brandy, Binky said eagerly, "What's my next assignment, kemo sabe?"

"If you are to play Tonto to my Lone Ranger," I told him, "you must demonstrate energy and inspiration. I suggest you investigate Rhoda, the faux nurse. Discover her last name and home address. Determine whether she is Ernest Gorton's inamorata or merely his employee. And what is her relationship to Oliver Whitcomb."

He was completely flummoxed. "How do I do all that?"

"Use your imagination," I advised. "Perhaps you might start by asking Rhoda for a date. Take her home to have dinner with the Duchess."

He blanched and began to tremble. "Oh golly," he said, "I couldn't do that. You're joking, aren't you, Archy? Tell me you're joking."

"I'm joking," I assured him. "How you do it is up to you. Just do it."

"I wonder if she'd enjoy birdcalls," he said thoughtfully.

"I'm sure she would," I said. "Try a cockatoo."

I apologize for that one.

I drove back to the McNally Building asking whatever gods may be why I had been saddled with a disciple who was such an utter goof. It wasn't that Binky was incapable of reasoning, but his gears had slipped a bit, just enough so his thinking was slightly skewed. I mean, he was the kind of numbskull who, informed that a friend had choked to death on a fish bone, was likely to inquire, "Broiled or sautéed?"

I arrived at my office to find a message that Mr. Horace Whitcomb had phoned and requested I return his call. The number given was Whitcomb Funeral Homes' headquarters in West Palm Beach, and I had to navigate through the queries of receptionist and private secretary before their chieftain came on the line.

"I hope I'm not disturbing you, Archy," he said.

"Not at all," I said. "How are you, sir?"

"I'm well, thank you," he said, his voice at once stiff and hollow. "But Sarah is back in the hospital."

"I'm sorry to hear that, Mr. Whitcomb."

"Well, it's only for more of those damnable tests, and I hope she'll be home by the weekend. But she's somewhat depressed, as you can imagine. She asked if I'd call and see if you have time to pay her a short visit. Just for a few moments, you know. I think it would cheer her immensely."

"Of course I'll visit," I said. "Immediately if hospital rules permit."

"You'll have no problem," he said. "Sarah is in a private suite." He gave me the hospital name and address. "Thank you so very much, Archy," he said huskily. "I know my wife will be delighted to see you."

Errands of mercy do not come easily to yrs. truly, and I find hospital visits particularly difficult. In fact, I *loathe* hospitals. Most of them look like fortresses or warehouses, and then there's that deplorable hospital odor. No matter how much wild cherry spray they use, one still imagines an underlying scent of sickness and sheet-covered bodies on gurneys.

And also, of course, there's your own behavior to sadden you: the stretched, mirthless grin and a complete inability to keep the conversation casual and comforting. How Florence Nightingale and Walt Whitman did it I shall never understand.

But off I went to visit the hospitalized Sarah Whitcomb. Naturally I could not arrive empty-handed, but I decided against flowers; she was sure to have plenty of those. I stopped at a gift shop and found a windup music box. There was a tiny porcelain lady in a formal gown on top and she twirled as you heard a plinked "I Could Have Danced All Night." Kitsch? It was, but I hoped Sarah would find it as amusing and evocative as I did.

I guessed Horace Whitcomb was paying horrendous daily rates for that private two-room hospital unit, but my first impression was that I had entered a motel suite. An upscale motel, to be sure, but there was still the hard, impersonal look: everything gleaming, everything of assembly-line sleekness including framed floral prints bolted to the walls and an excess of vinyl and Formica.

The bedroom was a little better, a little softer, and Mrs. Whitcomb lay in a bed covered with gaily patterned sheets I was certain she had brought from home. She was lying still, her skull now covered with a blue medical cap. Her head was turned and she was staring out the window at the endless sky.

"Sarah," I said softly.

Slowly—oh, so slowly—she moved to face me and her bright smile was almost enough to cause me to lose my cool and blubber.

"Archy!" she said. "What a sweetheart you are to come visit an old, decrepit lady like me."

"Neither old nor decrepit," I said. "Madonna wanted me for the afternoon, but I told her I had a better offer."

Her eyes squinched with merriment but her laugh seemed to cause pain. "Kissy," she said.

I leaned to kiss her cheek and then pulled up a small armchair covered with a trompe l'oeil fabric depicting the Colosseum. Just what I needed.

"Getting along, are you?" I asked. It was the best I could do; I was acutely uncomfortable.

"Getting along," she said. "Right now I'm very drowsy. I think they've given me something. If I fall asleep while we're talking, I hope you'll understand."

"Of course," I said. "But before you snooze, here's a little nothing I brought for you."

I unwrapped the music box, wound it up, and set the porcelain dancer twirling.

Sarah's reaction was unexpected. Tears came to her eyes and she reached out a quavery hand.

"It's beautiful," she breathed. "Just beautiful. Thank you so very, very much. But how did you know?"

"Know what, dear?"

"When I was a young girl I loved ballroom dancing. I even entered contests and won prizes. In those days it was all waltzes, the fox trot, the two-step, and if you were very daring, the tango. Thank you again, Archy. It's the loveliest present anyone has ever given me."

"I admit I cherish the tune," I said. "I like songs with a melody. But that's hardly a weakness, is it?"

"If it is," she said, "it's one more ailment to add to my long, long list."

She seemed to be fading, her voice dimming. I had to crane to hear what she was saying.

"Oliver tells me the two of you had lunch."

"We did indeed," I said. "A splendid luncheon."

"Oliver likes you," she said and looked at me awaiting the expected response: "And I like Oliver."

When I cannot lie I prefer to finesse. To be perfectly honest (well, no one is *perfect*), I didn't much like Oliver Whitcomb. So I merely murmured, "That's very kind of him," and Sarah accepted that.

"What I asked you to do," she said with some effort, "and what you promised to do, was to investigate the hostility between my husband and my son. Have you discovered anything?"

"Nothing conclusive," I told her. "I think it may be just a generational conflict. Each man has his own standards. And I know I don't have to tell you how far and how fast the world has moved in the past fifty years. Sarah, it may be just the difference in their ages that causes their disagreements."

She looked at me a long time in silence and then her eyes closed. I thought she might have fallen asleep but she hadn't.

"Archy," she said faintly, "I think you are an intelligent and sensitive man."

"Thank you," I said. "I wish I could agree."

She waved that away with a flap of a palsied hand. "But I think there's more to the situation between Horace and Oliver than a difference in their age. Something else is going on that's tearing them apart. I sense it. Archy, I love my son, love him more than anything else in this world. I can't stand the thought of him being hurt, and especially by his father. I am telling you these things because you're not one of the family and because I trust your judgment and discretion. I know I don't have much time left and I want you to be witness to this: If I ever have to choose between my husband and my son, God forbid, I will side with my son. Do you understand what I'm saying?"

What she had said had been spoken in tones of such sad finality that I knew she had given the problem much anguished thought and had come to her decision with sorrow and regret.

"I understand, ma'am," I said gravely.

"But I still hope that with your help I can bring them together again. You will try, won't you, Archy?"

"I'll try," I promised again.

"I'm falling asleep now," she whispered. "I can feel it coming on."

"I'll leave," I said, rising. "Sarah, be well and may all your dreams come true."

"Thank you," she said in a tattered voice. "Play the music box again for me."

I departed to the tinkly notes of "I Could Have Danced All Night."

21

It had been a shaking experience, not only to visit a doomed woman but to be plunged into the midst of what was obviously a familial crisis. So it was curious—as odd to me as it must seem to you—that during my drive back to the McNally mini-estate on Ocean Boulevard I could not concentrate on the Whitcombs' travails but only on how they might mirror my own relations with my parents.

I arrived home, slid the Miata into our three-car garage, and went looking for mother. I found her in our little greenhouse talking to her begonias, and she looked fetching in a flowered apron that swathed her from neck to knee.

I followed her about as she watered her darlings, pinching off a dried leaf here and there, and told her of my visit to Mrs. Sarah Whitcomb in the hospital.

"That was very sweet of you, Archy," momsy said approvingly. "I do hope you brought her a get-well gift."

"I did indeed," I said and described the music box.

Mother was delighted and said she'd surely visit Sarah or at least phone to gossip awhile. I said I was certain Mrs. Whitcomb would welcome a call.

All this chitchat was stalling on my part, you understand. What I really wanted to do was ask mother, if circumstances demanded a choice of her sympathy, love, and understanding between her husband and her son, which of us would she choose? You can see how deeply I had been affected by Sarah Whitcomb's dilemma.

But I could not bring myself to ask the question. It would be an excruciating decision for her to make, I knew, but even worse I felt that even posing that louche query was an impertinent invasion of her privacy.

And so, after a time, I wandered away, none the wiser but reflecting how often children (myself included) regard their mother and father simply as parents and rarely make an effort to consider them as individuals or give a thought to their secret lives, what they had sought, won, lost.

I went upstairs to my digs still pondering the infernal complexities of family ties. I had told Mrs. Whitcomb I suspected the hostility between her husband and son might be a generational conflict. I did believe that was part of it but not the total answer.

Now, preparing for my daily ocean swim, I brooded about my relationship with my own father. There was certainly a generational factor at work there, but more a difference than a conflict. I mean, he wore balbriggan underwear and wingtips. I wore silk briefs and tasseled suede loafers. Big deal.

I knew I would never be as erudite as he, and in turn he was not as streetwise as I. There had been and would be disagreements between us of course—how could there not be?—but never dark looks, clenched fists, and muttered imprecations.

Not once had we treated one another with less than civility, however formal, and there's much to be said for it. And for a bemused love never verbally expressed but which was real and enduring. That I knew.

After my saltwater dip, the family cocktail hour, and dinner (shrimp and scallops sautéed with capers, roasted peppers and sundried tomatoes) I waddled upstairs with some effort and set to work bringing my journal current on the strange affair of the Whitcomb Funeral Homes. There was much to record, but none of my scribblings yielded a clue as to what was going on. All I had was an account of disparate facts and fancies that revealed no pattern or even a wild surmise.

I interrupted my labors to phone Connie Garcia, that paragon I had been neglecting shamefully. She was in a chipper mood and we gibbered for almost half an hour, exchanging tidbits of gossip and scurrilous opinions of close friends and local political muck-a-mucks.

"By the way," Connie said, "about an hour before you called, one of my spies reported she spotted your pal Binky Watrous wining and dining an orange-haired judy at a Lauderdale McDonald's."

"How does one wine another at a McDonald's?" I asked, reasonably enough.

"Just a figure of speech, doll. Anyway, my informant says she was all over Binky like a wet sheet."

"He was probably imitating a lovesick whippoorwill."

"No doubt," Connie said. "Just thought you'd be interested."

"Oh, I am. Mildly. Give you a call on Friday, Connie. Maybe we can tear a herring over the weekend."

"Let's," she said. "Before all the snowbirds arrive and we can't get a table."

We disconnected and I hung up thinking Binky Watrous, the wannabe Inspector Javert, was taking my advice to heart and displaying energy and inspiration. I was sure the orange-haired judy was Rhoda, Ernest Gorton's carrottop, but I doubted if birdcalls and a Big Mac would be sufficient to entice startling disclosures.

I finished my journalistic chores, skipped a nightcap and final ciggie, and went directly to bed. It wasn't that I was physically weary but the McNally neurons were churning and I sought sleep to deliver me from all the bedeviling puzzles encountered during the day. I hoped I might awake the following morn with an apocalyptic inspiration that would solve the Whitcomb case, reveal the whereabouts of Atlantis, and explain why our laundry always withholds one of my socks.

Such was not the case of course. I awoke Thursday morning, peered out my window, and saw a world swaddled in murk. I mean, the fog was so thick you couldn't see a foot in front of your face—which made things difficult for podiatrists.

Even worse, the weather mirrored my inner gloom. Sleep had brought no grand revelations; I was still mired in perplexity. Can you wonder why I was in such a grumpy mood and so silent at breakfast with my parents that mother inquired solicitously if I was coming down with something?

"Nothing serious," I assured her. "Just a galloping case of frustration."

"A lot of that going around these days," father remarked, which was his version of Wildean wit.

I arrived at the McNally Building about an hour later, having tooled the Miata slowly through the swirling mist. I sulked in my office and wondered what to do next. Felo-de-se was one possibility, but I rejected it.

I was saved from a fatal attack of the megrims by a phone call from Sgt. Al Rogoff.

"How're you doing, buddy?" he asked.

"Surviving," I told him. "Barely. And you?"

"Lousy. This miserable fog. We've had more crashes than I can count. Mostly fender-benders but a few bloody messes. Listen, when can you and I get together?"

"You have information about Ernest Gorton?" I said, suddenly on the qui vive.

"Some," he admitted. "And some questions for you. I should be home by four o'clock. How about dropping over to my chateau around then?"

"I'll be there," I promised.

I arrived at his mobile home later that afternoon, bearing a cold six-pack of Molson ale. He put out a bowl of honey-roasted cashews and we settled in. Al's place always reminds me of a slightly tatty's men's club: lots of oak furniture, worn leather, and a total disregard of the trendy and uncomfortable. It made you want to kick off your shoes, and I did.

We sipped a little ale, popped a few cashews, talked lazily of this and that. Then the sergeant got down to business.

"About Ernest Gorton," he started. "You told me a client thinks this guy is clipping him and that's why you wanted a trace. Was that the truth?"

"No," I said.

"Didn't figure it was," Rogoff said equably. "You lie even when you don't have to—just to keep in practice."

"That's what Connie Garcia keeps telling me."

"She's right. Okay, sonny boy, let's have it: what's your interest in Ernest Gorton?"

"It's a long story."

"We have a six-pack; take your time."

I told him about the Whitcomb Funeral Homes investigation. Not everything of course. I said nothing about the conflict between Horace and Oliver, the anguish being endured by Sarah Whitcomb, or my uneasiness about the role Sunny

Fogarty was playing. Al had no need to know. But I did give him the bare bones, including Oliver's close friendship with Ernest Gorton and the activities of Dr. Omar K. Pflug and Rhoda, who was no more a nurse than I was a nuclear physicist.

I finished speaking. The sergeant opened another ale, took a deep draft, and looked at me reflectively.

"Beautiful," he said. "I just love these swamps you drag me into. Nothing as simple as a post office massacre or a terrorist plot to blow up City Hall. You only get involved in the wheels-within-wheels cases."

"That's not fair," I protested. "When this thing was first brought to our attention, both my father and I thought it was nothing. Now we both think it's for real."

"Yeah," he conceded. "It does sound like something is going down."

"That seems plausible to me."

Rogoff's smile was cold. "Let me tell you about Monsieur Gorton. From what I heard from my Miami pals, this guy has megabucks. They say he's got green eyes: all he sees is money. He's into everything rancid you can think of. Drugs, money laundering, ripoffs of high-priced labels, prostitution, guns. Is that enough for you? If not, how about this one: He's also suspected of killing horses."

"Of *what!?*"

"Rich no-goodniks who own a valuable Thoroughbred, trotter, or jumper that's not performing up to snuff want the animal put down so they can collect the insurance. Gorton has the rep of providing experts who can make the slaughter look like an accident."

I gulped. "That's nice," I said.

"Oh yeah," Al said. "Sweet people."

I recalled what Binky had told me about Oliver and Gorton

flying to Ocala to inspect a horse. But I related nothing of that to Rogoff. It might have been an innocent trip. Maybe.

"He is one active villain," the sergeant continued. "And the kicker is that he's never done time. Archy, the man is no dummy. He's got layers of management, and if his soldiers or sub-bosses have to take a fall, he provides money for their defense and takes care of their families while they're inside. Loyalty up and loyalty down. I mean, the guy's got a tight organization. It's not as big as the Mafia or the Colombian drug cartels—although he's worked with both of them—but his outfit is lean and mean. He's been busted a hundred times and always walks away singing 'Who Cares?' "

"A charmed life," I observed.

"Yeah," Al said. "But what the hell, it's rumored he has local pols on the pad. Now here he is palsy-walsy with the chief executive officer of a chain of funeral homes that's shipping north a lot of dead people from Florida. What's going on?"

"He's getting rid of his victims?" I suggested.

Rogoff thought about that a moment. "Maybe," he said.

"Illegal immigrants? He's charging for airlifting them north in caskets? No, scratch that. They'd probably never survive in sealed containers packed into an airliner's cargo bay."

We looked at each other and both of us shrugged.

"Two problems," Rogoff said. "One: What is Ernie boy doing? And two: Why is Oliver Whitcomb apparently cooperating? Blackmail?"

"Perhaps," I said, but I didn't think so. I was beginning to get a glimmer of Oliver's motives, but I didn't want to mention it to Al; he'd be convinced I had played too many games without a helmet.

I stayed for an additional hour. We each had another ale and wolfed cashews while we reviewed again all the known facts and discussed possible scenarios that might account for them. Our conclusions. Zero, zip, and zilch.

I drove home in a weighty mood. I believed I knew Oliver's reason for cultivating a friendship with such a scurvy knave as Ernest Gorton, but I shared Sgt. Rogoff's bewilderment as to what exactly those two wiseguys were doing.

Later, of course, I realized what Rogoff had told me about Ernest Gorton that afternoon contained sufficient clues to solve the mystery. But at the time neither the sergeant nor I was perspicacious enough to see it.

I blame it on good ale and honey-roasted cashews.

22

It had been a curiously condensed day—Rogoff had given me a great deal to ponder—but it wasn't over yet. I was in my belfry, preparing to descend for the family cocktail hour, when my phone began ringing. For some peculiar reason I thought it a particularly insistent clangor and was briefly tempted to ignore it. But who can resist a ringing phone? I picked up.

"Oliver Whitcomb, Archy," he said, positively burbling with bonhomie. "How you doing, fella?"

"Very well, thank you," I said. "And you?"

"Got the world on a string," he said breezily. "Listen, Mitzi and I just decided to have a spur-of-the-moment minibash tonight. Nothing fancy. Very informal. Very casual. Come as you are. We'll have a few drinks and laugh it up. You're cordially invited. Can you make it?"

I didn't hesitate. "Sure I can. Thanks for the invitation."

"Great! Anytime after nine o'clock. Binky Watrous promised to show up. You have our address? If not, we're in the Boca book."

"I'll find you."

We hung up and I decided Oliver was making a determined effort to be friendly. My ego is not emaciated, as you well know, but I could not believe he sought my palship simply because of my sterling character or aftershave lotion. The lad was eager for my attendance at his "minibash," but for what reason I could not then have said. Four hours later I knew.

All of which explains why, at about nine-twenty that evening, I pulled into the white graveled courtyard of the Whitcomb mansion in Boca Raton. There were already a dozen parked cars but the one that caught my eye, other than Binky's moldering Cabriolet, was a custom-made silver Cadillac stretch limousine. That thing was so long it should have been articulated with a separate driver to operate the wheels of the rear section.

A thug in chauffeur's garb was leaning against the front fender, smoking a cigarette and staring at the heavens. Trying to locate Cassiopeia, no doubt. His uniform was shiny silver to match the car's finish.

I strolled over. "Quite a yacht," I observed.

He looked at me without interest. Brutish chap. "Yeah," he said.

"How on earth do you turn a corner?" I asked.

"It ain't easy."

I made a guess: "Ernest Gorton's car?"

"You got it," he said, flicked his cigarette butt away, and yawned in my face. Mr. Congeniality.

I entered the tessellated front door, disappointed that I wasn't greeted by a periwigged flunky in knee breeches. As a matter of fact, I wasn't greeted by anyone but heard a cackle of talk and laughter coming from a chamber at the end of a marble-floored entrance hall. As Binky had told me, everything in this polished dwelling seemed to be constructed of mirrors, stainless steel, white leather, and tinted glass. Obviously "brown furniture" was anathema to the younger Whitcombs.

I entered a crowded living room with a wet bar along one wall with enough bottles on display to grace a luxe hotel. Few guests paused quaffing to inspect the newcomer, but Oliver came bustling forward to shake my hand heartily and give me a welcoming grin.

"Great you could make it," he said. "Just great! What do you think of our place?"

"Impressive," I said.

"You don't think it's too architectural, too stark?"

"Not at all," I lied. "If it ain't baroque, don't fix it."

His laugh was almost a roar and he clapped me on the shoulder. "You've got a great sense of humor, Archy," he enthused. "Great! Listen, I'm not going to introduce you to all these fun people. Just mingle and introduce yourself. The bar is open for business, but you'll have to mix your own poison. Live it up!"

He was trying too hard.

He drifted away and I headed for the pharmacy wondering if I was a fun person, qualified to mingle with this pot-smoking assembly most of whom looked ten years younger and a hundred years more with-it than I. I was certain they could identify all the current rock stars, which I couldn't. But I consoled myself with the thought that not one of them could name America's greatest war song, which I could. In case you're wondering, it's a 1918 classic entitled "Would You Rather Be a Colonel with an Eagle on Your Shoulder or a Private with a Chicken on Your Knee?"

I mixed a very mild vodka and water at the bar, reckoning it was going to be a long night. Then I turned to inspect the other guests. I spotted Binky Watrous in one corner sitting on the lap of Mitzi Whitcomb. Yes, *he* was sitting on *her* lap. I don't believe Sherlock Holmes ever did that with Irene Adler.

In another corner I saw Ernest Gorton looking as rumpled as he had the first time we met. He was wearing an undoubtedly costly three-piece suit of black silk, Italian cut, but it was so wrinkled I could only conclude he slept fully clothed. He had one meaty arm about the bare shoulders of the orangy-haired young woman I had last seen in the office of Dr. Omar K. Pflug—Rhoda, the carrottop, wearing a tight sheath of silver sequins, to match Gorton's stretch limo, I supposed. The man had an incredible lust for color coordination.

Following the host's instructions, I circulated assiduously, introduced myself, and met a great number of people I devoutly hoped I would never meet again. I suffer from *snobisme,* as you may have guessed, and I found the Whitcombs' guests agonizingly superficial. Conversation? Complete piffle, concerned mostly with holidays taken or planned, new *in* restaurants in Palm Beach County, the latest local political scandal, which movie heroes were gay, and the possibility of curing impotence by acupuncture. I shan't go into details about *that.*

And so I had another drink, or two, simply to endure until I could make a decent departure. Binky had vanished with Mitzi Whitcomb before I had a chance to speak to him. I wasn't even certain he was aware of my appearance. He had the glassy look he gets when he's addled by unrequited love or a surfeit of beef Stroganoff.

But Ernest Gorton was mindful of my presence.

"Glad to see you, Archy boy!" he shouted, clamping one of those fleshy arms about my waist. "Having fun?"

"A plenitude," I assured him.

"Love the way you talk," he marveled. "Just love it! Hey, you got time for a private confab?"

"Of course."

He looked around the living room. More invitees had arrived, the decibels were rising. In addition, despite the air conditioning, the atmosphere had become fuggy with the smell of burning grass. Oliver's friends, I concluded, definitely did not smoke cigarettes from packs labeled with the Surgeon General's warnings.

What truly surprised me was the expression of distaste on Gorton's phiz as he inspected the scene. If Al Rogoff's information was accurate, these fun people were Ernie Boy's customers. But there was no mistaking the contempt in his glower.

"Let's get out of this circus," he said. "We'll talk in my buggy."

He led the way outside to the Cadillac limousine. Some buggy! The glittery chauffeur was still leaning against a fender.

"Take a walk, Jake," Gorton said gruffly. The bruiser nodded and moved away.

We entered the wheeled cathedral. You don't crouch or slide into a car like that; you step in reverently, resisting an urge to cross yourself. We sat in the back, and I noted a little refrigerator, a little bar, a little TV set, a little cellular phone and fax machine. If that car had a little Port-o-John you could have lived there comfortably and never emerged.

"I got some Martell cognac here," Ernest said. "Okay by you?"

"Excellent."

He poured our drinks into outsized crystal snifters. Good cognac should be as much inhaled as tasted, and one ounce is a gentleman's tot. But he must have poured at least three ounces into each glass, and I had visions of enrolling for the 12 Steps the very next day.

"Have I got this right?" Gorton said abruptly. "Your father is an attorney but doesn't do litigation. You started out to be a lawyer but got kicked out of school. You're single and live with your parents. You drink but you're no doper. You do investigations for your father's firm. How'm I doing?"

"You're correct," I acknowledged, realizing he had gone to some trouble to learn my record. But I supposed that was one reason for his success. He was careful and he was thorough: a man of many talents, most of them feculent, and an overwhelming greed.

"I got a proposition for you," he said. He paused to give me an arctic grin. "An offer you can't refuse. I got this business in Miami. Import-export, like I told you. I got some good lawyers, courtroom guys, who know how to protect my interests. But my business is getting so big I need a sharp operator, someone who knows the laws but at the same time knows how to ask the right questions. I mean, I'm into a lot of things, this and that, and I'm always getting these business projects thrown at me. They all require an investment of capital on my part. You know? Now what I need is someone who's got the know-how to evaluate these deals. Do they have a profit potential or are they just scams? I think you're the man to handle the job."

He paused and we both continued to sip our brandies. I was listening attentively to his pitch. Oh, he was good! If he was a legitimate businessman his spiel would have made sense to me. But I knew he was proposing a no-show job. An experienced hustler with his background would never depend on someone else to make his investment choices.

"It's very kind of you to make the offer, Ernie," I said.

"I like you," he continued, tapping my knee. "I genuinely and sincerely like you. Of course you'd have to move to Miami. But that's no problem, is it? I have points in a couple of lush condos and I could fix you up with a flashy pad. What I'm talking about is a salary of fifty grand a year. Under the table if that's the way you want it. How does that grab you?"

"Tempting," I said. I looked down at my glass and saw to my horror it was almost empty. If I were required to take a Breathalyzer test at that moment, I'm sure a siren would wail, bells ring, and the U.S. Marine Band would launch into "Stars and Stripes Forever."

"Well?" Gorton asked. "How do you feel about it?"

"A generous proposal," I told him. "But surely you don't expect an immediate answer. It's an important decision and I want to give it a lot of thought."

He patted my knee again. "That's another thing I like about you, Archy. Most of the guys who work for me got sushi between their ears, but you know how to *think.*"

"Thank you," I said humbly. I know how to do humble.

"How much time?" he said. "I need help and I can't wait forever."

"A month tops," I told him.

"Make it two weeks," he said, the demon bargainer.

"All right," I agreed. "I'll let you know within two weeks."

We finished our cognacs and, with some effort, heaved ourselves from those cushioned thrones and exited.

"Coming back to the party?" Gorton asked.

"I don't think so," I said. "You've given me a great deal to consider. I better go home and get started."

He nodded. "I'll be in touch," he said and stalked back to the Whitcomb Museum of Modern Schlock and all those fun people.

I drove home slowly and cautiously. Despite the Brobdingnagian brandy I had consumed, the McNally gray matter (it's really a Ralph Lauren plaid) was surprisingly lucid and functioning. My conclusions?

Misconceptions: I had originally tagged Ernest Gorton as a two-bit grifter. I now saw him as a criminal Machiavelli and definitely not a man to be trifled with. I had also erred in assuming he and Oliver Whitcomb were equal partners and equally culpable in whatever their mischievous enterprise might be. But I now judged Gorton to be the leader and instigator.

I had no evidence of that—it was all supposition—but I thought it logical and believable. Of one thing I was absolutely certain: Ernest Gorton was aware of my discreet inquiry and was attempting to buy me off. He had first tried to bribe me with a case of wine, probably to test the level of my venality. Rejected, he had then upped the ante with an offer of fifty thousand a year. I could not help but suspect the Oliver Whitcombs' "spur-of-the-moment minibash" had been organized at Gorton's urging (or command) simply to give him an opportunity to subvert me.

I wondered how he had learned of my investigation. Binky Watrous may have revealed too much to Mitzi Whitcomb while romancing that lubricious lady. He might have boasted of his role as my assistant. That peabrain trusted everyone. He had never recognized the existence of evil in the world. Since he was nice, he assumed the entire human population of the planet was also nice. I'm sure he'd condemn an ax murderer of nothing more than bad manners.

But if Binky had not queered our game, there was another way Ernest Gorton may have become aware of an investigation into his activities. I was convinced other personnel of the Whitcomb Funeral Homes—especially those three nouveau riche directors—were deeply involved in the plot. Oliver could hardly organize and conduct a scheme of such magnitude without inside assistance. And perhaps his fellow conspirators had noted Sunny Fogarty's digging into records of Whitcomb's out-of-state shipments of human remains.

It was even possible, I reflected gloomily, that my visits to Sunny's condo had been observed. Jeepers, her apartment (including the bedroom? Gulp!) may have been bugged, and the efficient and painstaking Ernest Gorton knew exactly what was going on. I waggled my head angrily at such fears; I was becoming as paranoid as father and I initially thought Ms. Fogarty to be.

Before I fell asleep that night I was assailed by yet another fear. If I continued to resist Ernest's bribes and blandishments—as I fully intended to—what might be his final solution to end my prying? I didn't care to dwell on that. I don't have Binky's Pollyannaish philosophy; I did not think Mr. Gorton was a nice man.

23

Friday was bloomy. The fog and overcast had blown away, and an azure sky looked as if it had been through a wash-and-dry cycle. More important, my anxieties of the night before were banished by sunshine; the customary McNally buoyancy was working its wonders and I was ready for a fight or a frolic.

I awoke in time to breakfast with my parents, and what a treat it was! The previous evening we had feasted on a roasted Butterball turkey and on Friday morning Ursi Olson started using leftovers by serving creamed turkey on biscuits. Scrumptious! And a little dab of mild salsa instead of cranberry sauce didn't hurt.

Invigorated by the matutinal bracer I drove to the office singing another of my favorite songs: "It's a Sin to Tell a Lie." Loved the tune; totally disagreed with the lyrics. I was no sooner at my desk than Connie Garcia called.

"Archy," she wailed, "we can't have dinner this weekend."

"Oh? Got a better offer, have you? Kevin Costner?"

"You silly," she said. "One of my Miami cousins was in an

accident. Her car was totaled and she's in the hospital with broken bones and God knows what else."

"Ah, what a shame," I said. "Can I drive you down?"

"You're sweet to offer, but I wouldn't think of it. I'm taking an afternoon flight."

"Then how about lunch?" I suggested. "You better have something before you start out."

"Well . . . okay," she said. "But I'm so shook I probably won't be able to eat. It's Gloria—the girl who got hurt—and you know she's my favorite cousin. We're practically like sisters."

"Tell me about it at lunch," I urged. "The Pelican at noon?"

"Thank you, Archy," she said, and I could hear she was close to tears. A very emotional woman, our Connie.

I parked my mocs atop the desk and fell to brooding about the Whitcomb case. Well, perhaps brooding is a bit excessive; what I actually did was review everything I knew and everything I surmised about that strange affair. I tried to make sense of what was happening, but none of the scenarios I devised sounded the clarion call. I could not find any coherence in all those incongruous facts and fancies.

There was one fact I did not have. I also had no idea whether or not it might prove significant. Probably not. But while conducting a discreet inquiry I like to collect as many snippets of skinny as possible, even if most of them prove to be the drossiest of dross.

I could have obtained the information I sought by calling Sunny Fogarty. But because of my suspicion that rogues were at work in the hushed environs of the Whitcomb Funeral Homes I thought it prudent not to phone her office.

And so I spent half an hour calling Air Cargo Services at

three national carriers. At the end of this chore, having been shunted from one department to another, I had an answer to my query. Human remains in a coffin, properly gift-wrapped for air shipment, weigh approximately four hundred lbs.—an interesting factoid that will enable you to enliven conversation at the next cocktail party you attend.

I was preparing to depart for luncheon with Connie when I was delayed by a phone call.

"Al Rogoff," he said brusquely. "Can you make lunch at twelve-thirty?"

"No, I cannot," I told him. "I have a prior engagement."

"Who with—one of your tootsies? Cancel it."

"I do not have a date with a tootsie," I said indignantly. "And I refuse to cancel."

"All right, all right," he said. "Don't get your *cojones* in an uproar. Suppose we come over to your office at two o'clock."

"*We?*" I asked. "Al, are you suddenly using the royal plural pronoun—or may I expect a visit from two or more persons?"

"Two of us."

"And who will be the other visitor?"

"You'll find out," he said and hung up.

It was such a weird conversation I wondered if Rogoff wasn't already out to lunch.

Connie was seated at the bar when I arrived at the Pelican Club. She was gazing mournfully into a glass of Evian and definitely drooping. I gave her a hug, a cheek kiss, and hustled her to our favorite table in the dining area.

Priscilla came bopping over, took one look at Connie, and said, "What's wrong, honey?"

My paramour gave her a brave smile. "Family troubles, Pris. My favorite cousin got smashed up in a car accident in Miami. I'm flying down to see her this afternoon."

"Aw, that's rough," Pris said, instantly solicitous. "I hope she comes out of it okay. Listen, I think you better have a stiff wallop and then some solid food."

"Me, too," I said.

"You!" she scoffed. "You need a stiff wallop like Missouri needs another flood. How about vodka-rocks first and then a big platter of Buffalo chicken wings with Cajun-style rice and maybe a beer to put out the fire."

"Excellent medicine," I told her. "Thank you, nurse. And don't forget the Rolaids for dessert."

Connie was eager to talk during that luncheon and I was content to listen. She told me more about her extensive family than I had heard before. Most of her relatives were Marielitos and were succeeding admirably in their new homeland. For instance, Gloria, the injured cousin, managed a boutique, and her father had opened a Cuban art gallery.

Listening to Connie chatter on about parents, grandparents, uncles, aunts, cousins, and all their progeny, I began to comprehend part of the attraction this woman has to me. Perhaps the major part.

She is physically alluring—but so was Mrs. Agnes Snodgrass, my homeroom teacher in the sixth grade. She has inexhaustible brio—but so did Eve Arden. She has wit and sensitivity—but so did a dozen other women with whom I had briefly consorted.

I think my abiding affection for Connie is due to her ordinariness. I don't mean that as a put-down, of course, for she is a lady of quality, feisty and passionate. The ordinariness I refer to is the life she lives. You must understand that most of the women I dallied with, or who dallied with me, were encountered during the course of my discreet inquiries. More often than not they had lives of noisy desperation.

When I begin to believe that *all* women are like that, Consuela Garcia offers a healthy dose of normality. Quite simply, she restores me to sanity. Her world consists of the basics: family, job, friends—and me. You may find normality a bore; I found it a blessing. In fact, in the treacherous and sometimes violent world in which I moved, my attachment to Connie may well have been my salvation.

Professor McNally's next lecture on Psychopathology in Intergender Relationships will be held on Tuesday at Radclyffe Hall.

By the time we finished lunch, Connie's spirits had been elevated if not restored to their usual vertiginous heights. I had lent a willing ear to her nonstop monologue, but I cannot claim credit for her recovery. I think it was the Cajun rice that did the trick.

We parted outside. Connie held me close, looked at me sternly, and said, "I may be gone for a few days or a week. You'll behave, won't you?"

"Don't I always?"

"No," she said.

We paid mutual lip service and she promised to call me from Miami. Then she was gone. I watched her drive away. I had a sudden, mercifully brief attack of guilt and contrition. Don't ask me why.

I was a few minutes late getting back to the McNally Building and looked into the reception area to see if my visitors had arrived. They had. Sgt. Al Rogoff, in uniform, was seated next to a tall chap in civvies who was wearing sunglasses so dark they were practically opaque. Both men looked grim.

I made a brief apology for my tardiness and led them up to my model office—model in the sense of being a miniature, *not* an ideal. The three of us squeezed in and Rogoff introduced his companion: Special Agent Griffin Kling from the FBI office in Miami. He was built like a pencil and looked as if he had once been an artiste of the slam dunk. He took off those menacing specs before he shook my hand. I wished he had left them on; his eyes were pale and hard.

I got him seated in the swivel chair behind my desk. Al took the folding steel chair reserved for visitors. I stood.

Kling wasted no time. "Two nights ago," he started, "I was having a few belts with a friend of mine who's with Metro-Dade homicide. He told me he had received a query from Sergeant Rogoff here regarding Ernest Gorton. The reason my pal mentioned it was because he knows of my interest in Gorton. That creep's been Number One on my personal Most Wanted list for more than five years. I know he's into everything rotten, but I've never been able to nail him. On top of that, about a year ago I was running an informant, a nice young kid who got racked up on a minor drug rap. We turned him and he was paying his dues until he got smoked. Gorton ordered the kill—I'm sure of it—but I couldn't pin it on him. That slime has become a real—" He paused helplessly. "What's it called when you can't get something out of your mind?"

"An idée fixe?" I suggested.

"Is that what it is?" the FBI agent said. "Well, I got it. I want to see Gorton put down so bad I can taste it. So when I heard Palm Beach was asking questions about this shark, I drove up here hoping to find out something I can use. But Rogoff says it's not official business and not something he can tell me. He claims it's your baby and if you want to give me what you've got, it's okay with him, but he can't without your say-so. How about it?"

I was grateful for Al's discretion. He had acted honorably, knowing what his uncooperative attitude might cost him.

My first reaction was to refuse to reveal anything about the Whitcomb affair to the FBI. But then I realized those shipments of coffins across state lines might possibly have shattered federal laws. In addition, it would do no harm to have a colleague in the Miami area, Gorton's home territory.

I was silent for such a long time the Special Agent became impatient.

"Do you know exactly what Gorton is doing in this neck of the woods?" he demanded.

"Not exactly," I admitted. "But I'd wager it's something illegal."

"You'd *wager?*" Kling said, blinking.

"That's the way Archy talks," Rogoff advised him. "You'll get used to it."

"How about a quid pro quo?" I asked the FBI man. "I'll tell you what I know if you'll promise to keep Sergeant Rogoff and me promptly informed of any developments resulting from my information."

He rose to his feet and extended a hand to shake mine once more. "Done," he said and sat down again.

I told him what I had previously related to the sergeant: the unexplained increase in Whitcomb's income, those puzzling out-of-state shipments to the same consignee in New York, Boston, and Chicago: the Cleo Hauling Service. I also mentioned Ernest Gorton's close relationship with Oliver Whitcomb, CEO of the funeral homes.

As before, I said nothing of the equivocal roles being played by Sunny Fogarty, Horace, and Sarah Whitcomb. But I still had the feeling the drama being enacted there had a peripheral but perhaps meaningful connection to the criminal activities at the mortuaries.

"That's all you've got?" Griffin Kling said when I finished my recital.

He had taken no notes but, staring into his stony eyes (an easy trick if you concentrate your gaze on the bridge of the nose between the eyes), I knew he had missed nothing and would forget nothing.

"It's all I have," I assured him.

He nodded—but I was certain he didn't believe me. He was a hard man and wouldn't testify the sun would rise tomorrow until he saw it.

"All right," he said. "There are a few things I can do immediately. I'll contact our offices in New York, Boston, and Chicago and request they trace ownership of the Cleo Hauling Service. And if they can spare the manpower—excuse me; the personpower—I'll ask them to tail the Cleo trucks when they pick up coffins at the airports."

"I'm betting those trucks aren't delivering to funeral homes or cemeteries," Rogoff put in.

"I'm betting the same thing," Kling agreed. "But all that out-of-town stuff is going to take time. Meanwhile there's something I can do. Gorton's front is a legit import-export company. Mostly he brings in wood furniture from South America. The business seems to be clean. It better be; we've persuaded the IRS to do an audit every year. Anyway, Gorton has a warehouse out near the airport where he keeps his furniture inventory until it's sold and trucked out. I think I'll request twenty-four-hour surveillance on that place, either by a stakeout or concealed TV cameras. How does that sound?"

"Makes sense," Al said.

"Has the warehouse ever been searched?" I asked.

The agent's smile was as cold as his eyes. "Twice," he said. "By me. I thought he might be bringing in drugs in hollowed-out parts of the furniture. I struck out; the furniture was just that; nothing hidden in holes, panels, or anywhere else. Now I figure the vermin isn't a smuggler; he's buying his stuff directly from the cartels, cash on delivery in Miami."

"Are drugs his main source of income?" I said.

"Only a part of it. I'm convinced he's into guns, brand-name ripoffs, money laundering, and maybe even counterfeiting. Lately there's been a flood of the queer in South Florida. I tell you this Gorton is a world-class nasty and he's going to take a fall if I have to chill him myself."

There was no mistaking the triple-distilled venom in his voice. Rogoff and I traded a quick glance. We both knew how unpredictable and potentially dangerous a lawman can be when obsessed by a private vendetta.

Special Agent Griffin Kling apparently realized he had said too much. He rose abruptly and donned his black sunglasses. "I'll be in touch," he said crisply. "I'll keep you up to speed on what's happening in Miami, and I hope you'll let me know of any developments up here."

"Of course," I said.

There was another round of hand-shaking and the two men departed. I reclaimed my swivel chair and stared down at my desk blotter where, I saw, Kling's nervous fingers had ripped every match from a book and then had shredded the cover into jagged strips. Obviously a stressed man and I wondered if I had made an error of judgment in welcoming his assistance.

Doesn't W. S. say something about having a long spoon when you eat with the devil? I must look it up.

24

What a delightful Friday evening that was! Because nothing happened to roil the McNally equanimity. Father stirred up a pitcher of excellent gin martinis at the family cocktail hour and Ursi Olson served *cervelli con uova* for dinner. That's calves' brains with eggs, and if you haven't tried it, don't knock it.

I went up to my hidey-hole, played a cassette of Sinatra's "Duets," smoked an English Oval, sipped a very small marc, worked on my journals in a desultory fashion, and suddenly realized I was happy. That always comes as something of a shock, does it not? I mean, you have problems, troubles, frustrations, and then you realize how gossamer they are and you're content to be breathing. Of course it may have been the calves' brains, Sinatra, or the brandy that brought on my euphoria, but whatever the cause I welcomed it.

Connie Garcia phoned around nine o'clock to tell me her cousin's condition had stabilized and doctors were hoping for a complete recovery. Good news. My belle amour said she'd probably remain in Miami for three or four days, and when she returned she definitely expected an orgy à deux, both gustatory and physically frolicsome. I gave her a verbal contract.

And so to bed. Not forgetting to spread my arms wide to the ceiling and murmur, "Thank you, God." That's as serviceable a form of prayer as any, innit?

Saturday turned out to be an equine of a different complexion, and I was rudely wrenched back to the demands and insecurities of reality. I slept late and awoke with vague hopes of a lazy, laid-back weekend. Maybe some tennis, a round of golf, a game of poker, perhaps a gimlet or two or three. Look, Mr. Holmes had his cocaine and I have my Sterling vodka. Which of us is to be more severely censured?

I bounced downstairs to a deserted kitchen. Father, I reckoned, was on his way to his club for 18 holes with a foursome that had been playing together for so many years I swear they now communicated solely with grunts. Mother and Ursi were probably out shopping for provisions.

I had a jolt of Clamato, toasted a muffin I slathered with peach preserve, and boiled up a pot of instant black. I was on my second dose of caffeine when Jamie Olson came wandering in and planted himself down across the table from me. He was smoking his pungent old briar and in self-defense I lighted my first cigarette of the day.

"Got a raccoon," he reported glumly. "Pried the lid off the trash can. Made a nice mess."

"I thought the new can we bought was supposed to be raccoon-proof."

"Supposed to be," he said. "Wasn't. Them animals are smart buggers. Could work a combination lock, I have no doubt. Any coffee left?"

"Maybe a cup," I said. "Help yourself."

We sat awhile in silence, sipping and smoking.

"Jason," he said finally. "The Whitcombs' man. We hoisted a few together yesterday afternoon."

"Good," I said. "Learn anything?"

"Some. Like I told you, Jase is no blabbermouth when it comes to his family. But he admitted things are rough these days between father and son."

"Did he give any reason for their *casus belli?*"

"Their what?"

"Conflict. The reason for their dissension."

"I think it's money."

"That's odd," I said. "Both Horace and Oliver are loaded."

"Uh-huh," Jamie said. He was quiet a long time and I waited patiently. There was no point in trying to hurry our houseman; he had his own pace, more an amble than a stride.

"Want me to guess?" he asked finally.

"By all means."

"It's Mrs. Whitcomb. From what Jason said, she's fading. He doesn't think she's going to make it. Mebbe—I'm guessing now—she's got more cash than husband or son. And that's what the squabble's about. Who inherits."

I looked at him, astonished. "Jamie," I said, "you're a genius."

"Just guessing," he said. "Told you that."

We said no more on the subject. We cleaned up the kitchen and then I raced upstairs to flip through my professional diary, wanting to verify a vague memory. I found it: Father had told me that for tax reasons, Horace had transferred a majority of shares to his wife.

Jamie had been almost right. Sarah didn't have more cash than husband or son, but she held controlling interest in the Whitcomb Funeral Homes. That was the cause of the antagonism: Who would end up a lion and who a lamb?

You may think it inexcusably crass and unfeeling for husband and son to be concerned with inheritance while wife and mother is expiring in a motel-like hospital suite. If you feel that way, you have had little exposure to the basic motivations of human behavior. They are not depraved, y'know; they are simply *human.*

I phoned Sunny Fogarty, hoping to find her at home on a gorgeous Saturday morning.

"Archy!" she said. "I was just thinking about you."

"Thank you," I said. "And I, you. Sunny, I'd like to see you briefly as soon as possible. I have a few questions."

Short silence. "But not on the phone?" she said. No dummy she.

"Correct. And not at your home or mine. You know Mizner Park in Boca?"

"Of course."

"There's a bookstore. Liberties. Do you think you could be browsing at noon?"

Pause again. "Is it important?"

"It is."

"Then I'll manage," she said. "Archy, you're being very mysterious."

"I'm being very paranoid," I told her. "I'll explain when I see you. I'd love to ask you to lunch, but I don't think it would be wise. We'll chat a few moments and then go our separate ways."

Third pause. "All right, Archy," she said. "I trust you."

That was comforting. And somewhat daunting.

I had pulled on casual and rather raddled duds that morning, but now, preparing for a clandestine rendezvous at a smart bookstore, I decided something spiffier was called for. If you think me inordinately vain, you're quite right. I donned an aqua polo shirt of Sea Island cotton, slacks of go-to-hell fuchsia, and a jacket of properly faded madras. No socks. The loafers were cordovans with floppy tassels—which drive mein papa right up the wall.

It really was a splendiferous day and all during that exhilarating drive south to Boca I lustily sang "Enjoy Yourself—It's Later Than You Think," which pretty well sums up my basic philosophy.

I found Sunny Fogarty standing before the cookbook section at Liberties. She was leafing through a volume on soufflés. I joined her and selected a treatise entitled *Wild Game Stews.* That tells you something about us, does it not?

We stood shoulder to shoulder and conversed in hushed tones.

"What's this all about, Archy?" she said tensely.

Speaking rapidly, I gave her a succinct account of Ernest Gorton's apparent involvement in illicit activities at Whitcomb Funeral Homes and what I interpreted as his attempted bribery to convince me to end or soft-pedal my investigation.

"He's aware of my inquiries," I told Sunny. "No doubt about it. And I think his information originated from within your office."

She nodded. "I've suspected someone has been listening in on my calls. I know positively my personal files have been searched. And our computer records have been tampered with."

"The villains are probably aware of your suspicions and investigation. What concerns me is that I fear they also know you have requested assistance from McNally and Son. They may even have observed my visits to your home. I don't wish to alarm you unnecessarily, but you may be under surveillance and perhaps your apartment has been bugged."

Her face grew increasingly grim. "Yes," she said, "that's possible."

"I think it best you use a pay phone whenever you wish to contact me," I went on. "I really shouldn't have called you at home this morning, but I had no choice. That's why I selected a public place for our meeting and suggested we forgo luncheon just in case you might have been followed."

She accepted these dire warnings with admirable stoicism, and I saw again what a strong woman she was. I didn't want to add to her strain by relating what I had learned from FBI Special Agent Griffin Kling about the nasty proclivities of Ernest Gorton. After all, Sunny had no need to know; she had quite enough on her plate at the moment.

"Archy," she said in a toneless voice, "you said on the phone you had questions."

"I do. Two of them. First, have you heard anything recently about the condition of Mrs. Sarah Whitcomb?"

"Not good," she said, her face suddenly frozen. "Mr. Horace told me the doctors give him no hope. First they talked about years, then it was months, then weeks; it spread so swiftly. Now I'm afraid it's days."

"Dreadful," I said. "A lovely woman."

"Yes," she said. "She's been good to me, so understanding when my own mother became ill. I'll never forget her kindness."

"How is Mr. Horace taking it?"

"He's trying to cope. But he's hurting."

"And Oliver?"

"I wouldn't know about him," she said curtly. "What's your second question?"

"Financial. Does Whitcomb hold a large cash reserve?"

She looked at me. "What an odd thing to ask. Will it help your inquiry?"

"I can't swear it will, but it might."

"I shouldn't reveal our balance sheet," she said. "After all, we are not a public company. But I'll take the chance. As I told you, Archy, I trust you. Up to about six months ago our cash balance was nothing extraordinary. About average for the past several years. Then those out-of-state shipments suddenly ballooned, and so did our cash reserve. I put most of it in three- and six-month Treasury bills. I can't give you an exact figure, but it's considerable. Is that what you wanted to know?"

"It is," I said, "and I thank you."

We replaced our books on the shelves and smiled quizzically at each other.

"Archy," she said, "what you told me about people possibly being aware of our, uh, connection and my apartment being bugged, I guess that means you shouldn't come over again."

"I'm afraid that's what it means," I agreed. "Until we bring order out of chaos."

She sighed. "I'll miss you, Archy," she said.

Was I imagining it or did I detect a note of relief in her voice? I decided I would never understand this enigmatic woman.

Sunny departed first and I watched her go, thinking what a stalwart figure she cut. I waited a few moments, then wandered out into the midday sunshine. I toured Mizner Park and found a German restaurant I hadn't known existed.

After inspecting the menu posted in the window and being panged by hunger—my customary state—I popped inside for a platter of plump potato pancakes with hot sauerkraut. There are those who like a spicy ketchup on their latkes; I prefer apple sauce. I also had a stein of an excellent chilled lager.

I headed homeward reflecting that after my Teutonic

snack I was in no condition for tennis, golf, or any other physical activity more vigorous than a game of jackstraws.

But the McNally aptitude for creative delusions had not been impaired and Sunny Fogarty's answers to my two questions began to form the spine of a theory explicating Oliver Whitcomb's role in what was happening at the funeral homes. I still didn't know exactly *what* was happening but had no doubt that, to paraphrase Woollcott, it was immoral, illegal, and fattening—to Whitcomb's bank account.

I spent the remainder of Saturday afternoon sharpening my solution to one part of the Whitcomb puzzle. A rereading of the jotted notes in my journal persuaded me that, as I had remarked hopefully to Sunny, order was beginning to emerge from chaos.

I must admit right now that my elegant scenario turned out to be wrong. Not totally wrong, mind you, but half-wrong. In my defense I can only plead guilty of making a case from insufficient evidence.

Well, what the hell, Columbus thought he had landed at Calcutta.

25

I accompanied my parents to church on Sunday morning. This rare event, I confess, was not due to a sudden upsurge of religiosity. Actually I was hoping for another glimpse of that Amazonian contralto in the choir. Sad to say, she was not present.

Could she be ill? If so I would have been happy to hasten to her bedside with a jar of calf's-foot jelly or a crystal decanter of chicken soup. But of course I didn't know her name or address.

I mention this ridiculous incident merely to illustrate my addiction to fantasies that sometimes engross me. Fortunately, few of them are ever realized.

I returned home in a grumpy mood and immediately began making phone calls hoping to arrange some action on the courts, links, or even around a poker table. But all the pals I contacted had already made Sunday plans; I was odd man out, an unwonted and disturbing role.

Finally, in desperation, I phoned Binky Watrous. He sounded as if he had just undergone several hours of CPR.

"Binky," I said, "why are you breathing like that?"

"I'm fortunate to be breathing at all," he said hollowly. "Archy, when I signed on I had no idea the job would entail so much wear and tear on the old carcass."

"Let me guess: You partied last night with Mitzi and Oliver Whitcomb."

"With them and a gaggle of other fruitcakes. It was a traveling party: here, there, and everywhere. I think at one time we might have been in Fort Pierce, but I can't be sure. Those people skitter around like characters from that Christmas ballet, 'The Ballbreaker.' "

"Binky," I said gently, "it's called 'The Nutcracker.' "

"Oh," he said. "Well . . . whatever. Archy, you know what I need right now?"

"A new head?"

"It would help, but before I have a transplant I'd like a very big, very strong, very peppery Bloody Mary."

"So mix one."

"I can't. The Duchess decided I've been imbibing too much and she's put our liquor supply under lock and key. Guess who's got the key. Not me. And the saloons aren't open yet. Archy, if you have a soupçon of charity in your heart, help me!"

I sighed. "All right, Binky. Drive over and I'll give you an injection."

"I can't drive over."

"Why not?"

"I don't have a car."

"You didn't total it?"

"No, but I left it somewhere."

"Binky, where did you leave your car?"

"I can't remember, but I'm sure it'll come to me after I take my medicine."

"If you don't have a car, how did you get home last night—or this morning?"

"Someone must have delivered me."

"Who delivered you?"

"I don't remember."

"Binky," I said, "everyone knows that before you are allowed to become a private eye you are required to take and pass a peculiarity test. You have just qualified. Hang on, old buddy. I'm on my way."

I went into the kitchen and hurriedly prepared a quart thermos of iced Bloody Marys. I remembered to take two plastic cups and set out for the Duchess's rather grungy residence on South County Road. Binky was waiting for me outside, slowly to-ing and fro-ing with hands thrust deep in trouser pockets, his head hanging low. The poor lad did appear to be one short step away from rigor mortis.

"You have my plasma?" he croaked.

I nodded.

"Not here, not here," he said hastily. "The Duchess is probably watching from her window and cackling at my torment. Let's vamoose."

I had no desire to chauffeur this shattered hulk to the McNally home even for the purpose of resuscitation. Nor did I wish to park on the beach where a gendarme might become outraged at the sight of a desperate young man swilling from a quart thermos. So we ended up in the vacant parking area of the Pelican Club, which had not yet opened for business.

I poured Binky a cup of Bloody Mary and he gulped greedily.

"More!" he gasped.

"In a few moments," I said sternly. "If you are willing to overindulge you must be ready to accept the consequences."

"What was I to do?" he demanded, enlivened by the stimulant (it was the horseradish that did it). "I couldn't sit there like a lunkhead, could I, when everyone else was swigging or smoking. By the way, her name is Starlight; I remember that."

"Whose name is Starlight?"

"Ernie Gorton's carrottop, Rhoda Starlight."

"You're jesting."

"Well, her real name is Rhoda Flembaugh, she told me, but Rhoda Starlight is her stage name."

"Uh-huh," I said. "And what stages has the lady graced lately?"

"Mostly tabletops in nudie clubs," Binky said, staring longingly at the open thermos. "But she says she's not doing that scene anymore. Claims she's self-employed."

I poured him another cup and one for myself. I felt I needed it and deserved it. Actually, I was pleased with Binky's report. Despite his intemperate roistering he had managed to collect a few nuggets that might prove to be meaningful.

"But I don't think so," he said, sipping his second drink slowly with beamy satisfaction.

"Don't think what, Binky?"

"That Rhoda is self-employed."

"Oh? And what makes you think that?"

"She spent a lot of time chatting up some of the more exciting birds at the party. I got the feeling she might be recruiting."

"Recruiting?"

"You know. Luring them into a life of ill repute."

I didn't laugh or even smile. I'm proud of that. I said, "Binky, do you suppose she works for Ernest Gorton? That she's his CEO in a call girl ring operating in this area?"

He looked down into his empty plastic cup. "I guess it's possible," he said finally. "Archy, I really don't like these people. They're not top drawer."

"No," I agreed, "they're not."

We shared the watery remains of the Bloody Marys and then I drove him home.

"What I'm going to do," he declared, "is get into bed and sleep nonstop for forty-eight hours."

"A wise decision," I told him.

We pulled into his driveway, and there was his battered MB Cabriolet. Binky whimpered with delight, hastened to his heap, and patted the dented hood.

"Hiya, baby," he crooned. "Did you come home to daddy?"

Disgusting.

I accomplished nothing of importance during the remainder of that day. I futzed around my quarters, read the newspapers, leafed through a few mags, smoked two cigs, listened to a Hoagy Carmichael tape, dined with my parents (we had roasted salmon with a basil sauce), returned to my mini-suite and took an hour's nap, rose to shower, watched the last half of a Dolphins game, attended the family cocktail hour, supped with my parents (we had spaghetti bolognese), returned upstairs and listened to a cassette of Ella Fitzgerald singing Cole Porter, picked up my journal and put it aside, croaked out a chorus of "Just One of Those Things," and decided I had done enough work for one day.

Exciting, huh? Have your eyes glazed over?

I have detailed that litany of ho-hum activities to prove my life is not all harum-scarum adventures, brief moments of violent action, and the pursuit of loves, both requited and un-. I mean, I do have periods of soporific ennui. The only reason I mention it is that I hope it may give us something in common. Surely you've had times with nothing better to do than count the walls.

Sleep came swiftly, which was a blessing because my dreams were rather racy—improbable but racy.

A phone call awakened me on Monday morning.

"H'lo," I mumbled.

"Aw," Al Rogoff said, "I bet I woke you up. And it's only eight-thirty. I'm frightfully chagrined. Can you ever forgive me?"

"No," I said. "What's it doing outside?"

"The sun is shining, birds are twittering, God's in His heaven and all's right with the world. Satisfied?"

"Sounds good. I may eventually arise. And what is the reason for this reveille?"

"I got a call from that FBI guy Griffin Kling. He's keeping his part of the bargain. He says his offices in New York, Boston, and Chicago traced the registration of trucks owned by the Cleo Hauling Service. It didn't take them long—but why should it? They probably made one phone call. Anyway they got a name. Didn't you tell me there was a fake nurse working out of the office of that flaky doctor?"

"That's right."

"The name you gave me was Rhoda. Got a last name?"

"I do now. Her stage name is Rhoda Starlight. Apparently her real name is Rhoda Flembaugh."

Sgt. Rogoff whooped with delight. "Kling says the Cleo trucks are registered in the name of Rhoda Flembaugh. How do you like that?"

"Love it," I said. "Just love it."

"What's the connection between this Rhoda and Ernest Gorton?"

"Very close," I told him. "I think she's his madam running a call girl ring in this area. She's been observed recruiting."

"Yeah? Observed by whom?"

"Binky Watrous."

"That's like saying she was observed by Daffy Duck. But she and Gorton are definitely connected?"

"Definitely."

"I'll call Kling and give him the good news. That guy is sweating to cut off Gorton's family jewels. He's still working on who eventually gets those coffins Whitcomb is shipping out. Keep in touch."

He hung up and I swung out of bed yawning, pleased with the way the day had started. It seemed to me we were webbing Ernest Gorton. I had little doubt we could snare that villain and he would plea-bargain by betraying Oliver Whitcomb and his cohorts. Gorton knew all the tricks of survival in his corrupt milieu.

I drove to the McNally Building musing on the role of Griffin Kling in this affair. The FBI agent struck me as a very odd chap indeed. I admire Sgt. Al Rogoff as an estimable law enforcement officer, and one of the reasons is that he never lets his emotions and prejudices influence his professional judgment.

But I sensed Kling was a man haunted by furies. Somehow he had settled on Ernest Gorton as a symbol of everything wrong in the world. If he could bring Gorton down, it would mean not only the end of a single criminal career but would be a blow against the forces of evil and a victory for decency, cherry pie, and white socks.

I arrived at my office to find a message requesting I phone Horace Whitcomb at home. I hesitated a moment, wondering if I should first inform my father. But then I decided to call and discover why Mr. Whitcomb was phoning the drudge of McNally & Son.

"Archy," he said, "I apologize for bothering you."

"No bother at all, sir."

"Oliver is with his mother at the moment and I'm at home. I'll go to the hospital at noon after Oliver leaves."

Of course it was possible Sarah was allowed only one visitor at a time. It was also possible that husband and son, or both, had no desire to meet at the bedside of the stricken woman.

"Could you come over for a short time?" Horace asked, and I detected a note close to desperation in his voice. "I hate to burden you with my problems, but I really need to talk to someone personally involved."

Moi? Personally involved? That was enough to send a frisson jittering along the McNally spinal cord.

"Of course, sir," I said. "I can be there in twenty minutes."

"Thank you," he said, and I thought he sounded weepy.

It took a bit more than twenty minutes, for traffic was horrendous that morning. But eventually Mr. Horace and I were seated on his terrace, gazing out at the sun-sequined lake and brunching on coffee and mini-croissants with lemon butter.

"And how is Mrs. Sarah feeling?" I inquired.

He tried to control his distress but failed; his eyes brimmed. "She's dying," he said, and my hope for a felicitous day went into deep six.

26

I had no idea what to say; I'm not good at commiseration. But it was not compassion he was seeking.

"I have a confession to make," he said, looking at me steadily now, patrician features sagging with a mixture of sorrow and shame. "It concerns the illegal activities taking place at the Whitcomb Funeral Homes."

"Sir," I said, and it was my turn to be desperate, "don't you think it would be wiser to discuss this matter with my father? He is, after all, your attorney. I have no legal standing whatsoever."

He gave me a gelid smile. "Your father is completely trustworthy, I know, but he can be a rather intimidating man."

I could not disagree with that.

"Besides," he went on, "you have been the one conducting the investigation Sunny Fogarty requested."

Curiously, I was not unduly shocked by the revelation that he was aware of her initial consultation with McNally & Son and my resulting discreet inquiry.

I told Mr. Horace as much. "It seemed incredible to me," I

said, "that Sunny should recognize something illicit was going on and you not know of it. But she insisted the suspicion of wrongdoing was solely hers, you hadn't a glimmer and were not to be informed of my nosing about."

He sighed. "Please don't blame Sunny. She was merely following my instructions faithfully, as she always has. Of course I knew something unethical and probably illegal was going on. It's *my* business, Archy, as it was my father's and grandfather's. I know it as well as I know my collection of ship models. If the placement of a potted palm is changed in any of our homes I notice it at once. What I'm trying to say is that Whitcomb Funeral Homes are my life. You may think it odd that mortuaries can constitute a full and rewarding existence, but they do. I have nothing for which to apologize."

"Sir," I said, "if you suspected skulduggery was going on, why on earth didn't you conduct a quiet internal investigation and then, if your suspicions proved valid, call in the police?"

He looked away from me, gazing somberly over the spangled lake. "Archy," he said, "I love my wife. I love Sarah with a devotion so deep and so intense that sometimes I wonder if I shall be able to carry on after she's gone. God damn it!" he shouted suddenly. "Why couldn't I have become ill instead of her? It's not right! It's not fair!" Slowly he calmed. "I do not tell you this to ask for your sympathy or pity but to explain why I acted the way I did. As much as I love Sarah, so does she love our son. I don't mean to imply she loves me the less, but Oliver is and always has been precious to her. We tried to have more babies but didn't succeed, and so my wife lavished all her maternal love on our only child."

I could guess what was coming but wanted to hear him say it. I knew it would resolve some of the riddles that had been gnawing at me.

"And then," he said, turning to look at me directly again, "I became aware of our unexpected increase of income during the past six months. I asked Sunny Fogarty to look into it. We agreed something very troubling was going on."

"The huge number of out-of-state shipments?" I suggested.

He nodded.

"You might have told me from the start," I said. "Instead, Sunny tried to make me believe it was my discovery."

"I apologize for that," he said. "It was a scurvy thing to do but had to be done. Because it became obvious to Sunny and me that the chicanery taking place could not succeed without the active participation of our three chief funeral directors and my son, who is supposed to oversee the day-to-day operations of the entire business."

"Why didn't you confront Oliver and demand an explanation?"

"I couldn't!" he cried. "Don't you see it was impossible? My wife became ill about five years ago and her condition has steadily worsened. She has accepted that with more fortitude and grace than you or I could muster, I assure you. Could I go to that terminally ill woman and tell her our son was probably a thief and I was turning him over to the police? Could I really do that? Tell her the child she loved so very much was a criminal?"

I lowered my head. "A horrible dilemma," I murmured.

"Yes," he said. "Horrible. I could not devastate my wife's final days, nor could I allow Oliver to continue his depredations against an honorable business that's been in the family for three generations. I talked it over with Sunny Fogarty, and we decided our only option was to proceed against Oliver with an outside investigation in which I apparently played no part. It would be an inquiry by McNally and Son, our attorneys, and whatever was uncovered would be strictly a legal matter. Then I could assure Sarah I would do everything I could to aid our son's defense. It wasn't much of a solution to my problem, was it, but I saw no other choice."

"I can't think of anything else you might have done, Mr. Whitcomb. Booting Oliver out of the company would have destroyed your relationship with your wife. I should tell you she is aware of the hostility between you and Oliver. But she has no idea of the cause of the conflict. I doubt, from what you tell me, she could ever be convinced her son capable of criminal behavior."

"Thank God for that," he said fervently. "If it's possible to die happy—and I'm not sure it is—it's what I wish for my wife: that she may quietly and peacefully slip away without pain and with her love for me and her son intact. She deserves nothing less."

We were silent for a few moments. I had no hint of what he was thinking, but I was brooding on the infernal complexities of living: enduring disappointments and tragedies, coping with problems and challenges, seeing ambitions thwarted and hopes deferred—just spending your ration of days doing your damndest to hang on to your sanity.

Mr. Horace straightened up in his chair, squared his shoulders, and took a deep breath. I could not interpret his expression; sadness and resolve were mixed.

"Archy," he said, "what I've told you this morning has been a sort of preamble to what I must say now. Sunny Fogarty has kept me informed on the progress of your investigation. I gather that Ernest Gorton is involved in what's going on."

"It certainly appears so."

"He sounds like a loathsome character."

"He is that, sir."

"My son's close friend," he said bitterly. "Sunny also told

me you believe this Gorton knows of your investigation and has attempted to buy you off."

I nodded.

"If Gorton is aware of your relationship with Sunny, do you believe she is personally at risk?"

I hesitated a beat or two. "I think her double-checking of your files and computer records is known to the perpetrators. I think it probable her office calls are monitored and her home phone may be bugged. Yes, I believe she is under close observation, but whether or not her safety is threatened, I simply cannot say."

"Can you swear it's impossible?"

"No, sir, I can't swear that."

"Then it is possible?"

"Yes," I said softly. "Considering what's at stake and Ernest Gorton's reputation, I must admit it's possible."

"That's what I feared," he said tonelessly. "And it's why I ask you now to end your investigation immediately. Sunny and I will end our inquiries as well."

I was astounded. "Mr. Whitcomb," I burst out, "you can't do that!"

"I can," he said, "and I will. You are an employee of the legal firm that represents Whitcomb Funeral Homes, are you not? I intend to write your father requesting your inquiry be ended. If it is not, I shall terminate our association with McNally and Son."

I glared at him furiously. "You realize that such a course of action will in all probability allow what is apparently a crime in progress to continue."

"I know that."

"And the suspected criminals, possibly including your son, may then succeed in utterly destroying what you have described to me as an honorable business that has been in your family for three generations."

"I know that also. But the personal safety of Sunny Fogarty, a devoted employee, takes precedence. If her life is at risk—and you admit it is possible—I'd rather surrender than see her harmed."

My fury slowly cooled to admiration. He had obviously wrestled with this quandary for many sleepless hours and had come to the only decision he could live with. It was a high-minded decision. It was also an impossible decision.

"Sorry, Mr. Whitcomb," I said, "it can't be done."

His face grew stony. "And why not?" he demanded.

"For two reasons, sir. First of all, you refer to me as an employee of McNally and Son. I am that and it pleases me. But regardless of your relationship with our firm, I shall continue my inquiries no matter what."

"Even if your father orders you to stop?"

"Even if he does. But I doubt if that will ever come to pass. He knows me better than you do, Mr. Whitcomb. And you don't know my father either. Yes, he can be an intimidating man, but he is also an extremely upright man. Never in a million years would he order me to end a criminal investigation. And I have absolutely no intention of doing so, whether as an employee of McNally and Son or as a private snoop. I have my standards, sir, just as you have yours."

He was silent, staring at me.

"You may or may not believe what I have just said," I continued. "But now let me give you the second reason why your proposed cancellation of the investigation is out of the question. This is information Sunny Fogarty did not relay to you because I didn't tell her."

I then related the involvement in the affair by Sgt. Al Rogoff of the Palm Beach Police Department and Special Agent Griffin Kling of the Federal Bureau of Investigation.

"Both men are experienced law enforcement officers," I told Mr. Horace, "and no way are you going to persuade them to end their digging. Agent Kling in particular is positively ferocious in his intent to end the criminal career of Ernest Gorton. Kling is a driven man, and I assure you any plea to end his crusade will be ignored."

Mr. Whitcomb drained his coffee, and when he replaced his cup it clattered on the saucer.

"I suppose you think me a fool," he said dully.

"No, sir," I said, "I don't think that. But events have been set in motion and they have an inexorable momentum you cannot stop. Until the matter is concluded—successfully, let us hope—Sunny Fogarty must take her chances, and so must you, I, Oliver, Ernest Gorton, and everyone else even remotely connected. We are all pawns, Mr. Whitcomb."

"Yes," he said with a twisted smile, "aren't we? And especially Sarah."

I didn't know what he meant by that and didn't ask.

Unexpectedly he yawned, stretching his arms wide, and I realized my guess of sleepless hours of worrying had not been amiss.

"I started the whole thing," he said ruefully. "Told Sunny Fogarty to look into it. And now see what's happened: my son a deceiver, Sunny's safety at risk, my business threatened, the FBI involved. I have been hoisted by my own petard."

"I don't think that expression particularly apt, sir," I told him. "It implies self-destruction, and you're far from that."

"Perhaps," he said, not really believing it. "What do you propose to do now?"

"Continue what I have been doing. Sniff about, ask questions, listen to what people say and observe what they do, wait for things to happen. And sometimes give them a nudge."

"It's an art," he said. "What you do."

"Not quite," I said. "More of a craft."

Silence again, a long silence while he scrabbled at crumbs on the tablecloth. "My God," he said in a low voice, "we do manage to mess things up, don't we?"

I feared he was losing his nerve and it alarmed me. "Sometimes it seems so, Mr. Whitcomb," I said, "but one never knows, do one? I mean, think of those lads who fought the men-of-war in your collection."

That brightened him. "Yes," he said, "you're right. Have you ever heard the apocryphal story of what happened when John Paul Jones was battling the *Serapis* from the bridge of the *Bonhomme Richard?* His ship was riddled, on fire, sinking, decks awash with the blood of dead and dying sailors. Jones was called upon to surrender and shouted back, 'I have not yet begun to fight!' A Marine marksman high in the rigging looked down at the destruction below and said, 'There's always one son of a bitch who never gets the word.' "

We both laughed and I hoped he would be that son of a bitch, though naturally I didn't mention it. I thanked him for the morning's refreshment, we shook hands, and I departed. I drove slowly back to the McNally Building, thinking that for all his candor, his revelations and confessions, he had not yet told me the complete truth. The man was concealing something that troubled him mightily. I was convinced of it, but what that secret could be I had no idea. I had the dizzy notion it was the keyword in a perplexing crossword puzzle. Ferret it out and everything would become clear: solved and elegant. Or so I thought.

I descended into our underground garage, parked, and

hopped from the Miata. Herb, our security guard, came lumbering over, his big dogleg holster flapping against his thigh.

"Hey, Mr. McNally," he said, "you got a visitor. A lady."

"Banzai!" I said. "Where is she—in the reception room?"

"Nah," he said, jerking a thumb. "Over there."

I turned to look. A new white Honda Accord. Very nice. I started toward it and the driver's window came purring down. I leaned and peered within. There was no mistaking that tangerine hair: Ms. Rhoda Starlight/Flembaugh.

"Hi there!" she said brightly.

27

"Treat a harlot like a lady and a lady like a harlot." Who said that? I have no idea, although it sounds like the Earl of Chesterfield advising his son. But I resolved to follow this counsel, so when Rhoda gave me a Cheshire cat grin and patted the seat beside her, I obediently circled the car, entered, and immediately became aware of the scent she was wearing. Stirring. One might even say invigorating—and I do say it.

"Arky," she said. "I can call you Arky, can't I?"

"If it pleases you. Actually my name is Archy."

"Of course. Archy. We met once before, didn't we?"

"We did indeed. Briefly. In Dr. Pflug's office."

"Oh, *him,*" she said disdainfully. "Ernie calls him El Jerko. Isn't that funny?"

"Hilarious," I said.

"Well, I shook that turkey," she went on. "I'm self-employed now. My own business."

"Good for you."

She dug into a bulging wallet, extracted a business card,

and handed it to me. The engraved legend was simplicity itself: "Rhoda. Physical Therapy for Discerning Gentlemen." This was followed by a phone number and, wonderful to behold, a fax number. No address.

"Are you a discerning gentleman?" she asked.

"I try," I said modestly. "I don't always succeed."

She laughed and clamped a warm hand on my knee. "Ernie has told me so much about you I just knew we had to become better friends. Are you busy this afternoon?"

"Unfortunately I am. An appointment with my trichologist for the repair of a small tonsure."

"Golly," she said, distressed. "Does it hurt?"

"The pain is excruciating," I said, "especially when the wind is from the east."

"Then how about tonight?" she inquired. "You could come to my place or I could come to yours. No charge. It'll be a freebie."

"Rhoda," I said, "you are an extremely attractive young lady and your beauty is exceeded only by your generosity. But there is something you should know: I am engaged to be married to a woman I have known for several years. I love her dearly and have sworn to her my undying devotion and absolute faithfulness."

The hand on my knee didn't relax. "She doesn't have to know, Arky."

"Archy. But I'll know, won't I, and it will make me feel like a cur."

"You must love her very much."

"I do, I do!" I cried, and if I could have wiped a tear from my eye or stifled a small sob I would. I have no shame—as you well know. "Rhoda, she means the world to me and I could not live with the thought of betraying our love. Have you ever felt that way?"

The warm hand was withdrawn from my knee. "No," she said sorrowfully, "but I've dreamed of it. Some guy who would really turn me on and we'd make it together. I mean, I'd cook and clean for him and everything. But you're right; if I found out he was cheating on me it would spoil the whole deal."

"Of course it would. I knew you'd understand how I feel."

"Yeah," she said, "I can see where you're coming from. I hope you make it. Right now my life's the pits."

I felt a momentary twinge of guilt at the way I was misleading this poor, brainless lass—but I really had no choice, did I?

I opened the passenger door and prepared to withdraw.

"Rhoda," I said, "I hope you find the true love you're seeking and start a new life."

"You really believe that could happen?" she said hopefully.

"Of course it could," I assured her. "You must think positively."

"What does that mean?"

"Be confident that better times are coming."

"Yeah," she said determinedly. "I've got to keep thinking better times are coming. Thanks, Arky."

I stood there and watched the white Honda Accord exit from the garage. I felt dreadful. I had tried to be a bucker-upper, but if I had given her a lift I knew it would be brief. Her life had fallen into a cast-iron mold and it would take a sledge to smash it.

Of one thing I had no doubt: Rhoda's unexpected visit and invitation had been ordered by Ernest Gorton. Her offer of a "freebie" was his Ultimate Bribe. The way his mind worked simply amazed me. He had decided his offer of a no-show job at a handsome stipend might be rejected. If money didn't work, sex was another option. And if that failed, I was certain he would resort to a threat of physical violence.

I began to appreciate Mr. Horace Whitcomb's fear of Sunny Fogarty being endangered. And I found myself sharing Special Agent Griffin Kling's fury at this brute's machinations. Ordinarily I am a "live-and-let-live" sort of bloke, but Ernest Gorton's evil designs caused me to question the latter half of that philosophy.

I hadn't totally prevaricated during my surreal chat with the carrottop. It was true I had an appointment with Herman Pincus, my tonsorial artiste, that afternoon. And it was a delight when he showed me, with the aid of two mirrors, that the bald spot on my bean was now boasting the fuzz of a hirsute peach.

I endured another hot oil massage, and Herman assured me it would not be long before my luxuriant locks were restored to their pristine glory. What a relief! You think me guilty of vanity? Of course I am. And so are you. Self-love is the only enduring passion. C'mon, admit it.

I returned to my office and found a message requesting I phone Al Rogoff instanter.

"Progress report," the sergeant said briskly. "I told Kling about Rhoda Flembaugh, Gorton's floozy, and he couldn't have been happier. He just called me. He ran a trace and she's got a record. Nothing heavy. Loitering for the purpose, lewd and lascivious behavior, and swell stuff like that. Anyway, Kling is going to pay her a visit and ask how come a nice girl like her is the registrant of trucks in New York, Boston, and Chicago used to haul stiffs."

"I hope Special Agent Kling is a discerning gentleman," I said.

"You hope *what?*"

I told him of my recent tête-à-tête with Rhoda. Al chuffed with laughter.

"That tootsie is something else," he marveled. "No charge to you, huh? You think Gorton put her up to it?"

"Of course he did. The scoundrel is determined to find my weakness and exploit it."

"He'd do better to offer you a mauve velvet fez."

"True," I admitted. "It might succeed. Let me know how Kling makes out with Madame Pompadour."

I had no desire for lunch that day, having pigged out with Mr. Whitcomb. But I thought a period of quiescence was in order after a hyperemotional morning during which I felt like a shuttlecock being batted about by people playing a game with no rules. Something tall and cold at the Pelican Club would restore the McNally aplomb, I reckoned—but it was not to be.

I was starting from my office when the accursed phone rang and I stared at it with loathing. I was briefly tempted to depart and let it shrill its heart out to an empty room. But then I dreamed it might be the White House beseeching my advice on how to handle the latest crisis in the Udmurt Republic. Or, better yet, it might be the Amazonian contralto from the church choir who had tracked me down and wished to become better acquainted. It was neither of course. The caller was Oliver Whitcomb.

"Archy!" he said, all false joviality. "Can we have a drink together?"

"When?" I asked.

"Now," he said. "The sooner the better."

"I was just heading for the Pelican Club," I told him. "Do you know it?"

A pause. "Yes," he said. "All right, if you insist."

I had suggested, not insisted, but I was in no mood to truckle. And so, half an hour later, Oliver and I were seated at a table in the almost deserted bar area of the Pelican. I had a depressing premonition the travails of my day had not yet ended and I was to be treated to another dose of someone else's angst. I wondered idly what it might cost to rent a confessional wherein I could ply my trade.

We had ordered gin and tonics, and Oliver gulped his greedily. I am proud to say I sipped genteelly—and frequently. Whatever was troubling the lad kept him silent a few moments, giving me the opportunity to eyeball his attire. He obviously had no "important funeral" scheduled, for he wore the threads of a Neapolitan toff. I have a fondness for rather assertive duds, as you well know, but Oliver's costume looked as if it had been created by a designer hooked on Crayolas.

"I visited mother in the hospital this morning," he said moodily.

"Oh?" I said. "And how is she feeling?"

He shook his head. "Not good. I wanted to have a heart-to-heart, but it was a no-go. She was hallucinating. Kept talking about ballroom dancing. Old stuff. I couldn't get through to her."

"A sad situation," I said—the most neutral comment I could devise at the moment.

Then his talk became so pizzicato it went beyond desperation and entered the realm of franticness.

"It's the will, y'see. Mother's will. She holds controlling interest in the business. Naturally I expect to inherit her shares." He stopped sputtering and looked at me expectantly.

"Naturally," I murmured.

"But I've got to *know*," he rattled on. "After all, it's my future, isn't it? I just assumed . . . But now I'm worried. So much depends . . . Have you seen mother's will?"

"No."

"Do you know what's in it?"

"No."

"I called your father. He said he can't release that information. Suggested I ask mother. But the woman can't talk sense. She's at death's door."

Death's door. A grisly cliché. Unless, of course, it's a revolving door.

"Archy, could you ask your father? About my mother's will."

"I could," I said stonily, "but it would do no good whatsoever. He'd never tell me and he'd be horrified by my asking."

"Yes? Well, how about this . . . There must be a copy in your office files. Could you sneak a peek? I need to make sure I inherit. There's a lot riding on this, Archy."

"Oliver, have you asked your father? He probably knows."

His laugh was harsh. "My father and I are not simpatico these days. Archy, will you do it for me? Take a quick look just to confirm I'm inheriting. I can't tell you how important it is to me."

If I were a courageous, stand-up chap I would have delivered a stern "No!" immediately. But he was in such an agitated state I feared that if I rejected his appeal he would launch himself across the table and go for my jugular with his incisors.

"I'll see what I can do," I said weakly.

"Good man!" he said, almost weeping with gratitude. "Good man! Do this for me and there's a nice piece of change in it for you."

We drained our glasses, shook hands, and departed. One drink. That's all we had. I swear.

I drove slowly home, pondering what Oliver had just unwittingly revealed about the motivation for his association with Ernest Gorton. The plot was becoming clear to me, as I'm certain it is to you.

I had time for a swim that afternoon prior to the family cocktail hour. It was during my languid wallow that I began laughing and succeeded in choking on a mouthful of the Atlantic Ocean. The reason for my mirth? In one day I had been promised a "freebie" by Rhoda Flembaugh and "a nice piece of change" by Oliver Whitcomb. My position as Chief of Discreet Inquiries at McNally & Son was suddenly offering an abundance of fringe benefits.

Dinner that evening was something that might tweak your salivary glands: mahimahi sautéed with fresh herbs, tomatoes, garlic, and olive oil so virginal I was certain it had taken a vow of chastity. Profiteroles for dessert. I restrained myself and had only four.

"On a diet, Archy?" father inquired. Sometimes the pater's sarcasm can nip.

I scuttled to my lodgment after dinner and set to work. I had been neglecting my journal shamefully and had a great deal to record since the last entry. I worked steadily and conscientiously, for I am not just another pretty face; when duty calls, McNally is ready to click heels and salute.

I was briefly interrupted by a call from Connie Garcia in Miami. She said she expected to return in a day or two, and it was welcome news; I missed that lady.

"Behaving yourself, laddie?" she asked.

"Don't I always?"

"No," she said. "I'll get a complete report on your activities from my spies when I come back."

"There's nothing to report," I protested. "The naughtiest thing I've done since you left was watching 'The Sound of Music' on TV."

"Liar, liar, pants on fire!" she scoffed and hung up.

I went back to my scribbling, labored determinedly, and finished shortly after eleven o'clock. I poured a marc, lighted a cigarette and began reviewing the entire account of the Whitcomb affair.

The role Oliver was playing now seemed evident to me, as was the hostility between son and father. The mysteries remaining concerned the curious behavior of Horace Whitcomb and Sunny Fogarty. And, of course, puzzle numero uno was the out-of-state shipments of coffins going to a hauling service obviously owned by Ernest Gorton even if he had taken the precaution of registering his trucks in the name of the tarty Rhoda.

I wrestled with that enigma through one more brandy and one more cigarette. I experienced no grand epiphany. Finally I gave up, disrobed, and went to bed. I hoped to dream of Gene Tierney but Maria Ouspenskaya showed up instead. Oh well, it could have been Hoot Gibson.

28

"I think the Duchess hates me," Binky Watrous said gloomily.

"Nonsense," I said, although I wasn't so sure. "It seems to me she's been the soul of forbearance. Got you out of that scrape with the belly dancer in Tulsa, didn't she?"

"Well, yes, but she makes me eat oatmeal for breakfast. I detest oatmeal and she knows it. But she insists. Says it'll build strong bones. Who on earth wants strong bones? Not me. I mean, what can you *do* with them? Got a cigarette?"

I shoved my pack across the desk. It was Tuesday morning and when I had arrived at the McNally Building I found Binky grumping about, obviously in need of a kind word. I took him to my office and offered what cheer I could.

"Still partying with Mitzi and Oliver?" I asked him.

That quickened him. "Mostly with Mitzi," he reported. "Oliver isn't around much these days. Apparently his mother is extremely ill and also Mitzi says he's got all these big deals cooking. And talking about deals, one of Whitcomb's pals wants me to put some money in a new product he's bringing out."

"Oh? What is it?"

"A cognac lollipop. A sure winner, don't you think?"

"Absolutely," I said. "Are you going to invest?"

"Come on, Archy, you know I have a bad case of the flats. But if I had a few bucks I'd certainly plunge on the cognac lollipop. It can't miss. I don't suppose you'd—"

"No," I interrupted, "I would not. All my cash is tied up in a gerbil ranch. Binky, has Mitzi ever said anything about Oliver's relationship with his father?"

He thought a moment. At least I believe he was thinking. It was hard to tell with Binky. He might have been dozing.

"Yes," he said finally. "Once she remarked that Oliver was the apple of his mother's eye and the lemon of his father's. That's not bad, is it, Archy?"

"No, not bad."

He snapped his fingers. "Something else. I almost forgot. There was a small party at the Whitcombs' last night. Well, it wasn't really a party. More like a gathering. Maybe six or seven people. Oliver wasn't there, but Ernie Gorton showed up. Stayed a few hours. Very friendly. Talked to everyone."

"Uh-huh. Was Rhoda present?"

"No, she didn't show up. Mitzi says Rhoda has her own business now. She even has a fax machine."

"Will wonders never cease?"

"Anyway, after everyone left, Mitzi and I were alone and she told me Gorton had offered her a job."

I roused. "What kind of a job?"

"She didn't tell me, but she said the salary was stupendous. That was her word: stupendous."

"Binky, did you get the feeling Mitzi was interested in working for Ernest Gorton?"

"Oh yes. Definitely. She was charged. She said Gorton has deep pockets. Deeper than her husband's."

"That I can believe," I said. "And then what happened?"

He looked at me, puzzled. "When?"

"When you and Mitzi were alone in the Whitcombs' home and she told you about Gorton's job offer."

"Oh. Well, then we went skinny-dipping. No, that's not strictly accurate. She did, in the pool behind their house, but I didn't. To tell you the truth, I had consumed a number of brandy stingers and feared if I entered the pool, clothed or unclothed, I would immediately sink to the bottom without the strength to rise."

"You must eat your oatmeal," I admonished. "So what did you do?"

"Just lolled on a lounge and watched her. There was a full moon and I had a terrible desire to howl. Mitzi really is an excitement, Archy. If I was loaded I'd plead with her to dump Oliver and share a glorious future with me."

"Very poetic," I said. "But the lady has a bottom-line mentality?"

"What a bottom," he said dreamily. "What a line. Archy, tell me something honestly. Do you think I've been doing okay in the discreet inquiry business?"

"Your efforts have exceeded my expectations," I assured him—a valid statement since my expectations had been nil.

He left my office a much jauntier lad than when he entered. You may think it was a silly conversation, but amidst all that dross I spotted a few sparklers confirming my theory about Oliver Whitcomb's activities and a few that were to prove of some significance in solving the riddle of Ernest Gorton's despicable schemes.

The brief encounter with Binky elevated the McNally spirits and I was in a hemidemisemi ebullient mood, thinking the day was starting out splendidly, when everything turned drear. It began with a phone call from Sgt. Al Rogoff.

"I'm at home," he said. "Kling is here. Can you come over?"

His numb voice alarmed me. "Something wrong, Al?"

"Yeah. The Lauderdale cops fished a floater from the Intracoastal last night. Rhoda Flembaugh. Shot once through the back of the head. An assassination."

I closed my eyes. I tasted dust. "All right," I said faintly. "I'll be right there."

I drove slowly and carefully. (I always do that after hearing of a sudden, violent death.) When I arrived at Rogoff's I found the two officers seated at the round oak table working on mugs of black coffee. I was offered a cup but politely declined. I know how Al makes coffee: boil a pan of water, throw in a handful of coarsely ground beans, let the mixture boil until it's the color of tar. The taste? "Battery acid" springs immediately to mind.

"Tell Kling about your meeting with Flembaugh yesterday," the sergeant said. "I've already told him, but maybe you can add something."

The FBI man turned those black sunglasses to me, and obediently I recited everything I could recall of my conversation with Rhoda. I added that I was convinced Gorton had sicced her on me in an effort to halt my investigation into his connection with the Whitcomb Funeral Homes.

"I hope the fact that I rejected her advances had nothing to do with her demise," I said—anxiously, I admit.

The Special Agent spoke for the first time since I had entered. He had not granted me even a "Hello" or a "Hi."

"No," he said, "don't blame yourself. I triggered the kill. What I figure happened was this: Rogoff told me the trucks of the Cleo Hauling Service were registered to Gorton's playmate. Late yesterday I looked her up and tossed a few hardballs. I got nothing from her. A squirrelly broad but smart enough to keep her mouth shut. We're checking the phone logs, but I'm guessing the moment I was out of her place she called Gorton and told him the Feds had been around asking about his trucks. He didn't like that and so he had her put down just to make sure she'd never spill."

"He did it?" I asked.

"Not personally," Kling said. "This is one careful shtarker. He doesn't do the heavy work himself. He knows plenty of crazy dopers who'll pop someone for fifty bucks. Meanwhile he's miles away when it happens."

"When did it happen?" I asked.

"We're waiting for the ME's estimate. Probably around midnight, give or take."

"Then you're right," I said. "Gorton was miles away. At a party at Oliver Whitcomb's home in Boca."

I told them what Binky Watrous had reported: Gorton had showed up, acted in a friendly manner, talked to several people.

The FBI man sighed and removed his cheaters. His pale eyes looked infinitely weary. "Oh sure," he said. "Setting up an alibi. That bastard doesn't miss a trick."

"Something else happened at the party," I said. "I may be imagining this but it makes a nasty kind of sense."

I related what Binky had told me of Gorton's job offer to Mitzi Whitcomb at a "stupendous" salary.

"If Gorton knew Rhoda Flembaugh was being taken out," I argued, "he'd need a replacement, wouldn't he? Someone to run his call girl ring in the Palm Beach area. Who better than Mitzi? She has a lot of moneyed contacts, many of them druggies. And Oliver, her husband, can't object because Gorton has him by the short hairs."

The two officers looked at each other.

"It listens," Al Rogoff said.

Kling nodded. "I'll buy it," he said. "I like it because it's the way Gorton operates. He's a businessman, an entrepreneur, one hell of a manager. He's always planning, looking ahead, figuring angles and percentages. If he had gone legit he'd be a zillionaire today. Instead, he's dead meat. He doesn't know it yet but that's what he is—dead meat."

Once again I was shocked by the venom in his voice. I think even Al Rogoff was made uncomfortable by his intensity. If Kling had obviously been a religious fanatic I would have assumed he considered himself God's surrogate on earth. But in the absence of that motive I could only guess his passion sprang from professional hubris.

I must admit the man frightened me. I don't wish to imply he was irrational, a raving maniac, or anything like that. But he was suffering from a monomania so condensed it was consuming him. I was happy not to be the subject of his rabid vengefulness and wondered if Ernest Gorton knew he was the target of such an implacable nemesis.

I asked him if he had learned the identity of the final consignees to whom the Cleo Hauling Service was delivering all those caskets.

He donned his dark sunglasses again and paused a long moment. I think he was considering how much to reveal.

"Preliminary stuff," he said finally. "There was one drop at a Boston funeral home reported to have mob connections. Another delivery was made to a private home in Westchester County in New York. The owner is a wheeler-dealer with a lot of loot in offshore banks. We're still working it, but so far there's no pattern."

"Where do we go from here?" Rogoff said.

"Since the Flembaugh woman got whacked," Kling said,

"we've put twenty-four-hour surveillance on Gorton's warehouse. The phones there and in his home and office have been hung. But I don't expect anything from that. The guy loves to use pay phones—and never the same one twice. A dummy he ain't. You want a prediction?"

Rogoff and I looked at him.

"Why not," Al said. "I even believe horoscopes."

"In the next two or three days the body of a young doper will be found in the Miami-Lauderdale area. Either he'll have his throat cut or maybe a slug through the ear. The local cops will have no suspects and no motive."

"But you will?" I said.

"Sure," Kling said, almost cheerfully. "The corpse will be the guy who popped Rhoda Flembaugh. That'll be Gorton's work—cutting his link with her killer. I told you he's a smart piece of dreck, didn't I?"

There didn't seem anything more to be said, and after a few moments I departed even more depressed than when I had arrived. I gloomed we were all spinning our wheels while Gorton went his merry way, doing exactly what he had set out to do. In other words, we were playing a reactive role but that vile blackguard was calling the shots—literally and figuratively.

In such a despondent mood I really had no choice but to drive directly to the Pelican Club, hoping to convert the McNally spirits from the torpid to the fizzy.

I lunched alone at the bar. Priscilla brought me an excellent salad of shrimp and chicken with a few chunks of pepperoni tossed in to give it a kick. I also had toasted bagel chips and a few glasses of our house wine, a chardonnay that always reminded me of Fred Allen's quip about the Italian winemaker who was fired for sitting down on the job.

Lunch consumed, I discovered to my dismay that I had not

yet achieved the verve I sought, and I knew the cause: I could not forget the cruel extinction of bubbleheaded Rhoda. A great brain she was not, but I didn't believe there was malice in her. She was simply trying to survive and didn't succeed. I could only hope she had been totally unaware of her impending doom and had gone to her death laughing.

Musing on her sad fate, I went out to the parking area and discovered all four tires of my fire-engine-red Miata had been slashed. My poor baby was settled down on the tarmac like an exhausted bunny. It took only a sec for my bewilderment to become outrage. Then I may have uttered a mild expletive sotto voce.

I was examining the damage when a scuzzy gink strolled over, hands thrust into the pockets of a polyester leisure suit I thought had been declared illegal in the 1960s. He had a coffin-shaped face and eyes that looked like rusted minié balls. I had never seen him before and devoutly hoped I would never see him again.

"Took a hit, huh?" he said.

I nodded.

"Funny they should pick your heap out of all the cars parked here."

"Yes," I said. "Funny."

"Maybe someone's sending you a message," he said with a ghastly smile. "Think about it."

He stalked away and swung aboard a black Harley that looked as big and menacing as a dreadnought. I watched him roar out of the parking lot. He wasn't wearing a helmet and I wished him only the best—an uncontrollable skid, for instance.

29

I shall not bore you with a detailed account of my activities during the following afternoon hours; you might snooze. Suffice to say I returned to the Pelican Club and started feeding quarters into the public phone. I called a towing service, my garage in West Palm, a retailer of tires, a car rental agency, my insurance agent, and Sgt. Al Rogoff, who was incommunicable.

All I can tell you is that I functioned in a practical manner and shortly after five o'clock that evening was heading homeward behind the wheel of a white Acura Legend. It was okay, but driving a closed car gave me a mild attack of claustrophobia after years spent in a top-down convertible with the wind uncombing my hair and the Florida sun giving nourishment to all those hungry squamous cells on my beak hoping to become malignant.

I pulled into the graveled turnaround of the McNally faux Tudor yurt just as my father had garaged his Lexus and was heading for the back door, toting a bulging briefcase. He paused to watch me park and crawl out of the Acura. He gave me a bemused glance.

"Changing your religion, Archy?" he asked.

"Not by choice," I said grumpily. "Sir, can you give me some time tonight after dinner?"

"Regarding what?"

"The Whitcomb investigation."

One of those tangled eyebrows slowly lifted. "Is that why you're driving this vehicle?"

"Yes, sir, the two are connected. Tangentially."

"Very well. I'll see you in my study after dinner. Please try to make it short. I brought work home with me. Interesting case. Concerns an estate on conditional limitation. Do you know what that is?"

"No, sir."

"Nor do I—exactly. Nor apparently does anyone—exactly. That's what makes it interesting."

Which explains why, at about eight-thirty that evening, I was seated in the squire's study, occupying a leather club chair facing his magisterial desk. He didn't offer a postprandial glass of port or jigger of brandy and I was just as happy because I wanted to exhibit absolute lucidity—as likely a prospect as my becoming world champion of the clean and jerk.

Ordinarily I do not give the boss progress reports during the course of my discreet inquiries. He is only interested in the final results. Also, I suspect, he would rather not know the details of my modi operandi, fearing they might be an affront to his hidebound code of ethics—which, of course, they would be.

But there had been developments in the Whitcomb case of which he should be made cognizant since they involved legal problems he might be called upon to solve. Speaking rapidly,

I delivered a précis of what had recently occurred, including my meetings with Horace and Oliver Whitcomb. *Mon père* listened to my recital without interrupting, but when I had concluded he began pelting me with questions.

"Horace Whitcomb was aware of our investigation from the start?"

"Yes, sir. He is an alert businessman with a sharp eye for details. It was he who first noticed the inexplicable revenue increase and asked Sunny Fogarty to request our assistance since he didn't wish to distress his dying wife by a showdown with their son."

"And in the event of his mother's death, Oliver hopes to inherit a controlling interest in Whitcomb Funeral Homes?"

"I believe that's his hope, father. It's the reason why he's been building up their cash reserves, so he can start his expansion program the moment he becomes the majority shareholder."

The sire looked at me strangely. I can only describe his expression as one of grim and sour amusement. I had the oddest notion he was about to reveal something that might turn the Whitcomb inquiry upside down. But apparently he thought better of it and returned to his interrogation.

"And in his effort to increase Whitcomb's cash balance, Oliver struck a deal with this gangster Gorton?"

"That's the way I see it, sir."

"An illegal activity?"

"Undoubtedly."

"You feel Gorton is responsible for what happened to your car?"

"I'm sure of it. He ordered the kneecapping of the Miata. It was a message to me to end my prying or risk a more violent response."

"I don't like it," father growled. "I don't like it one bit. But

Sergeant Rogoff and the FBI agent are in pursuit of Gorton. Is that correct?"

"Yes, sir."

"Good. It's their job. Archy, I strongly urge you to cease and desist from any further inquiries into the schemes of Ernest Gorton. Is that understood?"

"Father, I can't cease and desist. I'm already involved and can hardly send Gorton a letter of resignation. In addition, Sunny Fogarty is in danger. I could not endure seeing her suffer the same fate as Rhoda Flembaugh. I simply cannot wash my hands of the whole affair and stroll away."

I knew the pater was concerned for my personal safety and I appreciated that. But if he had his ethical code, I had mine. No way was I about to give up this chase. Succumb to the crude threats of a wannabe Alphonse Capone? I think not.

The guv didn't argue, knowing it would be fruitless. He said, "Do you have any idea of the exact nature of Gorton's role in this matter? Why all those caskets are being shipped north?"

"No, sir. No idea whatsoever. At the moment."

"Getting rid of the victims of gang killings?"

"Possibly. I'm hoping the FBI investigation will give us a clearer picture of what's going on."

"During your last conversation with Horace Whitcomb," he said, switching gears on me, "did he agree our inquiry was to continue?"

"He did. After I convinced him it was impossible to terminate it as he had requested."

"Good. Keep a careful record of your billable hours, Archy."

And on that happy commercial note we parted.

I trudged upstairs to my third-floor cage reflecting I had not been entirely forthcoming with the author of my existence. It was true, as I told father, I thought Oliver Whitcomb had made a devilish bargain with Ernest Gorton in order to further Oliver's dream of creating the McDonald's of mortuaries.

But I suspected there might be another reason for their partnership: Gorton was a dependable source of all those "controlled substances" people stuffed up their schnozzles or injected into their bloodstreams. I did not believe Oliver was hooked, but I suspected many of his moneyed chums were. And it was those same stoned pals our hero wanted to keep happily dazed, for he was depending on them to help finance his grandiose plans.

But that was speculation and I could be totally wrong. I have been totally wrong before—as when I assured Binky Watrous he would suffer no ill effects from eating a dozen fried grasshoppers.

I knew I should work on my journal, bringing that magnum opus current, but the prospect of scribbling for an hour was a downer. I yearned for a more challenging activity, something that would set the McNally corpuscles boogying and enliven what had really been a dismal day.

And so, when my phone rang, I pounced upon it, hoping it might be Consuela Garcia announcing her return. In truth I missed my fractious fraülein. But it was not Connie; it was Sunny Fogarty.

"Archy," she said in a hushed voice as if afraid of being overheard, "I'm calling from a public pay phone. I'd like to talk to you tonight. Is there any safe place we can meet?"

I thought swiftly. I can do that, y'know. Not habitually but occasionally.

"Suppose I pick you up in half an hour," I suggested.

A pause. "But if I'm under observation," she said, "won't they recognize your car?"

"I'm not driving the fire engine tonight," I said blithely. "I have a white four-door Acura. No one in his or her right mind would ever link it with A. McNally, the registered playboy and bon vivant. Wait in the lobby of your condo. I pull up, you pop out and pop in, and off we go. It'll work."

"You're sure?" she said doubtfully.

"Can't miss," I said with more confidence than I felt.

"All right," she said. "I wouldn't ask you to do this if it wasn't important to me."

"Thirty minutes," I repeated. "White Acura sedan." And I hung up before she raised more objections. The lady seemed spooked, and I didn't blame her a bit. I had no desire for another encounter with that knife-wielding gent in the polyester leisure suit.

It went beautifully. Sunny was waiting, scurried to the Acura, and away we sped. I glanced in the rearview and saw no signs of pursuit. Certainly not a black Harley. That was comforting.

"Why don't we just drive down the coast and back," I proposed. "I have a full tank. Well, I don't but the car does, and I think we'll be more secure on wheels and in motion rather than holing up at some public place. Is that acceptable?"

"Fine, Archy," she said, putting a hand lightly on my arm. "It'll give us a chance to talk in private."

"You told me it was important."

"It is," she said. "To me."

Not another word was uttered while I headed for A1A and turned south. It was a so-so evening: scudding clouds, high humidity, a gusty breeze smelling of geriatric fish. It was the sort of dreary weather than would make a knight want to curl up with a good book—or one of the pages.

We were closing in on Manalapan when she finally spoke.

"Archy," she said, almost whispering, "I want to apologize."

"Oh? For what?"

"Mr. Horace told me he informed you that he knew of your investigation from the start. I'm sorry I misled you and your father."

"Perfectly understandable and forgivable," I assured her. "You were merely following the instruction of your employer."

"Yes, and he had a good reason for acting as he did. He didn't want his dying wife to learn he had discovered their son might be engaged in a criminal conspiracy. Mrs. Sarah loves Oliver so much."

"I cannot quarrel with Mr. Whitcomb's motive," I said. "I'm sure he did what he thought was best. But he set in motion an investigation that can't be stopped."

"He said the local police and the FBI are now involved."

"That's correct."

"Archy, do you think Oliver will go to jail?"

"It's quite possible, Sunny. As well as the other Whitcomb employees who are accomplices in the scheme."

"But what *is* the scheme?" she cried despairingly.

"We're working on it" was all I could tell her.

"You may think it an awful thing for me to say," she went on, "but I hope Mrs. Sarah won't live to hear her son has been imprisoned."

"Not so awful. A very sensitive and empathic hope. What is her condition?"

"Not good," she said gloomily. "The doctor says it's probably a matter of days. She's going, Archy."

My desire for an activity to enliven a dismal day was thwarted. I should have stayed home, I decided, and worked on my journal. This conversation was definitely spirit-dashing time.

We were almost down to Delray when I pulled into a turnaround and parked for a few moments. I did this because Sunny had started weeping, quietly and steadily, and it seemed unfeeling to continue driving while she was so distraught.

"And if that isn't enough," she said between muffled sobs, "my own mother is fading, and I don't know how long she has. Archy, everything is just falling apart. Everyone I love seems to be dying and I've never been so shaken and miserable in my life. I just feel my world is ending."

Then she turned suddenly to embrace me. Not passionately, of course; she was seeking solace and who could blame her. She buried her face betwixt my neck and shoulder, making little snuffling sounds like a child who's fallen and is hurting.

"Sunny," I said, hugging her firmly, "you're going through a bad time. But you're a very strong woman and I know, I *know* you'll survive intact. Are you familiar with Lincoln's philosophy, appropriate to all times and situations? 'This, too, shall pass away.' It may sound cold and hardhearted in your present state but do keep it in mind. I think you'll be surprised at what consolation it offers."

After a few moments we shared a chaste kiss, disengaged, and returned to Palm Beach. Sunny's head remained on my shoulder during that silent drive home, and occasionally she touched my arm or shoulder, as if she wanted to make certain I was there, to make contact with the living.

It had been a harrowing evening and I trust you'll be muy simpático when you hear that, arriving back in my belfry, I immediately poured a double brandy and flopped down behind my desk to sip and recover from that wounding conversation.

I discovered that, in my cowardly way, I didn't even want to *think* about my talk with Sunny Fogarty. And so I donned earphones and listened to a snippet of tape: Gertrude Lawrence singing the yearning "Someday I'll Find You." I played it not once, not twice, but thrice.

I finally went to bed in a deliciously melancholic mood, reflecting that Mr. Lincoln may have been correct.

But the memory lingers on, does it not?

30

We now arrive at a section of this narrative which I find, regretfully, somewhat embarrassing to pen. It concerns how I discovered the exact nature of Ernest Gorton's flagrantly wicked scheme.

I wish with all my myocardium I could claim my discovery was the result of deucedly clever deductive reasoning—akin to Mr. Holmes solving a case by noting a dog *didn't* bark. But I'm sure you respect me as a chap of absolute veracity, scrupulous and exact, not given to embroidering the facts. And so I must be truthful about what happened. I fear you'll find it ridiculous—and it *was* ridiculous.

It began on Wednesday morning when, as usual, I overslept. Upon awakening I immediately phoned my West Palm garage and was overjoyed to learn the Miata was re-tired, back in fighting trim, and could be reclaimed at my convenience. Good news indeed.

I breakfasted alone: a frugal meal of cranberry juice, black coffee, and a croissant sandwich of liverwurst, jack cheese, tomato, a slice of red onion, and just a wee bit of a macho mustard. Invigorating.

I was heading for the garage when mother came trotting from our little greenhouse. She was clad in Bermuda shorts and one of my cast-off T-shirts. Over this costume she wore a soil-soiled apron, as so many pistil-whipped gardeners do, and I knew she had been digging into or perhaps transplanting one or more of her precious begonias. We exchanged a morning kiss.

"Archy," she accused, "did you have onions for breakfast?"

"Not me," I protested. "It must be that new Polish mouthwash I've been using."

"Listen, darling," she said, "do you think you might get over to West Palm Beach sometime today?"

"That's where I'm heading right now, luv. To get my car out of hock."

"Would you do me a favor?"

"I'd go to hell fa ya," I said, "or Philadelphia."

She giggled delightedly. "That's cute. What's it from, Archy?"

"Beats me," I admitted. "One of those oddments rattling around my cavernous cranium. A song lyric, I think."

(Dear Reader: If you happen to know the source of that quote, please drop me a line. Much obliged.)

"Well, here's what happened," momsy went on. "I ordered some hanging scented begonia bulbs from a garden supply house. I specifically and definitely asked for the apricot basket but they sent the lemon which I already have. I want to return their package and request what I ordered or a refund. I have it all packed up and addressed. Could you take it to that mailing place in West Palm and send it out by UPS?"

"Of course I can and shall," I averred. "Give me the package and I'll be on my way."

An innocuous incident, was it not? Merely the incorrect delivery of lemon-scented begonia bulbs when apricot had been ordered. Who could have guessed that trivial business would lead to the solution of the Crime of the Century? Certainly not A. McNally, the demon detective who once again learned the importance of chance and accident.

It took me an hour or so to return my rental, bribe an attendant to give me a lift to my garage, and ransom the Miata. I paid for everything with plastic and kept a record of the extravagant cash tips I distributed. Papa might be interested in billable hours; I was just as interested in my next monthly expense account.

Then I set out for the mailing emporium to send mother's begonia bulbs on their way. I'm sure you have similar handy and useful services in your neighborhood. They pack and address shipments of all shapes and sizes, and send them off via United Parcel Service, Federal Express, Airborne Express, or whichever carrier you request. Of course one pays extra for this convenience, but it's well worth it to have the paperwork professionally prepared.

The mailing outlet was crowded when I arrived, and I wondered how the U.S. Postal Service could hope to compete with express shippers offering speedy delivery, sometimes overnight, of everything from a legal-sized envelope to a leather hippopotamus hassock swaddled in bubblewrap and encased in a carton that looked large enough to contain a Wurlitzer.

I sent off the mater's package by UPS, received a receipt for same, and wandered outside musing on the scene within and imagining what would have happened to our nation's commerce if we were still enamored of the Pony Express. I was climbing into my rejuvenated Miata when it hit me.

I cannot declare it was a stroke of genius or claim my sudden revelation gave me the urge to yelp with joy and execute a grand jeté, toes atwirl. My first reaction was a desire to smite my forehead sharply with an open palm, devastated by chagrin that I had been such a brainless ass I hadn't grasped it before. "It" being Ernest Gorton's odious machinations.

Instead of driving to my office in the McNally Building, I returned home, for there was work to be done to verify my sudden enlightenment. I cannot describe my mood as one of exhilaration. Grim would be closer to the bone—and admittedly a smidgen of humiliation at not having solved the puzzle sooner.

I climbed directly to my oubliette and, donning my reading specs, began poring through my journal, that scrawled compendium of the frivolous and the meaningful. What I sought, y'see, was evidence to lend credence to my theory. No, strike that. It was *not* merely a theory; it was a conviction, a certainty, not an opinion but a faith.

I found evidence aplenty to convince me I had lucked onto Ernest Gorton's crafty design. And you know, I found myself feeling a grudging admiration for the scoundrel. He had created a criminal enterprise at once simple, almost foolproof, and exceedingly profitable. It required boldness on his part, of course, but it was now obvious he was a man of unlimited audacity.

I jotted a page of brief notes: facts to substantiate my analysis of Mr. Gorton's illicit activities. Then I sat back and pondered what to do next. I knew my hypothesis must be brought to the attention of Sgt. Al Rogoff and Special Agent Griffin Kling—after all, the Gorton investigation was their baby—but I wasn't certain how to announce my discovery and which law enforcement officer should be the first informed. Cops are more protective of their territory than wolverines.

So, as is my wont, I dithered. And a very pleasant dithering it was, lackadaisical and pleasurable. Have you noticed I've made no mention of lunch? I had none. Skipped it completely by deliberate choice. Naturally I was famished, but I had recently noted the waistbands of my slacks were shrinking at an alarming rate, and I decided it was time to take a keen interest in my caloric intake.

I returned from a leisurely ocean swim to dress for the family cocktail hour and dinner. That night Ursi Olson served sautéed chicken breasts with grapes and grilled veggies. Dessert was cheesecake with a fresh blueberry sauce. I had two portions of everything—but then I had omitted lunch, hadn't I?

Despite that holiday afternoon and evening I had not ceased wrestling with the problem of what my wisest next move should be. By the time I retired to my digs after the cheesecake I had made my choice and phoned Sgt. Al Rogoff. I determined he should be present when I revealed my brainstorm. I might never be associated with Special Agent Kling again, but Al's continuing friendship and assistance were too valuable to cut him out of the loop.

I found him at home and he wasn't too happy at being disturbed by my phone call.

"Now what?" he demanded.

"What," I said, "is a complete, logical, and irrefutable explanation of Ernest Gorton's criminal involvement with the Whitcomb Funeral Homes."

"Yeah?" Al said, his voice sharpening. "You got a bright idea?"

"More than a bright idea," I told him. "It's the trut', the whole trut', and nothing but the trut'. Can you persuade Kling to drive up tomorrow? I shall disclose all to both of you then."

"Can't you tell me now?"

"No," I said. "I don't chew my cabbage twice."

"What an elegant expression," he said. "I must remember to use it—maybe in the next century. All right, I'll give Kling a call and get back to you. I hope you're not shucking me on this, because if you are, it's the end of the road for us, buddy."

"Not the end," I assured him, "but a new, more glorious era of a close and more trusting relationship."

"Bleep you," he said and hung up.

He phoned back in about forty-five minutes. "Okay," he said, "it's set. It took some fast talking, but Kling finally agreed to drive up tomorrow morning. Where do you want to meet?"

"Hadn't thought of it," I confessed. "Any suggestions?"

"Kling doesn't like restaurants. He thinks the salt shaker may be bugged. How about my chateau again? At noon."

"Fine," I said. "If you feel like it, order up some pizza and beer, McNally and Son will pick up the tab."

"Of course," he said. "Naturally."

We now fast-forward to noon on Thursday. Nothing unusual happened in the interim except that I awoke in time to breakfast with my parents (we had smoked salmon and scrambled eggs) and I arrived at my office at the traditional 9:00 A.M., shocking all the fellow employees I encountered and occasioning a few snide comments.

I worked dutifully at listing the billable hours father had requested and recording my own out-of-pocket costs. They would eventually appear on my monthly expense account, which was now beginning to rival the gross national product of Sri Lanka.

I arrived at Chez Rogoff just as the delivery lad was departing, and by the time I parked and entered Al's snug and pleasantly scruffy mobile home, he was setting out three medium-sized pizzas: meatball, pepperoni, and anchovy. He also provided Coors Light in frosted glass mugs: a welcome touch.

On this occasion Special Agent Griffin Kling rose to greet me and shake my hand. It was similar to receiving a benediction from the Grand Lama, even if he neglected to remove his semiopaque sunglasses. The three of us immediately began devouring hot pizza and swilling chilled brew. I could not resist casting a furtive glance or two at Kling. Have you ever seen anyone chomping a slice of meatball pizza while wearing black specs? An unsettling sight.

Curiously it was he who offered the first revelation.

"We have Gorton's warehouse under twenty-four-hour surveillance," he told us. "Last night around midnight a semi pulls up and starts unloading. The sign on the truck says it's from the Cleo Hauling Service of New York. We got all this on videotape. Okay? So then they start unloading the truck, carrying the cargo inside the warehouse. You know what? Caskets. All colors, plain, fancy, whatever. They had to be empty because two men were handling each one easily. No forklifts. Maybe twenty coffins. The truck was unloaded and took off. Now what do you suppose was going on?"

I laughed. "Easy," I said. "Mr. Gorton is such a shrewd money-grubber he was having the empties returned."

Rogoff looked at me. "What the hell are you talking about, Archy?" he demanded.

I took the page of notes from my jacket pocket, spread it alongside my pizza plate, and began my presentation.

"Al, you told me Gorton isn't tied to the Mafia or the Colombian drug cartels but he's worked deals with both. He knows how they operate, he knows their problems, and he figured a way to make them an offer they couldn't refuse.

"What he did was set up a service for the air-lifting of drugs, guns, and money to distribution centers in New York,

Boston, and Chicago. How is contraband ordinarily transported within the forty-eight contiguous states? By courier, car, van, truck, or small planes. But all those are easy targets for arrest and seizure. Individuals and trucks can be stopped and searched. Ditto private cars. And small planes need certification and are supposed to file flight plans.

"But our hero came up with a scam that couldn't miss. The deceased are shipped out of Florida at an enormous annual rate. Each casket is crated or placed in a carton clearly labeled 'Human Remains. Handle with Extreme Care.' Who's going to open a package like that to verify the contents?

"The dear departed depart from Florida in the cargo holds of legitimate airlines. The coffin, crate, and corpse weigh about four hundred pounds. Gorton learns all this from Oliver Whitcomb, who's in need of ready cash. Ernest realizes immediately that those caskets can be filled with guns, drugs, or laundered money, providing he doesn't exceed the usual weight by too much.

"Hey, maybe he was offering his customers flight insurance. If the plane crashed, the airline would have to pay, wouldn't it? But that's just smoke on my part. I think the way the scheme worked was this:

"Gorton makes a deal with Oliver Whitcomb. The original caskets are purchased through Whitcomb Funeral Homes. They're loaded with the goodies in Gorton's warehouse. Then they're trucked at night to one of Whitcomb's three mortuaries. The director in charge, working alone or maybe with a helper on the pad, crates the casket for out-of-state shipment.

"The phony death certificate is supplied by that zonked-out Dr. Omar Pflug. The paperwork and shipping invoices are prepared by the crooked funeral directors. Gorton pays for death certificate, coffin, crating, cost of the airlift, and probably a bonus. What does he care? He's making a lush profit from his clients, who are happy to pay mucho dinero for guaranteed overnight delivery.

"Ernest Gorton is operating a Coffin Air Express. The CAE. How does that sound?"

Special Agent Griffin Kling finished a slice of anchovy pizza and wiped his lips carefully with a paper napkin. He stood, turned his back to us, leaned to look out one of the small windows.

"You got it," he said tonelessly. And then he kept repeating obsessively, "You got it. You got it. You got it."

31

He finally quieted but still didn't turn to face us. Rogoff looked at me curiously.

"How did you happen to come up with that one, Archy?" he asked.

"Genius," I said.

"Luck," he said.

"A bit of both," I admitted. "The question now is, where do we go from here?"

Then Kling turned. I don't believe he had been listening to my exchange with Al.

"It fits," the FBI man said. "Our offices up north have checked out maybe a half dozen of the places that took deliveries from the Cleo Hauling Service. They're all no-goodniks. Funeral homes with bent-nose connections. Guys with records of security frauds. One hustler suspected of supplying guns to terrorists of all stripes. So when you tell me Gorton is running a ratty air express from South Florida, I'll buy it."

I was about to repeat my question of what happens next, but Kling would not be interrupted.

"The thing to do," he said, "is bust that warehouse."

I glanced at Rogoff and I swear he gave me a quick wink. I had the feeling we were both thinking the same thing.

"Sir," I said to Special Agent Kling, doing my humble bit, "I wouldn't presume to tell you how to conduct a criminal investigation—I'm the rankest of rank amateurs—but wouldn't it be better to seize the loaded caskets after they've been picked up by the Cleo Hauling Service at LaGuardia, Logan, and O'Hare? Then you'll have evidence of interstate shipment of contraband. It's even possible you may find Gorton's fingerprints on one or more of the coffins."

"Nah," Kling said decisively. "A waste of time. I smell blood. We'll raid the warehouse as soon as possible—maybe tonight if I can get the go-ahead. I hope Gorton will be there," he added with savage joy. "But even if we don't collar him and his soldiers actually loading the caskets, we'll pull in everyone in sight. Then we'll go looking for those funeral directors and that Oliver Whitcomb. We'll lean on them and I guarantee at least one of those bozos is going to cut a deal and talk. We might even be able to pin Gorton for snuffing Rhoda Flembaugh. This is the chance I've been waiting for. Listen, I've got to run. I want to get back to Miami and get the show on the road. I'll let you know how we make out. Thanks for the feed."

Then he was gone. Rogoff and I were left with a few cold crusts from the demolished pizzas. But the supply of beer hadn't been exhausted and we each had another mugful, slumping down and relaxing. Kling's presence was daunting; no doubt about it. The man was so perpetually intense it made my fillings ache.

"I don't like it," Rogoff remarked.

"The raid on the warehouse?" I said. "I don't either. The cart before the horse and all that sort of thing. He's not building a case methodically and logically; he's the proverbial fool rushing in where angels fear to tread."

"My, oh my," Al said. "We're full of folk wisdom today, aren't we?"

"Touché," I said. "But I didn't hear you making any objections while he was here."

"C'mon, Archy, think straight. I'm a Palm Beach copper who's supposed to warn guys who go jogging without a shirt. You want me to tell the FBI how to run a major case? They'd label me a redneck sheriff and put me on their shit list."

"But you don't approve of the raid on the warehouse, do you?"

The sergeant shook his head dolefully. "Kling has other options but he's so hyper about Gorton he's got to go for the muscle. I'm betting that bust will prove Murphy's Law in spades."

I drove away from Rogoff's assembly-line hacienda reflecting that his foreboding mirrored my own. I have confessed to you on several occasions in the past that I am a lad devoted to the frivolous and trivial. I simply refuse to take anything seriously. I have absolutely no absolute beliefs—other than grated ginger is wonderful on fresh oysters.

And so I found Griffin Kling's zealotry disturbing. I am willing to admit that fanatics have accomplished much of value in the history of the higher primates. Artists, for instance, and poets, composers, architects and such—monomaniacs all—have created wondrous things. But a distressing number of the obsessionally driven have engendered wars, inquisitions, pogroms, and general nastiness that prevent an international chorus of "On the Good Ship Lollipop."

Exhausted by such sober meditation, I decided the McNally spirits required a goose, and so I used my cellular phone to call Binky Watrous, that *homme moyen sensuel.*

(Short translation: a goofball.) Surprisingly he was at home and eager to chat.

"Golly, I'm glad you called," he said. "Listen, Archy, do you think I should grow a beard?"

"*Can* you?" I asked.

"Of course I can," he said, offended. "It might take some time, but I'm sure I could do it if I set my mind to it."

"I'm on my way to the Pelican Club," I informed him—a sudden decision. "Why don't you meet me there for a spot of R and R, and we can discuss your plans to cultivate facial foliage."

"You're on," he said enthusiastically. "The Duchess wants me to accompany her to a flügelhorn recital, but I shall tell her the demands of my job-training come first. Righto?"

"Righteo," I said, topping him.

Within the hour we were seated at a table in the bar area of the Pelican. I thought it wise to continue drinking beer, and Binky ordered a mild spritzer with a peppered Russian vodka as a chaser. Nutsy.

"I guess you heard about Rhoda Flembaugh getting murdered," he said mournfully.

"Yes, I heard."

"It rocked me. I mean, she was a wild one, Archy, but really quite nice. I was wondering if I should go to the gendarmes and tell them I knew Rhoda and we had shared a Big Mac or two. Do you think I should?"

"No," I said firmly. "Keep out of it, Binky. The police have a good idea of who ordered her killing, and your personal relations with the victim will hold no interest for them whatsoever. And speaking of your many and varied intimacies, are you seeing much of Mitzi Whitcomb these days?"

"Not really. I suspect she may be giving me the old heave-ho. I mean, the Whitcombs are still running their open house and I drop by frequently, but I think Mitzi is too busy working for Ernie Gorton to pay much attention to her most devoted admirer. Namely, me."

"Oh? What sort of work is she doing for Gorton?"

"I'm not sure but now there seems to be an amazing number of yummy young lasses lolling around the premises and just as many older guys wearing gold chains, silk suits, and face-lifts. I think Mitzi may be running a dating service. You know—introducing lonely singles to each other."

A *dating* service? What a goober my aide-de-camp was!

"That's possible," I said. "Or Mitzi could be selling subscriptions to the *Kama Sutra Gazette.*"

"Oh? What's that?"

"A new magazine. Profusely illustrated. Very *in.* Does Oliver attend these soirées?"

"Some," Binky said. "Not always, but occasionally. He's drinking an awful lot these days, Archy. I don't think he enjoys the idea of his wife working for Gorton."

"Uh-huh. And does dear old Ernie put in an appearance?"

"Well, he's been there every night I've dropped by. He doesn't stay long. Just pops in, says hello to everyone, has a private chat with Mitzi, and pops out. What do you suppose is going on, Archy?"

"Infamy," I said.

He finished his wine spritzer and started on the chaser.

"Binky," I said, "when we started our semi-professional association you more or less agreed to follow all my suggestions, instruction, and orders without question."

"Well, I have, haven't I?"

"You have indeed and I commend you for it. I now have another and probably final command. I want you to sever your relationship with Mitzi and Oliver Whitcomb, with Ernest Gorton, and all their snorting pals. You are not to visit the Whitcomb maison again or attempt in any way, shape, or form to contact the residents or guests thereof. In other words, Binky, cease and desist."

He was astonished. "You mean I can't even enjoy a jolly gibber with Mitzi on the phone?"

"I don't want you to even *dream* about her," I said sternly. "Momentous events have been set in motion, and I fear the Whitcombs, Gorton, and their coterie are quite likely to have their hilarity squelched and their lifestyle dampened by stalwarts of the law. Why, they may even be shackled and dragged off to durance vile. And this cataclysm may occur with a few days or a week at the most."

"What's going on?" he said indignantly. "You must tell me what's happening."

"I would if I could," I assured him, "but I have been sworn to secrecy. It involves plans by agencies and officials at the highest levels of the U.S. government."

"Gosh," he said, suitably impressed.

"What I definitely do not want," I continued, "is to have you caught in the wreckage and perhaps charged with misdeeds of which I know you are totally innocent. I'm sure the Duchess would be as horrified as I."

He became even paler, if such a thing were possible. "Oh no," he said hoarsely. "No, no, no. We can't have it. She's already threatening to cut my allowance. Insists I economize. I'm already buying underwear made in Hong Kong. What more does she expect?"

"Then you agree to end immediately all connection with Mitzi, Oliver, and their circle?"

"I agree," he said sadly and looked longingly at his empty glasses.

I felt he had endured enough of a shock to earn a refill and so I fetched him another spritzer and vodka from the bar.

Binky sipped his fresh drink appreciatively and then said, "You know, Archy, what you do—these discreet inquiries and all—it's for real, isn't it? I mean it's not all giggles."

"Of course it's real. Sometimes people get badly hurt. Sometimes people get killed."

"The trouble is," he said with abashment, "it's fascinating, isn't it? All the raw emotion and that sort of thing. I don't mind telling you it's a new world for me. I never realized people lived like that. Oh, I know there's plenty of mean things going on, but I supposed all the evil was committed by thugs in leather jackets and baseball caps. Now I find upper-drawer citizens with big bucks and mansions can be just as slimy as your average mugger. It comes as a bit of a shock."

I knew what he was trying to say. "You're such a tyke, Binky," I told him. "Frequently the people I investigate are moneyed, well educated, charming, and utter rotters. Class really has nothing to do with it. Net worth and beluga for breakfast do not prevent ignobility. Have you had your fill of discreet inquiries?"

"Oh no!" he said determinedly. "It may be an acquired taste, but as I said, it's fascinating. You're not going to fire me, are you, Archy?"

"How can I fire you when I didn't hire you?"

"No, but you let me help. And I did assist, didn't I? I admit I have a great deal to learn, but I'm certain my performance will improve as I gain experience. Can't I continue my on-the-job training for a while?"

As usual I temporized. I wasn't certain I wanted a geeky Dr. Watson walking up my heels but Binky was correct: he *had* contributed to the Whitcomb case.

"Let me think about it," I said. "When our current investigation is closed we can talk about it further. What will be the reaction of the Duchess if you keep working without pay?"

"She'll be delighted to get me out of the house," he said, "but not half as happy as I to be absent from that mausoleum. You've never been inside, have you, Archy?"

I thought a moment. "I don't believe I ever have."

"Then you're obviously not aware that every upholstered chair is equipped with an antimacassar crocheted by the Duchess."

"You jest."

"Not so," he said darkly. "About once a month, when she's not home, I swipe one of those disgusting rags and toss it into a distant trash can. It's driving her right up the wall. The Case of the Disappearing Antimacassars."

He cackled insanely and I feared he might be paddling a leaky canoe. The lad was a trial, I could not deny it, but neither could I ignore my very real affection for him, as one might have for a mentally disadvantaged brother whose main (and possibly sole) talent was birdcalls.

"Binky," I said, "about this beard you're thinking of growing."

"Oh yes!" he said, bright with anticipation. "What do you think?"

"I don't wish to be brutally frank," I said, "but let me be brutally frank. The growth presently on your upper lip which you claim to be a mustache is so fair, so almost colorless that it can hardly be seen in full sunshine. I fear a beard may exhibit the same gossamer quality."

"I could dye it," he suggested.

"And risk having it drip down your shirtfront when it rains? No, m'boy, I don't think a beard would suit you."

"Actually," he said, "I was hoping it might make me look more, you know, mature. I mean, you and I are about the same age but you look so much older than I do."

"Thank you very much," I said.

The remainder of our conversation was so absurd I'm ashamed to detail it here. Suffice to say I left Binky that afternoon with the horrifying realization I had just been chittering with a cartoon character from Boob McNutt.

32

The mood of that day had as many zigs and zags as the tail of an affrightened Halloween cat. And there was more to come.

I returned home and saw a swampy ocean in such turmoil I immediately decided to eschew my daily swim. Instead I ascended to my eighth heaven and recorded the day's events in my journal. I also had time for a sweet nap before preparing for the family cocktail hour.

But when I descended to the second-floor sitting room I found only mother present. She was seated in a wicker armchair and dabbing at her brimming eyes with a square of cambric.

"What is it, dear?" I said fearfully.

She looked up at me, her face wracked. "Mrs. Sarah Whitcomb passed away this afternoon."

"Oh," I said, feeling I had been punched in the heart. "Ah, the poor woman."

"Father called and said he's going to the hospital to see if he can assist the family. He doesn't know how long he'll be gone and suggested we start dinner rather than wait for him."

"Does he want me to join him?"

"He said nothing about it."

"Then I certainly shan't intrude. Her death was expected, mother, but it still comes as a blow. She was a brave lady."

"Yes. Very brave. Might we have a drink now, Archy?"

"Or two," I said. "Much needed."

I did the honors and stirred the martinis as I knew my father would—to the traditional recipe: a 3-to-1 mixture of 80-proof dry gin and dry vermouth. Not astringent enough for my taste but it was what my parents enjoyed and I had no desire to challenge their preference.

Nothing more was said until we both had consumed almost all of our first libation. I don't believe it enlivened us but it helped dull the pain.

"Archy," mother said, "do you remember the Whitcombs' party we all went to, the first big affair of the season?"

"Of course I remember."

"Well, I was talking to Sarah for a few moments. Just the two of us. And suddenly she asked me if you and father get along together. Wasn't that an odd thing to say?"

"Very odd."

"Naturally I told her that you and father get along very well, that you're quite close. And she gave me the saddest look and said, 'You're very fortunate.' I've remembered it because it was such a puzzling thing. Don't you think?"

"Yes," I said and rose to top off our glasses. We finished the dividend and started downstairs to dinner.

"I didn't know her very well," mother said. "She wasn't an intimate friend, you know, but I did admire her. I had the feeling she was an unhappy woman—and not only because of her illness. But she always had a smile. That's important, isn't it, Archy?"

"It surely is."

"Now you're going to tell me there's a song lyric that says it better."

"Of course," I affirmed and sang, "Smile, though your heart is breaking . . ."

"Yes," mother said, gripping my arm tightly. "That was Mrs. Sarah Whitcomb."

I think we both felt lost at the dining table without the presence of my father. He really was captain of our ship, and for all his foibles and cantankerousness we depended on him to chart our course. Moms and I were halfway through the crabmeat appetizer when we heard the sounds of the Lexus arriving and being garaged neatly and swiftly. A moment later the lord of the manor came striding in. His expression revealed nothing. He leaned down to kiss mother's cheek.

"Glad you started," he said to us. "I'll wash up and be down in a moment."

Well, it was more than a moment and I suspected he might have detoured to the sideboard in the sitting room for a quick wallop. Eventually he appeared, took his place at the head of the table, gobbled the crabmeat, and caught up with us while we were working on slices of beef tenderloin with purple Belgian bell peppers in a red wine sauce.

"How did it go, father?" the mater asked timidly.

He gave her a brief glare. He detests her addressing him as "father" although he frequently addresses her as "mother." Do you understand that? I don't.

"As well as could be expected," he replied to her question. "Arrangements were made. We'll all attend the funeral service. Burial will be private."

"Was Oliver present?" I asked him.

"Yes," he said, not looking at me but concentrating on his beef. "This sauce is excellent. Oliver was there but his wife was not. I thought that exceedingly strange. Archy, I'd like to see you in my study after dinner."

"Yes, sir," I said.

After dessert (apple tart with cinnamon ice cream) mother went upstairs to write the McNallys' letter of condolence to Mr. Horace Whitcomb. I followed father into his study. He closed the door firmly and went directly to the marble-topped sideboard. He poured each of us a snifter of cognac—not his best but good enough. He motioned me to a club chair and took his throne behind the massive desk. I thought his visage was now uncommonly grim.

"I didn't wish to mention this at dinner," he said, "because I feared it would upset your mother. But the scene at the hospital this afternoon was dreadful, simply dreadful. Horace and his son got into a shouting match that became so rancorous I feared it might result in physical combat. I was able to separate them and keep them apart, but the atmosphere remained one of vicious spite. Meanwhile the deceased was being prepared for transfer to a Whitcomb funeral home. The whole thing was unseemly, Archy, most unseemly."

"I concur," I said. "What was their argument about?"

"Horace accused his son of being unfeeling, inattentive, and cruel during Mrs. Sarah's illness. Oliver blamed his father for his infrequent visits, claiming Horace was guilty of deliberate malice in thwarting his plans for expansion. Both were almost incoherent in their fury. Extremely unpleasant." He said this wrathfully as if the bad manners of others were a personal affront.

"Deplorable," I murmured and sipped my brandy.

"Their conflict leads me to believe your investigation may be more decisive than you and I anticipated. Have there been any recent developments?"

"Yes, sir," I said. "The whole thing is unraveling."

I brought him up to speed on what had happened and was about to occur. He interrupted only once, when I described Ernest Gorton's stratagem of airlifting contraband up north in caskets within cartons labeled "Human Remains."

"Clever," father remarked, and I thought I detected a small smile of wry amusement.

"Very," I agreed and went on to detail the plan of FBI Special Agent Griffin Kling to raid the Gorton warehouse and, if evidence discovered warranted it, to arrest Oliver Whitcomb and others involved in the plot.

I concluded and there was silence for a mo. Then the old man rose to replenish our snifters. That was an indication of his perturbation. Ordinarily he would have asked me to play the butler.

"You obviously believe Oliver Whitcomb is guilty," he said when he was once again seated upright in his high-backed swivel chair.

"I do believe that," I said firmly.

"And his motive?"

"Oliver had grandiose plans for expanding the Whitcomb Funeral Homes into a nationwide chain, plans to which his father was bitterly opposed. Oliver knew his mother held a controlling interest, and he also knew she was mortally ill and he assumed he would inherit her shares since he was an only child and well aware of her devotion to him. So he decided to take action to realize his ambitions even before her demise. His first step was to build up the cash reserves of the Whitcomb Funeral Homes to have sufficient funds to cover initial expenses. He then intended to make a private offering of stock prior to the time he could go public and have Whitcomb shares listed. He believed when that happened he would become an overnight multimillionaire. The scenario has been used before, father, and sometimes it's succeeded."

"And sometimes, usually, it's been a disaster. But there was no way Oliver's game plan could possibly have succeeded."

"Oh?" I said. "Why is that?"

He rose abruptly from his chair and began to pace back and forth behind his desk, hands thrust into trouser pockets. His head was lowered, but I caught sight of his expression and thought he looked unutterably sad.

"If your hypothesis is correct, Archy," he said, "and I believe it may very well be, Oliver's aspirations were doomed from the start. You say he assumed he would inherit his mother's shares upon her death?"

"Yes, sir, I think he assumed that. Although recently he became rather antsy about it and attempted to bribe me to determine exactly what was in Sarah's will."

My father made a noise that sounded suspiciously like a snort. "He was correct to become, as you say, antsy." He stopped his pacing to face me with a bleak smile. "Oliver was basing his future prosperity on an assumption. When it comes to inheritance, Archy, assumption can result in disappointment, if not despair. I can now reveal something to you I thought unethical to reveal while Mrs. Sarah Whitcomb was still alive. I believe I've already informed you that for tax reasons Horace Whitcomb transferred a controlling interest in the company to his wife. I had a hand in the drawing up of that conveyance and made certain it was clearly stated that if Sarah should predecease her husband, her shares would revert to him. So as things stand now, Horace holds the majority of voting shares in Whitcomb Funeral Homes."

I don't believe my mandible sagged but I'm certain an ordinary bloke would have been rendered speechless, a condition completely foreign to my nature.

"Father," I said, my voice sounding strangled even to me, "what you've just told me means that Oliver's criminal conspiracy with Ernest Gorton could not possibly profit Oliver, that he took horrendous risks for no reason whatsoever and now must pay a serious penalty for his rashness."

"It would appear so," the squire said in his lawyerly way.

If I was startled by *mon père*'s revelation I could imagine what Oliver Whitcomb's reaction would be when he learned he had wagered his future on the turn of a roulette wheel which didn't include his number. I thought he'd do more than mutter, "Drat!"

"With your permission, sir," I said, not giving a reason for my request (knowing he'd guess it), "I'd like to bring this information to the attention of Sergeant Rogoff and Agent Kling."

Prescott McNally, Esq., fell into his mulling mood, one of those lengthy silences during which he carried on a slow mental inquiry, debating all the pros and cons of my suggestion. He goes through the same process when trying to decide if the flavor of a baked potato would be enhanced by a soupçon of pressed caviar.

"Yes, Archy," he said finally, "you have my permission to inform the authorities of Oliver's current status anent his inheritance—specifically the absence thereof."

"Thank you, father," I said, wondering if, in *his* will, he had bequeathed me his fondness for prolixity.

I left his study, trotted upstairs to my sanctum and immediately phoned Sgt. Al Rogoff. He wasn't at home but I found him at headquarters.

"What are you doing in the office at this hour?" I asked.

"Paperwork," he said briefly.

"I don't think so," I told him. "You know Kling's raid is going down tonight and you want to stick close to your direct phone or telex or computer network or whatever you defenders of the public weal are using these days, just so you can keep track of what's happening. Do you plan to sleep at your desk tonight?"

"I might," he said, and his tense tone warned me I better lay off the chivying.

"Al," I said, "there's something you should know, and if you have the opportunity I hope you'll relay it to Griffin Kling. I have my father's permission to reveal this."

I told him of Oliver Whitcomb's disastrous error in assuming he would inherit his mother's shares in the Whitcomb Funeral Homes. Instead, the controlling interest would revert to his father.

"If Oliver is arrested," I went on, "or even hauled in for questioning, I thought the revelation that his brief career as a master criminal has been a gold medal no-brainer and he never had a tinker's damn of achieving the result he anticipated—well, it might embitter him to the extent that in his angry frustration he'll be willing, if not eager, to implicate the other miscreants in the plot."

"Jeez," Rogoff said, "you're beginning to talk just like your father. But you're also a foxy lad. I catch what you're trying to say and it might work. If I get a chance to talk to Kling I'll tell him what you said. He'll need all the ammunition he can get. Archy, that Oliver—what a putz he turned out to be. I mean, he had a good job and a good future, a hot-to-trot wife, money in the bank, and a Boca mansion. But he wanted more, takes a stupid risk and goes for broke. What's with morons like that?"

"He's a man in a hurry," I said, giving him an instant analysis. "He's never learned to slow down, look around, and take time to smell the garlic."

"Yeah," Al said, "I know what you mean."

33

▲

I knew I should hitch up my pantaloons and labor at bringing my professional diary up-to-the-minute. But it had been such as chaotic day, I found the prospect of even an hour's donkeywork positively repellent. All I wanted to do was sit quietly, adopt a thousand-yard stare, and breathe through my mouth.

I was saved from that repugnant lassitude when Consuela Garcia phoned. My inamorata had returned!

I find it difficult to explain why the sound of her dear, familiar voice and the knowledge that she was once again a part of my daily existence energized and invigorated me. She really was a refuge of sanity and normalcy in a world that had lately seemed to me unbearably scuzzy.

We must have jabbered for almost an hour, and other than her cousin's improving health I don't believe our conversation included a single topic of importance. But chitchat can be pleasurable, y'know. I mean, it's not necessary that every dialogue be concerned with the International Monetary Fund or the endangered state of the Ozark big-eared bat.

Connie wanted to have dinner at the Pelican Club on Friday night and I happily agreed.

"Been behaving yourself, son?" she asked.

"I have been living an exemplary life," I declared, and I had—recently.

"I haven't had time to check with my tattlers but I shall, and I hope you're telling the truth."

"Connie, would I lie to you?"

Her laugh was so hollow it echoed. "See you tomorrow night, sweet," she said. "I warn you I might get mildly potted—I'm so happy to be back."

"In that case, suppose I pick you up around sevenish. Then you won't have to drive."

"Good thinking. You'll be the designated driver and I'll be the designated drinker."

"Um," I said.

After that bracing interlude I went to bed and descended into a deep and satisfying slumber.

It lasted until I was awakened by the persistent ringing of my bedside phone. I squinted to see the time: almost 4:30 A.M., and I knew it would be bad news. Who but Death calls at that hour?

"Rogoff," he said harshly. "Griffin Kling bought it."

It took a moment for my sleep-fuddled brain to comprehend. "He's dead?" I said stupidly.

"Him and another FBI agent. Two wounded. One perp out and three bleeding. That's the latest tally I got. Sounds like the O.K. Corral."

"Was Gorton there?"

"No mention of him. Archy, it was what you'd call a monumental balls-up. They're still trying to sort things out."

"Al," I said, "what are you going to do now? Hang around? Go home?"

"I guess I'll head for bed," he said dully. "I've had it for one night."

"Stop by," I urged. "I'll put on some coffee, maybe mix up an early breakfast. Okay?"

"Yeah, sure," he said gratefully. "I can use it. I'm shook. I didn't particularly like the guy, did you?"

"No," I said.

"But I respected him," Rogoff insisted. "He was a lawman. So am I. It's hard to take."

"I can understand that."

"No, you can't," the sergeant said. "I'll be there in half an hour or so."

I pulled on jeans and T-shirt and went padding downstairs barefoot. I glanced out the kitchen window and saw the sky had a dull, leaden, predawn look.

I put water on to boil and rummaged through the fridge for vittles Rogoff might enjoy. I selected eggs, a few slices of salami, an onion, and red bell pepper. I had started preparing a quasi western omelette when father entered the kitchen. I was happy to see he was wearing a seersucker robe I had given him on his last birthday.

He looked at me inquiringly. "Suffering from malnutrition?" he asked, and even after being roused from sleep he had the ability to hoist aloft one hirsute eyebrow.

"For Rogoff," I explained and told him of Al's report on the shoot-out at Gorton's warehouse in Miami.

"And the sergeant is coming here?"

"Yes, father. He's had a bad night. I think he's in need of sustenance."

"Of course. Do you mind if I remain and hear what he has to say?"

Typical Prescott McNally: couching a command as a request.

Al's timing was most felicitous. The omelette was beginning to crisp around the edges when his pickup pulled into our graveled turnaround. I slid a few slices of sour rye into the toaster as Rogoff came clumping in and shook hands with my father. He looked beat.

He washed his hands at the kitchen sink, removed his gun belt, and joined us at the table. Father and I didn't have anything but watched as he attacked his omelette, buttered toast, and steaming black coffee. He ate avidly as if he had consumed nothing but a single graham cracker in the past twenty-four hours. Not bloody likely.

"Good grub," he said to me. "Do you cater wedding receptions?"

"Sure," I said. "Also proms and bar mitzvahs. Al, I told father about that calamitous raid on Gorton's warehouse. Anything new since you phoned me?"

"Yeah," he said. "The chase is on for Gorton, Oliver Whitcomb, the three funeral directors and their stooges. That's why I've got to get back to headquarters instead of going home. Two of those directors live in the Palm Beach area. We're supposed to liaise with the FBI trackers when they get up here."

"They intend to arrest Oliver Whitcomb?" father asked.

"Yes, sir. I don't know if they have a warrant but with two agents dead they're in no mood to observe the legal technicalities. Besides, they have probable cause coming out their ears."

Hizzoner made a tch-tch sound. "This will cause Horace Whitcomb considerable pain. Naturally, sergeant, I shall say nothing to him about Oliver's predicament. He'll learn of the arrest soon enough. And then I expect he'll contact me to recommend an experienced criminal defense attorney to represent his son."

I looked at him in astonishment. "Father, Horace is well aware of what Oliver has been doing. After all, Horace initiated the inquiry that eventually ended Oliver's short criminal career. Are you suggesting that Horace will now aid his son?"

The old man stared at me sternly. "Of course. In any way he can. Oliver's illicit behavior has nothing to do with it. Horace Whitcomb is an honorable man, and this is family."

"Blood is thicker than water," Rogoff put in. "But not thicker than this coffee," he added, pouring himself another cup.

The idea of Horace helping defend his wayward son was incomprehensible to me, even though the senior didn't think it extraordinary at all. Perhaps I'll understand it when, if ever, I become a paterfamilias.

"Al," I said, "about Ernest Gorton—where are they searching for him?"

"They're looking for him here, there, everywhere. And I'll bet a million they'll never find him."

"Oh?" father said, interested. "Why not?"

"Look, counselor," the sergeant said, "this guy is a slime, granted, but a smart slime. Always one step ahead of the law and his competitors. Now don't tell me a shrewd apple like him wouldn't have a fail-safe plan in case things got hairy—which they have."

"How would he manage it?" I asked.

"Set up a residence and fake identity in some pipsqueak country that doesn't have an extradition treaty with the U.S. But I can't see Gorton spending the rest of his life in a jungle hut or beach shack. He's a guy who needs action. My guess is that he's got a beautiful villa and fake papers in some South American country. He changes his name and maybe even has plastic surgery. All this is going to cost plenty in bribes to local pols, but that's no different from how he was operating in

Miami. And he can afford it. So now he's a new man and can get back in the rackets again, in the country where he's living and in international trade in drugs, guns, money laundering, prostitution, and so forth. Believe me, we haven't heard the last of Ernest Gorton, no matter what his new name might be."

"A depressing prospect," my father remarked.

"Yeah," Rogoff said with a snarly laugh, "ain't it. Listen, I've got to get back to the salt mines. If anything important comes up I'll let you know. Thanks for the feed; it was just what I needed."

Then he buckled on his gun belt and was gone. Father helped me clean up the kitchen.

"Sir," I said, "if Oliver Whitcomb and the others are indicted and brought to trial, as they may well be, do you think I'll be called upon to testify?"

"I doubt it very much, Archy," he said, doing a good but not perfect job of hiding his amusement. "After all, what evidence do you have to offer?"

I reflected on that and acknowledged he was exactly right, as usual. I had no hard evidence to offer. Just guesses, suppositions, unsubstantiated hypotheses.

I returned to my interrupted slumber in a mood far from gruntled. It was an injury to my amour propre to realize that in the Whitcomb affair I had been a small cog on a large wheel. But even the absence of a single cog can freeze motion, can it not?

I awoke a little after 10:00 A.M. on Friday, feeling not at all refreshed and yearning for a few more hours of Zs. Before showering and shaving I sat on the edge of my bed and made a few phone calls—the first to Al Rogoff. He sounded uncommonly brisk for a man who had been conscious and functioning through a sleepless night.

"Well?" I demanded.

"We got 'em all," he reported. "Including Oliver Whitcomb. His father's been informed."

"What about Mitzi, his wife?"

"Picked her up, too."

"And Gorton?"

"Like I told you—he's long gone. Talk to you later." And he hung up.

My second call was to Binky Watrous. I obviously woke him up, which pleased me.

"What's happening?" he said groggily.

"Lots," I said. "The authorities have found Judge Crater, Amelia Earhart, Jimmy Hoffa, and have identified Jack the Ripper and the mountebank who wrote Shakespeare's sonnets."

"You're kidding."

"Have I ever? Listen, Binky, I don't think this will happen, but if any chaps with badges come around asking questions about the Whitcomb case, claim you know naught of the matter. This is a firm command."

Short silence. "You mean you want me to lie and tell them I'm totally ignorant?"

What a cue! "It's scarcely a lie, old boy," I said and disconnected.

My third call was to Sunny Fogarty's office. I was told she was not available. I then phoned her condo and let it ring seven times before giving up. Isn't it strange that one usually knows when no one is home? The ringing has an empty sound. I know it's ridiculous, but I'm sure you've had the same experience.

I went through my usual morning ablutions and dressed in a natty manner, hoping it might elevate my spirits. I donned an artfully wrinkled sky-blue linen sport jacket (no shoulder pads, of course), slacks of rust-colored covert, and suede loafers in a sort of tealish shade. The ensemble, I decided, was striking without being bizarre. I was certain my father would have a contrary opinion.

After a scanty breakfast (OJ, black coffee, and two croissants with heather honey) I drove directly to the McNally Building wondering if at that moment Ernest Gorton was flying to his hideaway abroad. Wherever he was heading I reckoned he was traveling first class. Sgt. Rogoff keeps assuring me it is gross stupidity to believe that in this world virtue is always rewarded and vice punished. Sad to say, he is probably correct.

I phoned my father when I arrived at my office and was pleasantly surprised to be put through immediately. I relayed Rogoff's most recent information.

"Thank you, Archy," he said formally, "but I am already aware of Oliver's arrest. Horace Whitcomb called a short time ago to tell me the news. He is coming over to discuss legal representation for his son."

"How did he sound?"

"Resigned, I would say, as if he had expected such an outcome to the inquiry he instigated."

"Father, what do you think will happen to Oliver and his accomplices?"

"I imagine there will be plea bargaining, but I fear Oliver and the others will serve prison sentences of various durations. I do not believe they will get off lightly. Two special agents of the FBI have been killed; the authorities will not be in the mood to be merciful."

"A sad situation," I said.

"It is," he agreed, "and I am glad McNally and Son will no longer be playing an active role in the affair. You will cease all your inquiries immediately." Thus ordained His Majesty.

"Yes, sir," I said, resisting a terrible desire to drop a curtsy.

34

Not quite, pappy. There was still a bit of unfinished business, a little tidying up to do before my record of the Whitcomb case could be closed. But before I could call her again, she phoned me.

"This is Sunny Fogarty, Archy," she said, sounding tearful.

"I tried calling you earlier, Sunny, but couldn't get through."

"I was with Mr. Horace," she said. "He's had a bad morning. I suppose you've heard what's happened."

"Yes, I heard."

"Archy, I'm home now. Is there any chance of your coming over?"

"Of course," I said. "Shall I bring us some lunch?"

"Oh no," she said. "Thank you but no. I'm really not hungry. But I do want to see you."

"I'll leave at once," I told her, hoping I might have the courage to ask her a direct and perhaps an insolent question. But if she answered honestly it would relieve an irritation that had bothered me from the start, a nagging as persistent as a vagrant lash on the eyeball or a fleck of lettuce snagged in one's bicuspid.

I think the way Sunny Fogarty dressed was part of the contradiction that puzzled me. A dichotomy, one might say—and I do say it. If it is true clothes make the man, clothes *are* the woman.

She met me at the door of her condo wearing a severely tailored pantsuit of black gabardine. But the jacket was unbuttoned to reveal a ruffled white silk blouse also unbuttoned in a manner I found disturbingly seductive. She ushered me to the couch in the living room and tried a brave smile.

"Quite a morning," she said.

"I can imagine."

"Archy, I'm having a chardonnay, but I suspect you might prefer something stronger."

"You suspect correctly," I said boldly, needing resolution to ask my impertinent question.

"Will vodka on the rocks do?" she asked.

"Splendidly," I said, and a few moments later she brought me a beaker of iced elixir that would have transformed a mild-mannered lemur into King Kong.

"How is Mr. Horace taking all this?" I said.

"Remarkably well. He has the funeral of Mrs. Sarah to arrange and now he must do what he can for Oliver. Plus reorganizing the funeral homes and hiring new directors and assistants. But he's a strong man and he's coping."

"I'm sure he's depending on you for assistance," I said. Crafty me—leading into the rude query I was determined to make.

"I'm doing what I can to help," she said evenly, "and so are all the other employees not involved in that dreadful business."

She rose from the armchair, removed her jacket, and

joined me on the couch. It could have been an entirely innocent maneuver, I agree, but one never knows, do one? She sat quite close and looked at me directly.

"Archy," she said, "I asked you to come over because I have an apology to make."

"Sunny," I protested, "you've already apologized. You admitted you and Mr. Horace were aware of Oliver's shenanigans before you asked McNally and Son for a discreet inquiry."

"No, no," she said with a small smile of rue. "This is *another* apology. A personal apology."

She placed a soft hand on my arm and answered the question that had been bedeviling me.

"I want to explain why I went to such lengths to protect Horace and why I may have misled you in the process. I even withheld things I knew and made you discover them yourself. It was all because I didn't want Horace to be hurt. You see, dear, he and I have been intimate for, oh, perhaps five years, ever since his wife became ill."

She paused and looked at me as if awaiting an expression of shock. But I was not shocked. Would you have been? I think not.

"Oh," I said, my suspicion confirmed. After all, there was the expensive condo, the new car she drove, those frequent payments for clothes and jewelry in her credit dossier. The lady was obviously living beyond her means, and the unexplained prosperity of others is always sufficient to ignite my penchant for nosiness.

"You mean a lot to me, Archy," she continued, "and it is important to me that you know why we did what we did. Horace's wife was dying. My mother is totally out of it and hasn't long to go. That's what brought us together. Can you understand it?"

"Not quite," I said, taking a deep swallow of my chilled plasma. "I must confess I'm an absolute klutz when it comes to grasping all the subtleties of he-she relations."

"It was grief, Archy," she said intently. "Like two people huddling together in a bomb shelter, comforting each other against the death outside. Of course we bedded; I won't deny it. But it was not passion; it was a sharing of sorrow—and fear."

"That's heavy," I said.

Sunny nodded. "I know but it's true. There was guilt, of course—there had to be guilt because his wife was still alive."

"Do you suppose she knew?"

"I believe she did. I like to think she approved—or at least accepted it with equanimity. She was a marvelous woman, Archy."

"She was indeed."

"Horace tried to compensate for his conduct by giving me gifts. It really wasn't necessary. I told him that but he insisted. Somehow it helped him deal with his guilt. Men are so strange. As for my guilt, I could endure it because I knew it was temporary; it couldn't last. The bombs were falling closer and closer. I think I need another drink. Are you ready?"

"Good Lord, no!"

She returned with a refilled wine glass and seated herself close beside me again.

"Two questions, Sunny," I said, "and I'd love to know the answers. There was once a Polish king known as Boleslaw the Bashful and I expect I shall go down in history as Coleslaw the Curious. First of all, did you grant me the pleasures of your bed just to ensure my continued cooperation in the investigation?"

She clamped my arm again, tightly this time. "Oh no!" she

said hotly. "Don't even *think* such a thing. I simply wanted us to enjoy. I wanted it to be purely physical, mindless, and fun. I wanted to surrender completely and for a brief, wonderful time forget all my problems and share joy instead of sorrow. Did I succeed?"

"Of course you did," I lied valiantly and have never uttered a more meritorious falsehood. "And now I must ask my second question: Will you marry Horace Whitcomb?"

Her grip on my arm slackened and she looked at me sadly. "You still don't understand, do you? Of course I won't marry Horace. It wasn't a mad, crazy love affair, a lust neither of us could resist. All we had was shared grief. And after that is gone, we have nothing."

This woman was too deep for me by far.

"Surely you have plans for the future, Sunny."

"Oh yes," she said determinedly. "I intend to stay with Whitcomb Funeral Homes until we have it functioning normally again. Then I'll leave and find another job. When my mother passes away I might move elsewhere. California perhaps."

"Mr. Horace will urge you to stay," I told her.

"He already has. But I want to put all this in the past and start a new life. Does that sound foolish?"

"Not at all. Romantic, but not foolish. What exactly are you seeking, dear?"

"I can't explain," she said. "I'm not sure myself."

I didn't believe that. She was a woman of secrets to the last.

There didn't seem much more to be said. Our final parting, a light embrace and kiss, was more bro-sis than he-she.

"Let's keep in touch," she said.

"By all means," I said.

Kindred liars.

I departed and aimed the Miata toward home and emotional security. I suffered one brief pang of remembrance: a vital woman, strong and zesty in bed.

I found my thoughts returning to what Sunny Fogarty had revealed of her relationship with Horace Whitcomb, described by my father as an honorable man. I believed Sunny had told me the truth—or at least what was valid for her. But I found her story so singular, so alien to my experience, that I could scarcely accept it.

And so, hewing to folk wisdom—"A boy's best friend is his mother"—I sought out Mrs. Madelaine McNally after I garaged my tumbril. I found her in our greenhouse.

"Mrs. M.," I said, "I'd like to take advantage of your superior acumen and ask help in solving an enigma that puzzles me."

She paused, brass watering can in hand, and looked at me inquiringly. "What is it, Archy?"

"Do you think it possible a man and a woman might form a close relationship—an intimate relationship, in fact—simply because both are suffering great sorrow in their personal lives?"

She didn't hesitate a moment. "Of course it's possible," she said promptly. "Grief does bring people together, you know. They cling to one another."

"Mother, I always thought passionate twosomes were based on physical attraction and shared interest in such things as opera, Bugs Bunny cartoons, ballet, and smoked provolone sandwiches on pumpernickel."

"Oh, Archy, people link up for so many reasons, and sadness is certainly one of them. Misery loves company just as happiness does."

I pondered that for a moment. "You're saying the motives for intimacy are many and varied?"

"Very many and very varied."

This was a fresh perception to me and I could not let it go. "Could a shared prejudice or hatred or bigotry be the motive for a man and woman cleaving to each other?"

"Of course," mother said matter-of-factly. "Even nasty people fall in love, Archy."

"I guess," I said gloomily, wishing I knew more than I did. But I consoled myself with the thought that Mr. Einstein probably had the same vain hope.

"Have I answered your question, dear?" she asked, not at all dismayed by the lesson she had taught me in the realpolitiks of love.

"You have indeed," I assured her, "and I thank you for it. By the way, I won't be able to join you and father for cocktails and dinner. Connie has returned from Miami and we're going out for a night on the town."

"That's nice, darling," she said brightly. "Have a wonderful time."

"I fully intend to give it my best shot," I vowed, kissed her velvety cheek, and left her asking a Merry Christmas begonia why it was drooping in such a shameful fashion.

The sea was paved that afternoon, but I was in no mood for a dunk. Nor did I have any desire to scribble in my journal and close out my account of the Whitcomb case. Instead, I lay on my bed fully clothed, stared at the ceiling, and suffered a severe case of weltschmerz.

I am not often depressed, being cheerful by nature, but recent events had brought me low. I was discomposed by so many people dancing about as if Walpurgisnacht would go on forever.

I suddenly realized what would cure my jimjams. I rose and called Connie Garcia, phoning her at the estate of Lady Cynthia Horowitz. I figured Connie had gone to work immediately to make up for all her absent days.

"Lady Horowitz's residence," she said crisply. "Consuela Garcia speaking."

"Archibald McNally speaking," I said just as snappily. "Is it on for tonight, hon?"

"You betcha," she said. "You pick me up at seven and off we go to the Pelican Club."

"Do me a favor, will you, Connie. I'd like to wear a dinner jacket. Will you get gussied up?"

Shocked silence. Then: "You want to wear a dinner jacket to the Pelican?"

"Yep."

"You'll be tarred, feathered, and ridden out of town on a rail."

"I don't care. It's something I must do. Will you humor me?"

"Say 'Please.' "

"Please."

"Say 'Please with sugar on it.' "

I groaned. "Please with sugar on it."

"Okay," she giggled. "I'll get all dolled up. It'll give me a chance to wear a neat coat dress I bought in Miami. It's white silk and makes me look like a vanilla Popsicle."

"Yummy," I said. "See you at seven."

Then I disrobed and went back to bed smiling for a much needed nap. If the Whitcomb affair had an almost operatic intensity, I was determined that evening would be as innocent and memorable as a pop tune. I don't know the lyrics of *La donna è mobile* but I can sing every word of "It Had to Be You."

35

When attending a formal affair in South Florida's clammy clime, I usually don a white dinner jacket, soft-collared shirt, and a tie and cummerbund of a modest maroon or even a sedate tartan. But not that evening.

I unzipped a garment bag to extract my black tropical worsted dinner jacket and trousers. The jacket had black satin lapels, the trousers black satin stripes, but the costume was really as conservative as a shroud. I also laid out a starched shirt, wing collar, onyx studs and cuff links.

I knew exactly what I was doing. The Whitcomb case had been such a raw and vulgar affair that I needed a healthy dose of convention to restore my emotional balance. My traditional uniform was one small step in recovering the comfort of custom. I have neither the gall nor the desire to deny the past.

Showered, shaved, and scented, I dressed in my formal attire, prized my feet into patent leather shoes, and descended to the kitchen. I moved rather stiffly, I admit, as if I were wearing a suit of armor and feared I might creak.

Mrs. Olson was preparing dinner and turned as I entered.

"Oh my, Mr. Archy," she said, awed, "you look so handsome!"

"Thank you, Ursi," I said, preening. "Do you think perhaps I need a boutonniere?"

She pursed her lips and regarded my costume thoughtfully. "Possibly," she said. "Something to add a bit of color to the black and white. But we have no fresh flowers available other than your mother's begonias, and they won't do."

"No," I said, "definitely not."

"I do have some fresh parsley available," she offered. "Do you think a sprig of that would help?"

"Just the thing!" I cried happily, and a few moments later I had a small bundle of that marvelous herb pinned to my lapel.

I had a hazy hope of how I wanted that evening to progress and end. And so I entered the pantry and searched the shelves bearing the McNally liquor supply. (The costly vintage wines are stored in a locked, temperature-controlled cabinet in my father's study.) I found what I sought: a bottle of Korbel brut. I slid it with two crystal champagne flutes onto the lowest shelf of our refrigerator.

Then I set out to rendezvous with the vanilla Popsicle.

Yikes! but Connie looked super, all slithery in white silk and with the excited, prideful look women get when they know they're splendidly dressed. Her long black hair was down and gleaming. The only jewelry she wore was the diamond tennis bracelet I had given her. What a glittery manacle it was!

I embraced her gently, not wishing to crush her coat dress.

"Welcome home, darling," I said. "I missed you."

"Did you?" she said eagerly. "Did you really?"

"Scouts' honor. I pined away while you were gone. Lost pounds and pounds."

She pulled away to inspect me. "I don't think so. Archy, you look spiffy, but what's that in your buttonhole?"

"Parsley."

"I hope you're kidding."

"I am not. It is a sprig of fresh parsley. It is decorative and should our dinner contain a gross amount of garlic, we can nibble on it to sweeten our breath."

She hugged my arm. "Nutty as ever," she said happily. "Let's go."

If Connie feared our finery would be greeted with raucous scorn by the raffish Friday night roisterers at the Pelican Club, she totally misjudged their reaction. Most of the lads and lasses beginning a bibulous weekend were clad in funky denim, leather, and T-shirts bearing legends ranging from the indelicate to the scabrous.

But when we entered, the chatter and laughter ceased as heads swiveled in our direction. Then many of our pals leaped to their feet and treated us to a vigorous round of applause interspersed with such cries of approval as "Oh, wow!" and "The baddest!"

Connie and I bowed graciously in all directions—royalty acknowledging their worshipful underlings. Then we paraded to the dining area where we claimed our favorite corner table. Priscilla came moseying forward to bring us down to earth.

"Going to a masquerade?" she inquired.

"None of your sass," I said sternly. "We merely decided the joint needed a touch of class."

"Gee," she said, "I wish you had warned me; I'd have put on clean overalls. Naturally you'll want champagne cocktails to start."

"Naturally," Connie said.

"I'll have to serve them on paper napkins," Pris apologized.

"All our lace doilies are in the laundry. I'm sure you swells will understand."

"Of course," I said loftily. "Noblesse oblige."

You would think, wouldn't you, that in view of our splendiferous attire we might dine on pheasant under glass or perhaps a roasted capon stuffed with minced hundred-dollar bills. But the Pelican Club was unable to provide such amenities, and Chef Leroy's special that night was pot roast with a fresh horseradish sauce so good it made one weep—literally.

Connie was at her magpie best during dinner, regaling me with trivia about her trip to Miami, the recovery of her injured cousin, the trials and tribulations of her multitudinous relatives.

Earlier in this account I suggested my attraction to this woman was due to her providing an island of normalcy in the sometimes violent sea I was called upon to navigate. I imagine some of you faithful readers must have shaken your heads sagely and thought, "That Archy! Just another example of his dissembling. He likes Connie because she's a dishy broad."

Well, yes, that was certainly part of it. But as mother has instructed me, intimacy is rarely simple. What human bonds are? Sgt. Al Rogoff once told me of a case he handled in which a woman bludgeoned her husband with a cinder block while he slept. Her reason? "He snored," she told the cops. But surely that was only one motive in a long, festering record of grievances.

We had shared a single dessert—a wickedly rich raspberry shortcake drizzled with Chambord—and were lazing over double espressos when Connie asked me what I had been doing during her absence.

"This and that," I said.

"I'll bet it was the Whitcomb case," she said. "It's been in all the papers and on TV every night. I'm sure you were mixed up in it because you asked me weeks ago about Oliver and Mitzi."

"I was involved," I admitted. "Up to my dewlaps. But there's little I can add to what you've already heard or read. It was a mess, Connie. Listen, do you know what I'd like to do now?"

"Yes," she said.

I laughed. "Later," I said. "There will be a short station break. Stay tuned."

We drove back to the McNally mansion manqué. It was a glorious night, almost completely cloudless with a wispy breeze from the northwest. The moon wasn't full, of course—that would have been too much—but there was enough showing to remind me of Guy Kibbee. It was a loverly stage set that convinced me I'd live forever.

I retrieved the chilled bottle of Korbel from the fridge and popped the cork. Carrying the bubbly and two glasses, I conducted Connie down the rickety wooden staircase to the beach. She asked nary a question nor made any objection. I led and she followed. What a sweetness!

She was wearing no hose and had only to kick off her suede sandals. But I had to pry off my patent leathers and peel away knee-high socks. I rolled up my trouser cuffs and we left all our footgear in the moon shadow of a palm. Before we started our stroll I poured each of us a glass of champagne. We linked arms before sipping. Cutesy? I suppose. But there was no one to see but God and I hoped He approved.

We ambled down to the water's edge where mild waves came lapping in. The ocean was still calm and it seemed layered with a pathway of aluminum foil leading to the rising moon.

"Oh, Connie said, staring out at the glistening sea and breathing deeply. She tilted her face up to the night sky. "Look at all those tennis bracelets!"

"Exactly," I said.

We wandered southward through warm froth that rarely doused our calves. The packed sand was cool and provided easy strolling. We saw the lights of fishing boats and the blaze of a passing cruise ship. Once we heard the melodious call of a seabird neither of us could identify.

"Binky Watrous should be here," I remarked.

"Bite your tongue," Connie advised.

We paused occasionally while I refilled our glasses.

You may think this barefoot ramble along a moonlit beach by a formally dressed couple sipping champers was a schmaltzy thing to do. But schmaltz is in the eye of the beholder—and you've never read a more disgusting figure of speech if you happen to know the original meaning of the word.

It was a fantasy and I was aware of it. After experiencing the crudity of the Whitcomb case I wanted to recapture the laughing elegance of a world I never knew and perhaps never existed: the clever, self-mocking era of Noel Coward songs, Fitzgerald novels, Broadway musicals, and William Powell movies. I was trying to re-create a madly joyous time I imagined.

"A penny for your thoughts," Connie said, "and not one cent more."

"I was thinking about dreams," I told her. "And how they shape our lives."

Then I described some of the dreamers I had met during the Whitcomb investigation:

Mrs. Sarah: Dying while listening to a tinkly music box.

Oliver: Driven by a fierce ambition to prove himself a money-spinner nonpareil.

Ernest Gorton: He of the green eyes with limitless greed and a vision of limitless wealth.

Mitzi Whitcomb: She saw a constantly expanding universe of young studs and giggles.

Griffin Kling: A man nurtured by a vengeful rage that eventually destroyed him.

Rhoda Flembaugh: She yearned only for a chance to change her luck.

I said nothing of Horace Whitcomb and Sunny Fogarty. But they too had their illusions.

Dreamers all.

Connie listened intently to my brief recital and suddenly shivered. "Archy," she said, "I'm getting chilly."

I set bottle and glass in the sand, took off my dinner jacket, and draped it about her shoulders. She looked enchanting.

"Let's go back," I said.

"Let's hurry," she said.

We turned and skipped along the strand under the spangled sky, silvered by moonlight, and hearing the sea's soft susurrus. We held hands and sang "You'd Be So Nice to Come Home To."

We had reclaimed our footwear and were preparing to board the Miata when Ms. Consuela Garcia declared, "I know what I want to do now, Archy. You?"

"I concur," I said.

"Then let's do it," she said.

And so we did.